The Code

The Code

Nick Thripp

Matador
9 Priory Business Park,
Wistow Road, Kibworth Beauchamp,
Leicestershire. LE8 0RX
Tel: 0116 279 2299
Email: books@troubador.co.uk
Web: www.troubador.co.uk/matador
Twitter: @matadorbooks

ISBN 978 1788038 065

British Library Cataloguing in Publication Data.
A catalogue record for this book is available from the British Library.

Printed and bound in the UK by 4edge limited
Typeset in 11pt Aldine401 BT by Troubador Publishing Ltd, Leicester, UK

Matador is an imprint of Troubador Publishing Ltd

For Hilary

'Everything we do is governed by a code. The art of harmonious living is to identify the appropriate code and abide by it. Breaking the code results in social failure, ostracism and, in a very few cases, unparalleled power and riches.'

– Prof Ernesto Mutande, Istituto Merluzzo,
Etra Panussenad (Trans: I Coglioni).

Chapter 1
ABBOTSFORD CEMETERY, 2007

What I thought were tears were only raindrops dripping slowly from her hood onto her cheeks. That made more sense. I doubted whether Rachel would have cried for anyone, least of all a detested ex-husband.

Her stony eyes turned towards me.

'Shall we go now?'

Nodding, I stepped away from the rain-sodden grave, and we started to trudge towards the car park. Wedges of clay stuck to my shoes. I glanced at the order of service. 'John Beart, 1954-2007'.

I tried to dislodge the clay before easing myself into my black BMW. Rachel didn't bother. She was already inside, staring ahead, clumps of red earth around her feet in what had been the immaculate foot well of the car.

We drove in silence to a pub we'd seen on our way

to the cemetery. Built in the 1970s, its mock Tudor beams, inside and out, gave it an air of false solidity. The smell of cooking fat permeated everything.

Apart from the funeral director and his staff, the only other witnesses to John's interment had been a handful of bored reporters who had soon abandoned the damp proceedings.

'Not much of a wake.' I raised my pint to my lips. A flicker of emotion crossed her face.

'More than he deserves.'

*

I gave Rachel a lift back to her flat, above an Asian food shop in Solhurst High Street. She paused when opening the car door.

'Do you want to come in?'

I wondered whether she was being polite. She'd spoken in that curiously intonation-free way in which some people speak a foreign language, her eyes no clue to her true feelings.

'Well?'

I realised I hadn't answered her question.

'OK. Why not?'

The curtains were still drawn and the sitting-room was dark. She switched on the bare overhead bulb, casting a dim light which left most of the room in shadow. In the gloom, I picked out a threadbare blue sofa, a pale grey armchair with a large brown stain on the arm, and another covered by a golden oriental throw. I looked around for some personal touches—paintings, photographs, books, magazines, anything. There weren't any.

From a cupboard she produced two glasses, and from the fridge a half-empty bottle of Bulgarian white wine. She saw my expression.

'It's all I've got.' She poured it out.

I took a sip and coughed.

'Like it?' she asked, raising an eyebrow.

'Rough as a badger's arse.'

A look of recognition flashed across her face at this favourite phrase of mine from when we'd been members of a wine appreciation group, and she smiled for the first time since I'd picked her up that morning. At fifty-five she was still an attractive woman and, in the flat's dim light, could easily have passed for fifteen years younger.

'Who would have thought it?' she said. I knew what she meant. We lapsed into a lengthy silence, during which I stared hard at my glass, not wanting to share what was going through my mind. It could have been so different. Perhaps… I suppressed the half-formed thought and drained the last of my wine.

'Best be off.' I hauled myself out of my armchair as she stared into the middle distance, her eyes glazed. I wasn't sure she'd heard what I'd said, or was even aware I was still there.

Chapter 2
SUNDAY, 29TH DECEMBER, 1963

I'd seen Mrs Beart before and felt nothing, but on 29th December, 1963, I fell in love with her.

My grandparents had taken me for Sunday lunch to Chez Antoine, and Mrs Beart, accompanied by a burly, thick-necked man, was sitting at a table in the corner. The man, his voice reverberating around the restaurant, ordered a bottle of wine.

'I've smelt more fragrant jockstraps,' he boomed on sniffing its bouquet. 'Bring me another.'

At first I thought the scene comic, but my eyes were drawn to Mrs Beart's face, where deep sadness seemed to lurk beneath her half-smile. The more I stared at her, the more bewitched I became. A week before, my best friend, Neil Wallington, had stumbled across a portrait of an almost-naked Nell Gwynne by Sir Peter Lely in a dusty art history book, and a succession of lustful boys had made their way to the school library to pore over it. What struck me now was that Mrs Beart bore an uncanny resemblance to Nell Gwynne. As I screened out the tedium of my grandparents' conversation, I felt an uneasy, pleasurable stirring in my loins.

To avoid embarrassment, I quickly redirected my thoughts to school and, in particular John, Mrs Beart's son, who was two forms below me at Bedlington House.

He had already earned Neil and me a caning from the headmaster by telling on us when we'd skived off a school cross-country run. Shortly after, also thanks to Beart, we received a pummelling from Ronald Carrot-Top and his Valley Park gang when they found out that Neil and I had knocked down a shelter they were building in the woods.

Fortunately, Roberts, my protégé in his class, tipped us off both times that Beart was the informant so, despite his tears and denials, we exacted full retribution.

The real problem was that Beart didn't abide by the schoolboy code, even though it was very simple. As Philip, my older brother, said to me the day I started at Bedlington House, there were only two things you had to avoid doing: sneaking and blubbing. Beart did both.

Chapter 3
JOHN BEART, 1965

Two years passed without my seeing Mrs Beart again, and the intensity of my daydreams, in which I'd been simultaneously her saviour, her protector and her slave, all gradually faded leaving only the memory of her in Chez Antoine and the persistently irritating presence of her son to remind me of her existence.

Though Neil and I, now both thirteen and in our last term at Bedlington House, became quite adept at avoiding Beart, sometimes it was impossible. Like that hot May afternoon when several of us bunked off to a secluded spot to drink alcohol and smoke cigarettes purloined from our homes, only to be busted by Mr Summerbee, the English teacher, and beaten with a gym shoe. We were puzzled how he'd found out, until Roberts, my ever-trusty informant, whispered Beart's name to me.

'It wasn't me, I swear,' Beart, his eyes filling with tears, whined to the kangaroo court we'd assembled. Of course, his refusal to own up only increased our anger.

I'm not sure who thought of stripping him down to his underpants and spreading his clothes around the wasp-infested orchard, but it was my idea to smear him with honey stolen from the school kitchen.

Then he was sent to Coventry for a week.

We were sure Beart would have learned his lesson, so it came as quite a surprise when, a week later, he sauntered up to me.

'I'll get you for that. And Wallington. You wait and see.'

He was such a little squirt I could have pushed him over, but I restrained myself. He walked off and joined a group of boys we called 'The Mollies', who started whispering, pointing in my direction and giggling. It was too much. About to launch myself at them, just in time I saw Mr Summerbee approaching. The Mollies were his favourites. He would take them on excursions after school and sometimes, so it was said, invite them to his houseboat to look at the mollies in his aquarium and enjoy a sumptuous cream tea.

I aimed a deft kick at a stone and sent it scudding into the bushes.

'He's a runt, a nothing, a nobody,' I muttered to myself.

Chapter 4
FESTON, 1965-68

Dean College, a gaunt Gothic mansion, rose from the marshland that lay to the north-east of Abbotsford, and was renowned for harbouring pathologically idle boys whose affluent parents were reluctant to consign them to the educational wasteland that was Valley Park Secondary Modern.

I'd failed to get into King Henry's School, my father's choice and where, gallingly, Neil had gained a place. Dean College accepted me without even an interview.

Bedlington House had prepared me well for Dean College. The combination of lazy, uninterested teachers with dubious moral and educational backgrounds, the vain and capricious prefects, and the atmosphere of summary and brutal punishment, were all reassuringly familiar. I knew how to survive and kept a low profile. When I wasn't at College, I was forced to make Feston the centre of my social life, thanks to the local bus service which ceased operations shortly after 8pm.

I'd grown up with most of the youngsters who lived in Feston. We started pairing off, not because of any great romantic inclinations, but because that's what everyone was doing.

Erica, who worked in the stationer's shop was, at the age of sixteen, my first serious girlfriend.

It was a cool, windy April evening when I saw her sitting on a bench at the edge of the youth club disco in a pink miniskirt with a duffel coat round her shoulders. She was filing her nails as her friends gyrated with their partners on the dance floor.

There was a convenient lull in the music between tracks.

'Hello Erica, long time no see. Remember me?'

She glanced up before resuming her manicure.

'Yes, I know you.' She was solidly built with brown eyes set too far apart and a nose like a small potato. Even in the strobe lighting, I could make out the freckles splattered across her cheeks.

My Generation started to blare out from two four-foot-high speakers.

'Do you like The Who?' I yelled above the noise.

'Don't mind them,' she mouthed.

I shifted my weight from one leg to the other, desperate for something else to say, while she examined her nails in the dizzying light for any minor imperfections.

'What about The Stones?' I screamed just as the track finished, and several pairs of eyes turned inquisitively towards me.

'All right, I suppose,' she muttered, her eyes fixed on the floor.

Satisfaction started playing and I grabbed her hand, dragging her onto the dance floor. There was no one else left and I was determined not to be the only one of my friends to end up as a wallflower. I strutted my Mick Jagger impersonation while she bobbed up and down round the handbag she'd placed in front of her.

At the end of the evening we clinched loosely and kissed. Her lips were limp and her breath smelled faintly of onions, but I was elated at having got off with her.

After a few months of fumbling, we ineptly consummated our relationship on the faded leather upholstery of my father's cherished Rover 90.

As the weeks passed, our couplings became less frequent. It wasn't a surprise when, one Wednesday evening, she met me on my way home from school and told me she couldn't see me the following Friday.

'I'm washing my hair,' she said, leaning against the bus stop.

'You washed it last night. You never do it more than once a week.'

She curled a long strand of it around her forefinger and shuffled her feet.

‘I’m seeing Ronald on Friday.’

‘What, Carrot-Top, the greengrocer’s boy?’ I’d had to endure Ronald and his gang’s insults again as I’d scurried past them at the station the previous week. ‘What can you possibly see in him?’

‘His hair’s auburn and he’s much more romantic than you. And he’s got a steady job. He knows all about vegetables.’

‘I’m sure you two will be very happy together then.’

I wasn’t sorry to be splitting up with Erica; what irked me was that she had chosen that thug. Still, I was determined not to let her see my annoyance so I gave her a broad smile, a farewell peck on the cheek and consoled myself by conjuring up images of the gingery and freckled offspring their union might generate.

Three brief and desultory relationships with other girls followed before I concluded that a few moments physical pleasure snatched in a sea front shelter or, if you were lucky, in a beach hut among the deckchairs, deflated rubber rings and furled up wind breaks, wasn’t worth the bother.

A life of celibacy beckoned.

Chapter 5
MRS BEART, SUMMER, 1969

My parents let slip the scandalous news that Mrs Beart had moved into a house in Earl's Court with her rich developer friend though, as I found out when I answered an advertisement in the newsagent's, she'd kept her ground floor flat in Feston. Shortly afterwards, arguing that it was the only job available, I overcame my father's objections and became her weekly gardener.

Though my brief was to cut the grass and keep things tidy, I couldn't help imagining how beautiful her garden could be, and how sensuously she would stroll through it, her dark hair streaming behind her and her skirt billowing in the fresh sea breeze.

So, after a lot of thought, I drew up a planting plan, costed it, and slipped my proposal through her letter box.

Her reply, enclosing a cheque, arrived in the post

three days later saying, 'Much appreciated, please go ahead', followed by an illegible signature.

I chose and bedded in the plants carefully. The garden would have white, blue and purple flowers continuously from Spring to Autumn. The bees would love it and I hoped she would too.

I saw her rarely. But, one Saturday morning as I trundled my lawn mower through the side gate, I caught sight of her huddled on a bench under the old pear tree, crying. I was on the point of withdrawing when she looked up and wiped her eyes with her sleeve. I mumbled something incoherent and she nodded as though she'd understood.

As I approached her, through the streaks of mascara I could make out the contours of a livid bruise on the side of her face. She didn't meet my gaze.

'I walked into a door.'

It was my turn to nod. She looked so delicate and tremulous I wanted to put my arm around her. Instead, we went inside and she offered me a cup of tea and told me John had won a maths prize at Beauhampton College, the well-known minor public school he attended.

Each week as I negotiated the side gate with the mower, I hoped to catch another glimpse of her. In all, I only saw her another half a dozen times while I was still her gardener. On the last occasion, her face was plastered with thick make-up, presumably to mask another injury. My heart was pumping so hard it pounded in my ears.

'What, I mean who...?'

Mrs Beart gazed at me, mesmerising me with her deep violet eyes so that the words tangled in my brain and I couldn't finish the question. She placed her hand on my arm.

'Nothing to concern yourself about, my dear. Would you like a cup of tea?'

★

Meanwhile, despite all expectations to the contrary, my academic career at Dean Court had taken off, at least relative to the other students. I was one of the few to pass as many as five O-levels and when I finally scraped two A-levels, my achievements were cause for celebration among the incredulous staff. The headmaster exhorted me to apply to university.

I pleaded with my parents to let me study horticulture. My father was adamant no son of his was going to end up as a 'labourer,' and my mother added, 'Working outside can't be very nice in the winter and, besides, if you get a good job, you can always buy a house with a lovely garden of your own.'

'I want to be the next Capability Brown,' I said.

My father snorted so vigorously that flecks of his catarrh speckled my sleeve.

'It's accountancy for you, and as you're so bloody clueless, I'm going to arrange it.'

I would have persevered had my mother not whispered, 'Please don't upset him or he'll get in a mood.'

Two days later my father announced he'd got me an interview in a local firm whose principal he knew through Rotary; all I had to do was avoid saying something stupid and the job would be mine.

After helping my mother with the washing up that evening, I was about to enjoy my new Cream album, *Wheels of Fire,* when my father thrust four days' copies of *The Financial Times* into my hands.

'You're virtually business illiterate. Read these.'

'But Dad—'

'Haven't got time to argue. Just do it.' He hurried towards the front door.

'I'll get onto it right away, Dad.' I marched upstairs, stuffed the newspapers into my wastepaper bin, opened my window and put my favourite single, *I Feel Free,* on at full volume instead. Then I peered out. My father, a stickler for punctuality, was dithering on the front path, torn between turning back and being on time for his Rotary meeting. I was relishing the sight until memories of Philip's fights with my father strong-armed their way into my mind. In the last of them, my brother had ended up in hospital with a broken jaw and had left home shortly afterwards. I took the single off the turntable and retrieved the newspapers.

Seconds later, I heard my father slam the gate shut behind him so I put the LP on – at much lower volume – and stretched out on my bed, immersing myself in Clapton, Bruce and Baker's virtuosity while I half-heartedly scanned the papers for something to comment on if asked.

I sent Mrs Beart a resignation note and started work with Kitson and Co. To my delight, I received a reply saying she expected to be around more at weekends and inviting me to drop in any Saturday morning.

Though I took her up on her offer more often than she might have expected, the welcome I received was always warm, if disappointingly maternal. She fed me tea and digestive biscuits, quizzing me about my plans and inflicting news of John's achievements on me, while I sat entranced by her grace and suppleness and intoxicated by her alluring fragrance. I yearned to know all about her; she evaded every question.

Chapter 6
KITSON & CO, 1970-1975

Time passed and I progressed slowly through the Institute's exams, suffering the ignominy of several retakes, until all my faith in their integrity was shattered when I passed the final one and qualified. I was now an accountant.

'I didn't think you'd do it.' My father took the Institute's letter from my hand. 'Wonders will never cease.'

But instead of congratulating me he buried himself in his newspaper, grunting every time he took exception to something in the leader column.

'Well done, dear.' My mother pointed the teapot at my empty cup. 'Have another cupper to celebrate.'

Celebrate! The word reverberated in my brain. I should be going out with my friends and getting drunk, except I didn't have any real friends now. Neil was away at university and I didn't particularly like anyone at work, except Ruth, who was always good for a laugh.

*

I'd probably still be at Kitson & Co now, if it hadn't been for Ruth.

I knew it was a mistake to become involved with the senior partner's secretary. A plump woman with full, creamy thighs and pendulous breasts, she had a penchant for wearing crimson lipstick and deep violet eye-shadow. She wasn't my type at all, but when unprompted, after a drink-sodden Christmas dinner, she stripped off and spread herself naked across her boss's large mahogany desk, inviting me to have her there and then, the prospect of sex and the irreverence of the location proved an irresistible combination.

It was Ruth who had suggested, with a broad wink, I walk back to the office with her to pick up some things she'd left behind. The building had been in darkness so it was quite a surprise, as I buried myself in Ruth's ample body, to hear Millicent's voice behind me. Millicent, a hard-bitten workaholic famed for her lack of humour and her unforgiving nature, was the firm's number two.

'What the dickens do you think you're doing?'

Even to my drink-befuddled mind, the language seemed archaic and the question fatuous. The two of us froze. I craned my neck to look at Millicent.

Seconds passed as I struggled to formulate an answer. Ruth started to giggle, like a spoilt child caught raiding the larder for chocolate biscuits. I shrugged my shoulders and turned my face back towards Ruth who was now jiggling around mountainously under me, convulsing with laughter. Thinking I might as well be hanged for a sheep as for a lamb, I resumed where I'd left off. Ruth's laughter became uproarious.

Millicent stormed out of the room slamming the door, and I knew my career at Kitson's had come to an end.

'She's bound to tell old Kitters,' I said as Ruth wriggled into her dress and I rearranged my dishevelled clothing. 'I hope you don't get into trouble.'

'Don't worry about me honey. If this desk could talk! I've got the goods on him and she knows it. I'm fire-proof.'

The next morning, I was summoned to Millicent's wood-panelled office with its odour of stale cigarette smoke. As I knocked and entered, my life became dream-like. Strangely disembodied, I watched the scene from the corner of the room.

From a near-empty silver cigarette box she took out and lit a Black Sobranie.

'Well,' she inhaled deeply, 'What have you got to say for yourself?'

The person wearing my suit apparently didn't have anything to say.

'Disgraceful behaviour, absolutely disgusting. It makes me sick to think about it.'

Silence, except for the heavy tick of the grandfather clock.

'Well?'

The office seemed to be coming to life slowly; far-off voices somewhere else in the building, a telephone ringing, a door slamming, a faint smell of coffee, the distant hum of the photocopier. Ruth must be carrying on with her work as usual. I wondered whether she had a hangover too.

'Have you nothing to say for yourself?'

No response. A shuffling sound in the corridor outside was followed by a knock on the door.

'Go away, I'm busy,' she shouted. The sound of footsteps retreated.

She drew heavily on her cigarette and looked down at some papers in front of her, as though they were relevant to the proceedings.

'I've decided against reporting this outrageous incident to Mr Kitson.' She exhaled a cloud of smoke. 'Let me have your resignation letter by lunch-time.'

'Will you give me a reference?'

Millicent stubbed the cigarette out in her overflowing ashtray. 'You'll get the reference you deserve.'

'You'll mention how well I got on with fellow workers then?'

'Get out!' she bellowed.

When it came to it, it was Mr Kitson who wrote the reference. I presumed Millicent hadn't been able to bring herself to describe what she'd witnessed and, ignorant of the recreational uses to which his office furniture had been put, Mr Kitson had no reason to qualify his comments.

★

My father was outraged. He couldn't believe I'd resigned without having another job lined up. I tried to bluff my way through by saying the firm lacked ambition.

He stared in disbelief.

'The only person who lacks ambition is you, you dunderhead. Don't expect me to support you while you loaf around.'

I looked to my mother, hoping for sympathy.

'It was such a nice job. You came home for lunch every day, just like your father. Now you'll probably end up working miles away, eating sandwiches and getting ulcers. Couldn't you say you've changed your mind?'

★

The months passed slowly as I made a succession of unsuccessful job applications. I spent most of my days working in the garden, receiving no thanks from my father and only simmering resentment from his gardener, who couldn't tell a hollyhock from a foxglove, and who had dug up my mother's freshly planted herbs under the impression they were weeds. In the evenings, with no money in my pocket I was reduced to sitting in one of the sea front shelters or, as summer replaced spring, wandering around the Civic Gardens, glumly inspecting the neat rows of begonias and busy lizzies and thinking how unimaginatively they'd been laid out. I'd stay out until past my parents' bed time when I knew it would be safe to return home.

Before turning off the light, I would flick through gardening magazines, often staying awake until the early hours, imagining the luxuriant gardens I could create. One night, around midnight, my father burst into my bedroom.

'What filth have you got there?' He wrenched *Amateur Gardening* from my grasp, then, with a look combining surprise and disappointment, let it drop to the floor.

'Don't make me spill my seeds, Dad,' I said, pointing to a free sample packet attached to the front cover. 'It did Onan no good at all.'

He glared at me and left without a further word.

★

I would slope off to Mrs Beart's flat most Saturday mornings – whenever I knew John wouldn't be there – and we would sit and drink tea and eat biscuits in her lounge, gossiping about the neighbours. Occasionally she would regale me with John's increasing academic and sporting successes.

'John's always been fond of animals,' she said one day. 'Only last week he saved a cat from drowning in the school swimming pool.'

It was all I could do to refrain from saying he'd probably thrown it in first.

'How's the job hunting going?' she would invariably ask, and I would shake my head until the day when, with a flourish and a bow, I announced a job offer from a City accountancy firm.

'Are you sure it's what you want?' Her voice was laden with concern. 'I've never seen you as an accountant. And after your last experience...'

I had told no one the reasons for my leaving Kitson's, and searched her face for a knowing look. It remained expressionless.

'Got to make a living somehow,' I sighed.

'Doesn't mean you shouldn't be true to yourself. Do you enjoy accountancy?'

All I could manage was a wry expression.

'Just make sure you don't spend your life doing something you hate.'

I wondered whether she was speaking from personal experience.

My father's reaction was rather different.

'At last! I thought you were never going to work again.' He stared me in the eye. 'Don't make a mess of it this time. Bone up on the finance sector and make sure you're fully prepared. I don't want you getting sacked again.'

'I told you Dad, I wasn't—'

'Pish!' he interjected. 'You didn't fool me.'

'Don't worry, Dad, I'll be well prepared.' And I meant it, though, in fact, I did nothing.

★

'Changed your mind about the new job yet?'

Mrs Beart, encased in a blue cashmere dress which accentuated the swell of her breasts, was standing outside the newsagent's holding a copy of *The Financial Times*.

'I'm a tad apprehensive.' I struggled to raise my eyes and focus on her face. 'And the commuting will be hell.'

'If you're absolutely determined, there are some consolations. At least you'll get away from this place.' She looked up the near-deserted street, wreathed in a sea mist. 'You might even get to like life in London. It can be quite exciting.'

I glanced down at the newspaper under her bare arm.

'About to invest in something?'

She shook her head. 'John's here this weekend. He's set on becoming financially savvy. Says it's a must in business. Reckons he's done pretty well out of it already.'

I could imagine the precocious John pontificating on share prices and boasting about investments; he'd be unbearable.

'I'm sure he'd like to see you, if you have time to drop in.'

I very much doubted it. The last time I'd seen Beart, Neil and I had been responsible for getting him caned. In our role as prefects we had uncovered his insurance scam, in which he would collect thruppence a week as a premium from every boy in his class and pay out a shilling for a detention and half a crown for a beating. I still remember his swearing he would get even with us, whatever it took, as he slunk into the headmaster's office.

'Bit busy,' I replied, dragging my gaze away from her entrancing violet eyes and directing it at the rack of periodicals by the shop's door. Colin Bell, wearing an England shirt, stared down at me from the front page of *Football Monthly*.

'Another time perhaps. Good luck then.' She stood on tiptoes to kiss my cheek and a shiver ran down my spine.

Chapter 7
LONDON, 1976

I wasn't short of agreeable company at Andrews Postlethwaite or AP, as it was known. At lunch-time, we'd go out and spend our fifteen pence luncheon vouchers on a desiccated sandwich from the small, unhygienic café run by a former Italian prisoner of war on the corner of the street. Sitting on wooden benches worn smooth by be-suited city bottoms, and breathing in the lingering smells of cooked meats and cigar smoke, we'd make fun of our managers, our clients and each other, and plan the evening's entertainment.

As my work-based social life took off, I frequently missed the last train home and found myself sleeping on the floor of an Earl's Court flat rented by Richard, another AP new hire. One morning, he drawled across the kitchen table, 'You spend so much time here, you ought to be paying rent. Ian's moving out next month. Want to move in?'

I accepted immediately.

★

'There is a God,' my father said.

'Will you be all right on your own, dear?' my mother asked. 'Who'll do your washing and ironing, and sew on your buttons?'

'You will, Mum. I'm going to bring everything home for you every fortnight.' Her face fell at my joke.

Richard and I had a lot in common, both regarding the office as a place of rest between hectic late nights at parties, wine bars or Jemima's, a club in Kensington where the disc jockey sat in a Jaguar XK140 suspended from the ceiling. Fortunately, work was never too demanding. Our supervisors were only slightly older and as bent on enjoying themselves, and the managers so old they had no clue.

We'd normally go to Jemima's after midnight when it started buzzing. One evening when I was there much earlier, I saw Neil accompanied by a tall slender girl with long dark brown hair. I knew he'd gone to Leeds University, although I didn't know what he'd done since. I walked over to them and Neil introduced me proudly to his girlfriend Samantha. Talk about coals to Newcastle. No one takes a girlfriend to Jemima's, the whole point being to pick a girl up and get her out before someone richer or better looking relieved you of her. Neil must be a real innocent. Samantha, on the other hand, with her lustrously piercing brown eyes, uneven smile and slightly chipped front tooth had a wickedly knowing look. Within minutes she'd placed her hand softly on my arm, leaning very close to me to speak, above the thrumming of the music, into my ear. I could feel her hazelnut-scented breath forming goose bumps on my neck, and had she not been with Neil, I could easily have fallen for her. However, I knew that once the cool operators came in, they'd flash their Rolexes and prise her away from him with talk of their Lotuses and Ferraris and that would be that. For old-times' sake, I wanted to look after him.

'Why don't we go somewhere quiet for a drink and a chat, and maybe come back later when it's livelier?' I mouthed my words deliberately at Neil. 'They allow re-entry if they stamp your hand.'

Neil gave a thumbs up. The effort of trying to make himself heard above the music was so great it was a relief to have an excuse to leave.

We went to a nearby wine bar. A small man with a tufty beard was singing Dylan songs in a thin, reedy voice and accompanying himself on the guitar.

Samantha looked even more desirable and I ached to reach out and place my hand on her smooth, golden brown arm. I restrained myself; she was Neil's girlfriend. That was part of the code by which I lived now. Different from the schoolboy code, but just as pervasive.

'How did you two meet?' Although I addressed the question to them both, I looked only at Samantha.

'I'm Neil's assistant.' Samantha smiled in a coquettish way. Blimey, I thought, he's podging his secretary.

'Who do you work for?'

'It's called Bed Sheets.' She breathed the words heavily.

Neil chipped in, his tone clipped. I imagined he'd been practising what he thought a thrusting business executive would sound like.

'Something I started; fantastic potential. Selling space in free news sheets, delivered to all the top hotels in London to place in their bedrooms. Next year we start in Manchester, the year after Leeds. A little gold-mine. Best of all, no competition.'

I glanced at Samantha. She was staring into the middle distance.

'What's more—' Neil said.

'Popping to the loo.' Samantha stood up.

'How long have you known her?' I asked Neil, my eyes lingering on her departing figure.

'Eight days.'

'Isn't screwing the staff a bit of a problem?' I said, trying to find a rationale to cloak my jealousy. 'Doesn't it piss the others off?'

'There aren't any others. Besides, it keeps the cost

down. I provide board and lodging, so I don't have to pay her as much.'

'Quite the hard-headed businessman,' I said, wondering who was really being screwed. Over Neil's shoulder, I could see her laughing and tossing her hair as she talked to the two men in shiny suits who had intercepted her on her way to the toilet.

His expression changed. 'Not really. In fact, I think I'm in love.'

I swallowed hard. Even I knew that Samantha was not a girl to love. She was a girl to have a good time with, to enjoy, to relish and to lose. I wondered whether to warn him, but one look at that bedazzled expression told me there was no point, and we lapsed into an uncomfortable silence which lasted until Samantha sashayed her way back to our table. As though a switch had been thrown, Neil started back into life.

'You'll never guess who I'm in contact with again.' He didn't pause for an answer. 'John Beart. He's an entrepreneur now. In fact, if it hadn't been for him, I wouldn't have been able to get my business off the ground. He paid in advance for a load of advertising. By strange coincidence, he's looking for an accountant to do some work for him. I ought to get the two of you together.'

'No thanks.'

'He's changed completely, you know. You wouldn't recognise him. He owns a posh flat and drives a flash car.'

‘So I heard.’

‘Are you still in touch with him?’

‘Just local gossip.’

I didn’t want to continue the discussion. The mention of his name conjured up the image of his mother in a kimono and brought back some recent memories which had left me in turmoil.

I emerged from my thoughts to find Neil staring at me. For a moment, feeling rather shaky, I wasn’t too sure where I was. Neil had obviously asked me a question and was awaiting an answer. I’d no idea what it was and, in my confusion, said ‘yes’, and gulped a mouthful of scotch, its rough warmth scorching my throat.

After more drinks, we exchanged telephone numbers and I made my way back to Jemima’s.

⋆

I lay awake all that night, my thoughts filled with Mrs Beart.

Following my mother’s relentless badgering, I’d paid a visit to my parents in Feston. Their house had all the charm of an old folks’ home; overcooked vegetables, suffocating central heating, and a mind-numbingly loud television that was continually on. Having cajoled me into coming, all they did was gaze at the box in the corner while he drank whisky and she played with a small sherry. There came a point on

Saturday evening when I couldn't take a second more of Bruce Forsyth and his woeful *Generation Game.*

Saying I wanted to stretch my legs, I strolled down towards the sea front, the road taking me past Mrs Beart's maisonette. As I drew near, I saw the light was on and peered through the brightly-lit window. I was in the shadows when Mrs Beart appeared at the door and threw something into the bushes. She ran back into the front room, where a familiar looking man pushed her onto the sofa. She fell with a shrill scream, then leapt to her feet, yelling abuse. She hurled herself at him, her flailing fists making no impression on his ox-like frame. He pushed her down again, this time even more roughly, stormed out of the room, barged through the front door, which he left open, and jumped into a black Mercedes parked opposite. A few seconds later he was roaring down the road, leaving a grey-blue cloud of exhaust vapour hanging in the night air. I was transfixed by the sight of Mrs Beart lying face down on the sofa, her shoulders heaving. Drawing a deep breath, I tapped on the front door and went in.

'Are you all right?'

Mrs Beart raised her head, her face wet with tears and her make-up smudged.

'Oh, it's you,' she said, curling up into the foetal position, and closing her eyes.

I dithered in the doorway.

'Can I make you cup of tea?' While it seemed

a feeble suggestion, even to me, to my surprise she nodded. I righted the standard lamp and tiptoed into the kitchen to put the kettle on.

When I returned a few minutes later, she was sitting up.

'Draw the curtains.'

I perched on the arm of the sofa as we drank our cups of tea. I could sense her steadying herself and trying to control her breathing.

'What did you see?'

I told her.

'He's a brute. I can't take any more of his violence, or his lying, or his womanising. We're through, finished—'

'How long has it been going on?'

'Years.' Her voice was dull and flat. 'Since the beginning really. I've always forgiven him before. Not this time. Enough is enough.' She reached under the sofa and pulled out a battered leather-bound notebook.

'It's all in here. I've always kept a diary, ever since I was a little girl.' She gulped loudly as she let it fall open to reveal pages crammed with spidery handwriting.

'Why did you put up with it?'

'John.'

'John made you stay with him?'

'No, of course not! He paid John's school fees, then he took him into his firm. Very generous, he was. I couldn't afford to upset him, so I put up with it, till now.'

Mrs Beart turned away from me and started to sob. I slid onto the sofa and put my arm around her. As her warm body sank against mine, her head turned towards me, our lips met, then our tongues, and we started caressing each other.

★

After making love, we lay curled up and I felt as though we were floating. I nuzzled her neck and breathed in her scent. It reminded me of sweet almonds with the faintest hint of something muskier in the background.

She stroked my hair and kissed my chest.

'I've always had a bit of a soft spot for you, you know. I never guessed we'd end up like this though. It's rather Lady Chatterley, isn't it?'

I looked hard into her deep violet eyes.

'I've always been in love with you.'

'Silly boy! What nonsense.'

I told her about the portrait, about my crush on her, how I'd wanted to hold her tight and protect her when I'd seen her battered face. She pulled me gently towards her.

'You darling, you're so sweet.' We kissed and I felt a thickening in my loins which gave way to a sudden sense of panic.

'Shit, my parents' supper!'

Mrs Beart stared at me.

'They'll be waiting for me to get back to eat their soused herrings.' I looked at my watch. 'I've been gone for hours. My father will go ballistic.'

I struggled into my clothes. Mrs Beart, barefoot and in her pale green kimono, came to the front door with me. I kissed her on the lips and, despite a surge of desire, pulled myself away. I looked back when I was at the gate. She waved, a delicate half-circling of her fine-boned wrist, and I forced a smile.

'See you tomorrow,' I shouted as I broke into a jog. I tried to rationalise my actions as I pounded home. However hard I tried, I couldn't quell the queasy feeling I'd acted like a prat and all through fear of my father. Those memories of my brother's heated arguments with my father came back to me; Philip's face livid with bruises, his nose parallel with his cheek and streaming with blood, one eye blackened and rapidly swelling, my father standing at the top of the stairs and yelling at him, my mother and I huddling together in the lounge. After many indignities, my brother had finally braved the no-holds-barred showdown which had ended with him first in Accident and Emergency and then homeless.

I clenched my fists, determined to be as courageous yet, at the same time, avoid a brawl.

As soon as my key entered the lock my father was at the front door, the smell of whisky heavy on his breath.

'Where the hell have you been?'

'Out for a walk.'

'You liar! Tell me the truth.'

My mother cowered in the sitting-room doorway.

'You're drunk.' I said, straightening up. 'Still, if you really must know, I've been with Mrs Beart.'

He slapped me hard across the right cheek. I breathed deeply, willing him not to strike me again.

'That harlot? What have you been doing there?' He pushed his chest up against mine. I was taller but he was much stockier. The veins in his face were purple and there were wisps of iron-grey hair on his cheeks. Even though my arms and legs were trembling, I stood my ground. I spoke slowly, trying to keep my voice low and calm.

'I've been working out a planting plan for her. I've got to go back there tomorrow to finish off the details.'

'You'll do no such thing. I'm not having my son hanging around with that trollop.' He took half a step back, his face puce and a globule of spit lodged in the corner of his mouth. 'In any case, tomorrow we're going to see Aunt Winifred in Glospool.' He stubbed his finger into my chest. 'You included.'

'I'm not coming.' My voice wavered and I took a deep breath to steady myself. 'I'm not a kid any more. You can't order me around. I'll do what I want.'

'We'll see about that.' My father turned on his heel.

My mother waited until he'd disappeared, then grabbed my sleeve. 'I've saved your supper for you.' She looked shaken.

'I'm not hungry,' I said, beset by a wave of nausea.

'Please come with us tomorrow, dear. He'll be unbearable if you don't.' Her grip on my arm tightened. 'He'll only take it out on me. You know what he's like.'

I didn't like being reminded that I'd been complicit in appeasing my father over the years, swallowing hard and trying to placate him when he picked on me and looking the other way when he vented his anger on my brother. What made me most angry, though not quite enough to prompt me to intervene, was seeing my father bully my mother. I'd never seen him hit her but I had witnessed him putting her down at every opportunity, belittling her views and criticising her if anything went amiss, whether it was her fault or not.

I looked around for some means of escape. I even thought of bolting back to Mrs Beart's and asking to spend the night there, and might have done so had my mother not still been holding tightly onto me, a lifetime's worrying etched into her forehead.

'Please dear, please, just for me.'

I felt her tremble as my father emerged from the kitchen and stomped upstairs without saying a word to either of us. A tear had formed in the corner of her eye. I couldn't bear it if she cried.

'Well, I suppose I could come for a while.' I pictured my dotty aunt and my spirits sank. Spending any time with her was an ordeal.

'Thank you, dear.' My mother's eyes were misty with relief.

*

Aunt Winifred was in a care home, twenty-five miles away. My father normally set off as early as possible. That day he seemed content to dawdle. He leafed through the *Sunday Telegraph* over breakfast, reading out articles supporting his contention that economic failure under the Labour Government was inevitable. He chuckled as he predicted widespread civil unrest, followed by an intervention by the army to restore order. Then he went outside, where he checked the car's oil level and topped up the radiator while engaging in a lengthy conversation with the retired estate agent next door. Sauntering back, he paused to pluck out a few dandelions from the cracks between the crazy paving on the front drive. My mother busied herself cleaning the already gleaming surfaces in the kitchen, while I perched on the edge of a chair in the sitting-room, scanning the sports pages and glancing at the clock every few minutes.

We finally left at 11.30, taking the meandering route through the lanes instead of the A road. We arrived just as the staff were serving lunch and were asked to come back at 2. My father drove us to a nondescript Victorian pub where we ate translucent slices of roast lamb smeared with grey gravy and surrounded by soggy vegetables. He drank three pints of bitter in quick succession while I nursed a half-pint and my mother sipped a sweet sherry. We left for the care home shortly after 2.30.

Aunt Winifred didn't recognise any of us. She'd been a nurse in the blitz and was busy reliving her experiences.

'You work on this one doctor, I'll bandage the little girl,' she barked, leaping from her chair and darting around the room, mumbling incoherently and shaking her head.

We lasted a couple of hours until the non-sequiturs, stultifying heat and smell of stale urine drove us out. There would just be time to get to Mrs Beart's if we left now.

'I think your mother deserves a cream tea, don't you?' My father brought the car to a halt outside a small café.

'Well, actually—'

My mother interrupted.

'What a treat!'

I dug my hands deep into the pockets of my jacket. Sometimes my mother's passivity angered me almost as much as my father's bullying.

The café was full of fat contented cats sprawling across most of the chairs. When, braving my cat allergy, I tried to move a warm bean-bag of a ginger tom so the three of us could sit down, the other customers stared and muttered their disapproval. The service was excruciatingly slow and it took half an hour for our order to be taken.

'Please don't do that dear, you're making the table shake,' my mother said, glancing down at my feet.

'Typical,' my father said. 'No consideration for others.'

I felt my body tense as I stifled the almost overwhelming urge to respond.

'Well, this is pleasant.' My mother looked round the teashop, her gaze settling on a row of Toby Jugs. 'I do like that one on the end, the one with the blue hat. So much character, so colourful.' She started humming softly to herself and stared into the middle distance. A few moments passed. I counted the number of people who were still waiting for their food, and noticed that at least one couple had come in after us and had been served already. My mother looked at me again.

'Please don't do that either dear. It puts me on edge.' She stared at my fingers, which were drumming lightly on the table. I slid my hands into my lap. My father glowered. Usually it was his legs that twitched or his fingers that drummed. Of course, she didn't complain then.

The owners, a brother and sister in their late sixties, continually brought the wrong dishes to everyone. I'd ordered a toasted teacake. A muffin arrived instead. I saw from the grandfather clock in the corner that we'd been waiting for our food for half an hour already, so I reckoned it best to accept it. My father thought otherwise and testily rejected the hot buttered scones brought to him in place of crumpets. The result was confusion and another twenty minutes' wait.

When the bill arrived, it was wrong by a few pence. My father insisted on its being corrected, citing the error as his reason for not leaving a tip. My mother and I started to sidle towards the door.

'Hold on.' My father nodded in the direction of the toilet. We shuffled back to our chairs and waited for him.

It was getting dark when we finally left, and we set off down a road I didn't recognise. We were surrounded by fields when the car started juddering. My father and I got out. The front right tyre was punctured and the spare was flat. I trudged back to the teashop to phone for help. It had closed. The village shop was also in darkness. The public phone box nearby wasn't working and the pub didn't open until 7 o'clock, so we had to wait.

When the pub opened, I phoned the AA and I tried to obtain Mrs Beart's number from the operator only to find she was ex-directory. My parents came into the pub. I couldn't face spending any more time with them so I went back to the car and sat on the back seat picking out, with my index finger, the faint brown stain left by Erica's virginal blood all those years before. Becoming involved with Mrs Beart might be crazy, but it was better than settling down with someone like Erica. I shuddered. Erica had bored me, and I'd irritated her; we would probably have frittered our lives away watching television and barely speaking to each other, just like my parents.

★

'You should always check your spare tyre when you do the others,' the AA man said, a disapproving tone in his voice. 'The number of avoidable calls we receive; all most cars need is regular care and attention.'

'I'll get my father,' I replied, 'So you can tell him yourself.' I went to the pub where my parents were sitting in silence.

'Quite right,' my father said on hearing the lecture himself. 'A regrettable oversight on my part; pressure of work and all that, you know how it is.' He slipped the AA man a folded pound note.

'Quite understandable, sir. Perhaps you could delegate some of these routine tasks.' He looked at me. I stared coldly back at him, and then at my father, whose obsequious smile had broadened into a self-satisfied beam. We got back into the car, my mother humming hymns softly to herself.

We finally arrived back at Feston at 9 o'clock and the last train left at 9.20. I raced in and packed a bag. My father drove me to the station and I made the train by thirty seconds. As I slumped against my seat, sweating heavily, I was acutely conscious I'd failed Mrs Beart. I imagined her looking out of the window, and then at the clock, and then sighing as the evening drew on and she realised the likelihood of my arrival was receding. Troublingly, these thoughts were interspersed with others in which she compared me unfavourably with previous lovers or, even worse, reprimanded herself for a foolish error of judgment which she would never repeat. And then I'd made a complete fool of myself with my unseemly exit. Why hadn't I ignored my parents for once and done what I wanted? An image of my mother's careworn face insinuated itself into my thoughts, and I struggled to rid myself of it.

When I got home, I wrote Mrs Beart a letter. It sounded dreadful, so I tore it up and wrote another, then another. I determined to wait until the next day. I tried one more time that Monday. The wording was still trite and sentimental, and I screwed it up and threw it away in frustration.

The longer I procrastinated, the more difficult the letter became to write until, finally, after half a bottle of scotch I scrawled something full of maudlin platitudes, stuffed it into an envelope and left it by the flat's front door so I wouldn't forget to post it.

The next morning, beset by waves of nausea, I decided to tear it up.

It was gone.

That evening Richard told me he'd posted it along with some of his own.

'God, Richard, I wish you hadn't.'

He looked puzzled.

'Thought I was doing you a favour. Who's Mrs Bart anyway?'''

'Woman I used to garden for. She wanted my

advice, and now I've given her some duff info.' Richard knew little of my life in Feston and nothing about Mrs Beart, and I wanted to keep it that way.

He looked at me closely. 'Everybody makes mistakes. Just pop another one in the post correcting what you've told her. I doubt she'll dig up the delphiniums before your second letter arrives.'

Phrases in the letter continued to haunt me for the next few days, and I prayed to a deity I no longer believed in to turn the mawkish drivel I'd written into something eloquent and noble.

The longer I didn't hear from Mrs Beart, the more convinced I was that I'd offended her or made myself appear ridiculous or, more likely, both.

Despite my mother's repeated invitations, I decided to keep away from Feston. I couldn't summon up the courage to visit Mrs Beart, and I'd no wish to see my parents. However, Mrs Beart continued to infiltrate my thoughts, often at the most inconvenient times.

My resolve was weakening when, one night, in a routine telephone conversation with my mother, she mentioned, in a scandalised voice, how Mrs Beart had taken up with a boy half her age. My father had seen them walking hand in hand along the Feston sea front. I asked who it was but all she could tell me was he had ginger hair.

I cursed myself. That could have been me, if only....

My heart filled with a mixture of self-loathing and jealous anger and I vowed never to see or speak to her again.

Chapter 8
REUNION WITH JOHN BEART, 1976

The noise of the telephone made me start. I opened my eyes and looked around. I'd been pretending to scrutinise a complex document for half an hour. It had been a good party the previous evening, although I'd drunk too much for a Tuesday and was paying the price.

'All arranged.' It was Neil's clipped tones.

'What's arranged?' His affected manner of speaking was beginning to irritate me.

'The meeting with John tonight.'

'John?'

'Don't piss around, mate,' Neil said. 'You agreed to meet him today. We talked about it in the wine bar. I'll be round yours about seven and we'll go together.'

'Where are we going?'

'Langhorne's.'

I inhaled sharply. 'Bit pricey, isn't it?' At my last meeting with my bank manager, the ugly topic of my overdraft had spoiled what otherwise would have been a reasonable cup of machine-vended coffee. 'Can't we go somewhere cheaper?'

'Don't worry, old son. He said he'd pick up the tab.'

Neil arrived at my flat that evening in his gold Ford Capri, accompanied by Samantha, swathed in a skin-tight bottle-green dress, cut low to expose her deep cleavage. I squeezed into the small back seat, and we set off for the West End, cutting back and forth between lanes and pushing in front of more cautious drivers. Neil's most daring manoeuvres were accompanied by a cacophony of car horns and expletives hurled in our direction through open car windows. Samantha, seemingly oblivious to the commotion, chatted away with Neil while I sank down into my seat, trying to ignore the imprecations and threats. We arrived at Langhorne's exactly on time and as we were getting out of our car, a red Ferrari Dino Coupe pulled up alongside and a head I didn't recognise poked out of its window.

'Hi Neil! Good timing! Let me get parked, and we can go in together.'

John's once chubby cheeks were now firm and peppered with blue-black stubble and his light brown hair had darkened. He approached, his movements sinuous and supple, and I realised he was now a good few inches taller than me.

He looked at me briefly as we shook hands.

'Long time no see.' He loosened his grip, then took hold of Samantha's hand, standing very close to her and fixing her with his eyes, which were the same shade of violet as his mother's. His handshake with Samantha lasted a moment or two longer than necessary. Neil beamed, apparently pleased his girlfriend was making such a good impression.

John ushered us into the restaurant and indicated, with a wave of the hand, where each of us should sit. I had the unnerving feeling of being with someone more mature and decidedly more urbane than I was.

The waiter came over and John ordered a double Southern Comfort on the rocks. I only ever drank the cheapest whisky, but I was intent on not appearing unsophisticated. I recalled my mother drinking gin and Dubonnet one Christmas and being considered very daring by her sisters, so without knowing what it tasted like, I ordered one.

John's limpid eyes fixed mine. 'I thought only Parisian tarts drank that,' he said with no hint of a smile.

Feeling myself start to blush, I recovered sufficiently to say, 'That's where I picked up the habit,' in a way I hoped would sound very worldly.

'My favourite city, Paris,' John said. 'Especially the George the Fifth. Such Art Deco luxury. I often take a suite there.'

Was he bullshitting? His expression gave nothing

away. I silently cursed him, and my ignorance of Paris, hoping he'd say something more obviously gauche so I could put him in his place.

The three of us pored over our menus. John left his unopened while he sipped his drink and gazed around at the diners at other tables, nodding at a few he recognised.

I was sure I could discern the trace of a smug smile playing around the corners of his mouth and guessed he was setting himself up to appear a regular there. I decided to say nothing.

'Aren't you eating, John?' Neil enquired, confirming my view that he was an innocent.

'I'll have my usual,' John replied in a self-satisfied tone.

I asked him what he'd been doing since school, and he told me he was in property development.

'Didn't you fancy university?' Neil asked.

'University is for mugs,' John replied. 'Why waste three years hanging out with half-stoned layabouts when you could be making your fortune?'

'There are stacks of parties at university, man, and loads of birds,' Neil said. The idiot must have forgotten for a moment he was with Samantha.

John peered at him.

'There are much better parties and more attractive women when you live in a penthouse and drive a Ferrari, believe me.'

I glanced at Samantha to see how she would

respond. She looked down at her menu and said nothing.

While Neil and Samantha were debating whether to share the Chateaubriand, John leant across the table and, in a low voice said, 'I hear you saw my mother recently.'

I felt the colour rise to my cheeks again, and my neck glowed with heat. What had she said to him?

'Yes, I did drop in on her,' I mumbled, trying to avoid his eye.

'She's had a very rough time, you know. Still she's coming through it all right. That bastard Smallwood won't be giving her any more grief.'

'Smallwood? Didn't he help you start out in—?'

'I hated him pushing her around, shouting at her, threatening her. Sometimes, he'd get really nasty and hit her.'

'Sounds horrible...'

'He won't have much of a business left now the tax people are onto his tricks.' John's face puckered. 'Could well face a spell inside.'

He took a sip of his drink.

'They raided him last week. Apparently,' he paused to emphasis the word, 'they received a tip-off a couple of weeks earlier.'

'A tip-off?' At times like these my mind seemed to take an eternity to get into gear. 'Who...?'

He smirked and I felt very stupid.

'Been planning it for a long time.' He looked down

at his fingers, which he stretched out and then flexed. 'Then when he dumped her it was time to stitch him up.'

He slammed his palm on the table making everything shake.

'By the time I've finished, they'll throw away the key.'

He leant even closer to me, his sleeve brushing my bread roll, his slightly sour breath hot on my cheek.

'No one messes with my mother and gets away with it.'

Though he sounded like a hammy actor in a second-rate film, the intensity of his stare unsettled me.

'Quite so,' I said, sitting upright to increase the distance between us. 'She's a fine woman.' An image of Mrs Beart, looking wistful, conjured itself up in my mind. Why hadn't I sought her forgiveness for that dreadful letter? I cursed myself for my cowardice. Or had my incompetence as a lover put her off? Perhaps she thought me ridiculous and was ashamed of what we'd done. Every time I thought of her, my mind went inconclusively and exhaustingly round in the same circles.

He leant back.

'Yes, she is. I owe absolutely everything to her. She taught me to stand up for myself. Once, when I was little, some bigger boys threw seaweed at me and made me cry. She told me get my own back.'

'And did you?'

A faraway look came into in his eye.

'One of them broke a tooth. The seaweed I threw had a stone tangled up in it. His father came over to complain and she told him he should teach his son not to start fights, and certainly not to whinge if he lost.'

The food arrived. My steak was smaller than I expected, and rarer. I didn't like these fashionable restaurants with their minute portions and their artistic arrangements. A rump steak should fill half the plate and be cooked through, not served still dripping with blood.

John steered the conversation around to business. He had it in mind to make a bid for a distribution company with depots in several towns and a head office in Wigan. He wanted me to look over the books and give him my assessment. I was in the process of finding excuses when he mentioned what he'd pay. I hesitated. I'd be able to clear my overdraft, buy a decent second-hand car and still have something to spare.

'How quickly would you want my report?'

'End of next week, latest.'

I thought of the parties I'd miss and the inevitable nights of hard work studying figures, an activity I disliked at the best of times. And worse still, I'd be working for him. The money, though, would solve so many problems.

'Well? Will you do it?'

Neil and Samantha stopped talking. All eyes were on me.

'All right,' I said, consoling myself that the deprivation wouldn't last long.

'Excellent!' He clapped his hands. 'Welcome aboard.'

Aboard what? I thought. I'm only doing a one-off job.

We agreed to meet at his office, and he gave me an address near St James's. I was intrigued by the opportunity to see evidence of his business empire, though I still harboured doubts as to whether he was a fantasist, and his wealth an illusion, or perhaps just an elaborate confidence trick.

I became conscious of Neil and Samantha watching us. Neil cleared his throat and raised his glass. 'A toast to your new accountant!'

I fingered the stem of mine for a moment. The others raised their glasses and I had no choice but to join in. John smiled broadly.

'Who would have thought we'd all be here together, after all these years?' he said.

Who indeed? I'd never been able to stomach him at school, and the prospect of working for him now filled me with foreboding.

Over coffee, Neil thanked John for his support for his own fledgling business, and the pair of them became engrossed in discussing the state of the advertising market.

I glanced at Samantha, who was staring intently at John, her eyes wide and her mouth slightly open.

'Penny for your thoughts?' I said.

'They're not worth a penny.'

Neil and John were plunging ever more deeply into the strengths and weaknesses of Neil's business model, the size of his potential customer base and the level of investment he'd need.

'What do you like to do in your spare time?' I asked Samantha.

'I like to go dancing.' She paused. 'And I do *The Times* crossword.'

'How long does it take you? Ten, fifteen minutes?' I'd never managed to solve more than two or three clues, and I thought she'd pick up from my tone that I'd realised she was joking.

'Often over an hour, though I get there in the end. Besides, there's not much to do in the office. Some days we don't get any post and the phone doesn't ring at all.'

She looked at Neil as though for confirmation. He was too busy explaining his gross margin forecast to notice.

'My dad used to let me help him with the one in *The Daily Telegraph*. Then I really got into them at university; I did an English degree, so I had plenty of time on my hands.'

'You went to university? Why the hell are you working with Neil? You could be on a graduate trainee scheme somewhere, ICI, Unilever, anywhere.'

'Filling in. Still haven't decided what I want to do, and Neil's newspaper is better than clerical work in some stuffy office.'

The conversation between Neil and John was tailing off. Neil's face was flushed, I didn't know whether from wine or from the passion of his sales pitch. John's was serene. He signalled for the bill. When it arrived, he left it lying on the table. Initially I suspected he wanted us to see how much it was. As it lay there, and the minutes passed, I was seized by anxiety that Neil had got it wrong, and John wasn't going to pay. Then John, barely glancing at the bill, threw a wad of notes onto the plate. You flash bugger, I thought. If it had been me, I would have checked every item.

'I trust you enjoyed the dinner.' He sat back in his chair.

'Delicious, thank you so much. Evening to remember. Fantastic restaurant,' Neil said. I smiled inwardly. He must really want John's help very badly.

'I adore this place,' Samantha said. 'And the company was great.'

John turned towards me. I paused, searching for the right words. Neil might feel the need to smarm up to him. I didn't.

'Very pleasant, thanks,' I drawled. 'Not sure it will tempt me away from my local Berni though.'

'I look forward to doing it again.' John's voice was almost a purr. 'It's been delightful meeting up with you two again.' He nodded at Neil and Samantha, then said to me more briskly, 'And a great pleasure seeing you again after all these years.'

The drive home would have been even scarier than the one there had I not been anaesthetised by large quantities of red wine. As it was, I lolled back in my seat, happily oblivious to the world land speed record that Neil was trying to set round Hyde Park Corner.

★

Analysing the business was easier than I'd expected. We had an audit client in the same field who was also struggling, and I was familiar with the market and the deficiencies in the business model they both used. It didn't take long to realise it was on the point of collapse and, if left to its own devices, would soon be dismembered by its rivals. The price being asked was disproportionately high, and I could find no redeeming features to counterbalance the many obvious negatives. As I didn't know anyone who could type proficiently, I wrote my report out in longhand, and looked forward to collecting my reward, which I'd been assured would be paid in untraceable cash.

★

A few days later I arrived at the address John had given me and was relieved to find that instead of being some luxuriously appointed modern office, it was only a few rooms squeezed uncomfortably into half the top floor of a dilapidated building in a neglected cul-de-sac. The ancient lift looked and sounded as though it could collapse at any stage as it wheezed its way slowly upwards.

When the door opened, I was met by a woman dressed in a navy suit and with her hair swept up into a neat bun.

'Samantha! What are you doing here?'

'I work for John now. It's nice to see you again.' She gave me a highly-scented peck on the cheek, before leading me along a narrow corridor and into a small office with a view of the brick wall opposite.

'John will be with you in a minute. Would you like a coffee?'

'White, no sugar,' I replied. 'How's Neil?'

'Neil? I think he's all right.' She bestowed a crooked smile on me, and my eyes fixed for a moment on that chipped front tooth. It contrasted with her sober attire and, if anything, the combination made her appear even more attractive. 'We're not together anymore.'

'Sorry to hear that.' I wondered how soon it would be decent to ask her out. 'I must give him a ring.'

'I'm sure he'd appreciate that. He was a bit upset. I'm–'

The door opened and John padded in wearing a

charcoal grey three-piece suit and a tie with a crest on it that looked as though it could have been from some army regiment. His black shoes shone brilliantly. I looked down at my battered M&S suit and scuffed shoes. John touched Samantha's shoulder and she swayed almost imperceptibly towards him, bathing him in the full crooked smile. A faint trail of perfume, I think it was Rive Gauche, wafted in my direction as, without looking at me again, she left the room and closed the door softly behind her. I realised with a jolt that Samantha was going out with John now.

'Well?' He draped himself over one of the two chairs in the room. 'What did you make of the business?'

'A turkey.' I sat on the other chair. 'Wouldn't touch it if I were you.'

I laid my report on the table and went through it page by page. He nodded occasionally, though he didn't ask me a single question. When I looked at his face I couldn't gauge his reaction.

'So, I suppose you'll move on to something else?' I was pleased I'd been able to demolish his plan so easily with my professional expertise. Somehow it seemed to restore the balance between us, diminishing him and enhancing me.

He stretched in a lazy, feline way, and yawned, exposing sparkling teeth. I felt a flicker of curiosity mixed with envy. How could he have such perfect teeth? My own mouth was filled with gunmetal-grey, evidence of a childhood spent indulging in sweets.

'On the contrary; I'm going to buy it and your report will help me get the price down.'

'You're going ahead after all I've told you? You must be mad.'

His predatory eyes fixed on me and I froze.

'Buying this business is going to make me rich. Don't assume that because you can't see something, no one else can.'

Seconds passed and no riposte came to mind.

He yawned, stretched again, and his tone mellowed.

'Thanks for your hard work. I'm going to ask Samantha to type it up, and then I need you to sign it and add your qualifications. Can you drop in tomorrow?'

Without waiting for my assent, he stood up and shook hands with me.

'Been good working with you. Samantha will see you out.'

I shuffled out, head bowed and brain buzzing. My assessment had been thorough. There was no reason for him to ignore it. In any case, how was he, without any relevant experience, going to turn around a business like that?

Samantha arrived to escort me to the lift. I felt no frisson of attraction when, guiding me round a particularly sharp corner in the corridor, she touched my arm. We reached the lift and she leant towards me, as though to kiss me on the cheek again. I took a step back and nodded curtly. I knew she was Beart's now, and that put me off her completely.

Chapter 9
FREEWHEELING, 1976

With the proceeds from my moonlighting fees, I bought myself a second-hand MGB in British racing green with beige leather upholstery. Though it was old, it only had 70,000 miles on the clock and I thought it would make me look cool.

I also talked Richard into going with me on a week's package holiday to Jesolo. We soon discovered all the Italian girls there already had Italian boyfriends, meaning we had to compete with the unattached locals, sun-tanned and laden with gold jewellery, for the favours of the usually lobster-red British girls. It was an unequal struggle. The UK's female contingent was clearly looking for a change in its sexual diet and preferred the charms of our slicker, more sharply-dressed Italian rivals.

Eventually, Richard and I found a quiet bar with a small garden at the back and spent our evenings there drinking grappa and playing cards. Pleasant enough, but I was relieved to get home.

*

The weather was warm and sunny on the afternoon of our return, so I rolled the MGB's hood down, and Richard and I set off for an old country pub. Our early holiday sunburn was maturing into a deep tan and our mosquito bites were fading, so when we saw some attractive girls through the window, we strode into the saloon bar to strike up a conversation, and discovered they were university students from Texas on an exchange at a local college.

Turning to Richard, I winked. 'Our lucky night.'

'Shooting fish in a barrel,' Richard whispered. 'If we don't score tonight, we should take a vow of lifetime chastity.'

Richard and I, much influenced by a recent nature programme on TV, decided to follow the same tactics as a pack of wolves in pursuit of a herd of musk oxen. First create some confusion, then separate one or two from the others, and then wear them down till their resistance weakened. The girls in question had been talking to some American guys wearing tee shirts and shorts emblazoned with surfing logos. We somehow managed to insinuate ourselves, extolling the virtues of Venice, or at least as many as we could remember from our couple of outings there. We were on safe ground. This was our new companions' first time abroad and we could have said anything. The girls seemed to soak it up, and the Beach Boy lookalikes faded into the background, muttering and casting occasional poisonous glances at us. Now I knew how those young Italian men felt when they'd routed Richard and me.

The difference between us and wolves was that we couldn't get the number we'd separated down below three. Then one of them, a small blonde with bright red lipstick said, 'I've always wanted to go to Chester, I hear it's so beautiful', and the other two joined in, screeching, clapping their hands and bobbing up and down. I'd never been to Chester, although in my mind's eye the name conjured up a scene of elegant timbered Elizabethan buildings a very long way up the motorway. One of the girls, Mary Jane, was leaning against me, her body warm and alluring. She looked round and smiled. Her perfect teeth were framed by soft and delicate pink lips, though, in the low light of the pub, I couldn't discern whether this was their natural colour or a subtle lipstick. Her green eyes sparkled with merriment.

'How about it, boys?' she said, and I'm sure she pressed a little harder against me. 'It would be such a blast.'

'We could take you to Chester one day,' I volunteered, hoarsely, 'although it's a sports car, so I could only fit a couple of you in.'

I'd already decided we'd leave Sara, the noisy and restless blonde, behind.

'Gee, I'm sure we could all squeeze in,' Mary Jane replied. 'We're only little, and it would be cosy.'

'Let's go now,' Sara said. 'It would be so cool to drive up there at night.'

'Yeah, amazing,' the other one, whose name I hadn't caught, added.

'Yeah, absolutely amazing,' they all seemed to be saying now.

'I'm not sure…' I rubbed my chin and viewed the three expectant faces looking up at me.

I sensed the Beach Boys closing in again and looked at Richard. He nodded. Why not? I hadn't really given the car a good spin, the next day was Sunday, and we'd nothing planned.

'All right. Let's go.' We drained our glasses and I led the group to my MG.

'What a darling little car. It would fit in the trunk of my dad's car,' Sara said.

'That's why I think I can only take a couple of you.'

'Bullshit,' Mary Jane said. 'Get in Richard.' As soon as he complied, she and the other girl plonked themselves on his lap, while Sara, with a nimble vault, squeezed into the space behind us.

The car's engine made a whining sound when I turned the key in the ignition. At the third attempt, it sprang into life, and we left a cloud of blue smoke behind us as I released the handbrake and we raced out of the car park.

We threaded our way through the country lanes, onto some arterial roads and finally onto the M1. I opened the throttle and the car gave a throaty roar. The girls whooped and I punched the air. All that slogging over Beart's report had been worth it. A night of unalloyed pleasure beckoned. This is what life should always be like. We drove at speed for about fifty miles, the roof down, the girls' long hair flying in the breeze, and the car rattling loudly. Conversation was difficult, although I could sense Richard squirming under the weight of the two women. He told me later he'd gone from lust to numbness to cramp within five minutes.

'Shall we stop for a break?' I shouted above the roar of the wind.

Richard and Mary Jane nodded. I didn't think the other two heard. In any case, we had a majority in favour. I pulled in to the next motorway services and parked. We tumbled out, the girls heading off in front and Richard walking with a pronounced limp behind.

'You can't still have a hard-on, mate.' I put my arm around his shoulder.

'I shall probably never have a hard-on again,' he replied. 'The blood supply there has been cut off for at least an hour. It'll probably drop off any minute now.'

We met up with the girls in the cafeteria and they

made room for us on the bench seat around their small table.

'How do you guys drink this stuff?' Mary Jane spat a mouthful of coffee back into her cup.

'I usually drink tea.' I replied. She lifted the cup out of my hand and took a small sip.

'Ugh! It's as disgusting as the other stuff, only it's a different shade of brown.' The other two girls pushed their almost full cups away from them, as though to avoid further contamination.

I gulped the last of my tea.

'Shall we be on our way?'

'You guys are really sweet, driving us all this way,' Mary Jane said, leaning against me.

Richard put on his best Jeeves voice. 'Entirely our pleasure.'

'Gee, I just love your accent,' Sara said, resting her hand on his arm. 'I could listen to it all night.'

Richard and my eyes met, and we struggled to suppress a smirk. This was going to be even easier than we thought.

The five of us, dancing arm in arm, returned to the car singing *I Get Around*. We climbed aboard. Mary Jane had just launched into *Good Vibrations* when I tried to start the engine. It emitted a sad whirring sound and died completely. Neither Richard nor I knew anything about cars. I opened the bonnet and peered inside. The lighting was dim and the engine was just a big, shadowy shape. It was Richard who noticed the black pool of liquid glistening under the car.

'We need more oil.' He pointed at the brightly illuminated service station in the distance, pushing me gently in its direction.

By now the three girls, in their light summer dresses, were shivering and huddling together.

I jogged off, returning with two large cans which I poured into the engine. I tried the ignition again. Nothing; it was dead. I found a telephone kiosk and phoned the AA. They'd be there in two hours.

'Gee, that's bad luck,' Mary Jane said. 'Such a cute little car.' The other girls nodded.

'Don't worry, ladies, we'll get you home somehow,' Richard said.

'Don't worry, guys,' Sara replied. 'We'll take care of ourselves. See you all around sometime.'

In turn, they pecked Richard and me on the cheek, before making off towards the lorry park where, only minutes later, I saw them clambering into an articulated behemoth. They gave us a cheery wave.

We stood staring as they pulled away. The driver's arm appeared through his open window and gave us a thumbs up.

'Bugger,' I said, and kicked the car. A chunk of paint and filler dislodged itself from the wheel arch, revealing a large patch of rust underneath. 'What was that about a vow of chastity?'

'Who needs to make a vow?' Richard replied.

When the AA man arrived, his examination was cursory and his diagnosis brief.

'Seized up. Must have had an oil leak for some time.'

'What can I do?' I asked.

'Call a garage and get it towed away; you'll need a new engine mate.'

'How much will that cost?'

'Blommin' fortune,' he replied, with a hollow laugh, and he mentioned a figure only slightly less than the car had cost.

He left us surveying the ruined remnants of my life in the fast lane. We wandered over to the lorry park and hitched a lift with an affable Yorkshireman delivering furniture to Surrey.

He dropped us off at Staples Corner just as a grey dawn was breaking. A fine drizzle drenched us as we plodded, shivering, to Hendon Central to await the first tube of the day.

Chapter 10
PROMOTION, 1979

'Have they told you they want to promote you?' Richard asked, his mouth still crammed with his cheese and pickle sandwich.

I flicked the debris he had sprayed off my jacket. 'You too?'

'Yep. Think you'll accept?'

I reflected on the question. 'Means more money.'

'And a lot more work,' he replied, brushing crumbs from his lap.

'They've told Digby and Rowlands they're going to promote them too.' Old Harrovians, they were both ex-public school snobs. 'If we don't accept we could end up working for them.'

'That settles it,' Richard said. 'I'm sure we'll be able to work things so we don't have to do too much.

We both accepted, and our promotions to Supervisor were announced. I decided to make the most of it with my parents.

'At last you seem to be getting somewhere,' my father said.

'Well done, dear,' my mother said. 'My sister was a supervisor in M&S before phlebitis made her give it up.'

Richard and I agreed to revamp our images. I invested in a new charcoal grey suit with a thin white stripe while Richard splashed out on a pair of gold cufflinks. We each bought a bright tie.

The buoyancy I felt on my first morning in the role had evaporated by lunchtime, and by the evening I was wishing I hadn't accepted.

'How are you finding it?' Richard said after a couple of weeks.

'Bloody awful. Work, work and then more bloody work. How is it for you?

'The same. The qualifieds need constant supervision and all those new graduates never know what to do. It's knackering.'

'And as for Houdini Walsh.' I spat his name. 'He's never there when needed and I always end up briefing the partner and the client.'

'Wish I could learn that trick,' Richard said. 'Still, we'll be managers one day. Then we can bugger off to play golf and leave everybody in the shit.'

'It's completely stuffed up my social life.'

'Sandra's none too happy either.'

One of the new graduates, a boy with fair hair and a round face, walked by. He didn't look old enough to shave.

'Is it me or are they getting younger?'

'You're turning into an old git, that's all. It's happening to us all,' Richard said.

'Fancy a beer after work?'

'Sorry mate. Can't tonight. I'm seeing Sandra.' Richard stared at the floor.

'Are you a man or a poodle?' I said, pushing his shoulder.

'Wuff,' he replied, sloping off.

Some days later I was auditing a distribution firm in the same field as John's. 'Has Beart's business turned around?' I asked the Finance Director.

'Only in the way an iceberg turned the Titanic round,' came the reply. 'Closed down last month with no warning. Everyone made redundant, and even people there for thirty years got diddly-squat. Brutal it was, absolutely brutal.'

Although I made sympathetic noises, I was intrigued. Asset stripping was all the rage, but what had he seen that I'd missed? The depots were all located in out of the way places, and the head office was a dilapidated building which probably qualified as a slum. I couldn't work it out.

*

After work, I used to go to the pub, and sometimes on to Jemima's, usually on my own as Sandra wouldn't let Richard accompany me now.

Sandra had virtually moved into our small flat,

which was now festooned with articles of women's clothing hanging up to dry. While Sandra's obsession with cleaning everything including the inside of the kettle irritated me, I did like the way the place smelled now. She cooked meals almost every evening, the aroma of roasting meat and fresh air supplanting that of take-away curries, pizzas and old socks. Richard's figure was already filling out, and he was slowing down in every way. He would spend his weekends doing the many trivial repair jobs we'd always ignored, or trailing round the shops, the domestic chains attached to his ankles clanking, to peer gormlessly and nod acquiescently at the things Sandra picked out. After years of rootless dissolution, he seemed as resigned to his fate as a terminally injured musk ox confronted by a determined wolf.

'Is this really what you want, mate?' I asked him one day over a pint in our local. 'Always making love to the same woman, always waking up with the same face in bed beside you, all that shopping instead of going to the footie, only ever going out to see romantic mush at the Odeon? Sounds like a life sentence with no remission.'

Taking a deep draught, he looked at me morosely.

'I sometimes ask myself the same questions.'

'So, what's your answer?'

'It's better than the alternative.'

'How can it be better than going out and enjoying yourself?'

He emitted a deep sigh.

'I don't want to grow into a sad old bachelor with breakfast stains all down my front.'

'Bet she wants kids. You'll be wiping bottoms and getting up at all hours to feed the little blighters in no time.'

'Well, as a matter of fact, we have discussed starting a family. I quite like the idea. After all, you can't go on living just for yourself forever.'

As I cleared my throat to debate the point, he looked up at the clock and gulped the rest of his beer.

'Better be getting back, mate. Sandra's cookery evening class finishes at nine. I said I'd give her a lift.'

Richard was not the only one of my peers to be settling down. The number who were still 'fully operational' was dwindling, making me feel older and lonelier, with the result I rarely went further than the pub.

It was on one of my rare visits to Jemima's, as I was nursing an expensive bottle of gassy American beer and surveying the writhing mass of sweaty bodies, that I noticed Samantha in the middle of the floor with a tall slim black girl with a strikingly angular profile. They were dancing close together while looking over each other's shoulders. I pushed through the crowds and into Samantha's field of vision. She looked right through me and I thought she must be trying to ignore me, though the surprise she showed when I touched her arm seemed genuine.

She introduced her friend, an Ethiopian whose name I couldn't catch. We walked to the side of the room where it was quieter, and I was taken aback to hear her relationship with John had petered out soon after my visit to the office.

'It's strange,' she said. 'He made me feel like the most important person in the world, then suddenly lost interest and I didn't see him again. What's even odder is that he sent my mother a huge cheque, even though he'd only met her once. She was really embarrassed.'

I was intrigued. I'd formed the view that Beart was only interested in himself. He must have had an ulterior motive. I raised my eyebrow theatrically.

'Yes,' Samantha continued, 'she was a bit broke and was going through a messy divorce from my stepfather. John insisted she hire a decent solicitor. She said she couldn't afford it, and then, hey presto.' She flicked a fine strand of hair away from her eye.

'By the way, how's Neil?'

'Fine, couldn't be better,' I replied, though I hadn't seen anything of him for some time. I made a mental note to contact him the next day. Conversation was difficult and I was conscious that both women were glancing around from time to time. I stayed just long enough to see Samantha and her friend dancing with a couple of Arabs and went home to bed feeling dejected. Life was not turning out as I'd wanted.

Chapter 11
RACHEL, 1979

AP sent me on an advanced course on Trust Law, possibly the most boring topic ever studied. When qualifying, I'd scraped through a paper on it after two attempts and not thought about it since. Trusts, however, were coming into vogue again, and I'd been selected to be the specialist in this area. At least it meant a week away from the office.

The course was held in St Hilda's, a hotel as dark and forbidding as a Transylvanian castle, and fog and driving rain made my journey through the Derbyshire countryside that Sunday afternoon perilous.

My new car, a second-hand Austin 1300 with eighty thousand on the clock, struggled up the steep hills. I arrived in the middle of a tumultuous storm which lit the sky every few minutes. A male receptionist with all the charm of Lurch checked me in and, in a gravelly voice, directed me to my room.

We met in the bar for pre-dinner drinks and I scanned the fifteen other participants; thirteen males and two females, one tall and faintly reminiscent of Olive Oyl, the other small and blonde, although with rather a forbidding mien. We filed through to the icy private dining-room and six or seven of the men scrimmaged to sit next to or opposite the blonde. Those who lost out sat near Olive Oyl. I chose a seat at the other end of the long oak table, between an Australian whose only topic of conversation was rugby, and a thin man with bad acne scars, who confided in me that it had always been his dream to specialise in tax and, once he'd mastered Trust Law, he would study for the Taxation Institute's exams.

The course was billed as 'intensive'. We ate every meal together, spent all day in the same room, and if we wanted a break in the evening, we could go for a drink with each other, or worse still, with the lecturers, in the hotel bar. Trust Law was the topic of every conversation. We were in the middle of nowhere, and the weather remained consistently brutish.

I kept myself to myself. I found no kindred spirit among the men, and the women were continually surrounded by fawning admirers. Olive Oyl had already teamed up with a man with a Frank Zappa moustache and horn-rimmed glasses. While the small blonde was still unattached, she was clearly out of my league. She'd told us at the introductory session she'd been awarded a hockey blue at Cambridge and had won a prize in her final accountancy exams. She worked for one of the biggest, most prestigious practices, already attaining the rank of manager.

We'd spoken superficially a couple of times and I didn't think it worth investing further energy in getting to know her, especially as Mike, one of the lecturers, followed her around like a lapdog, his tongue hanging out so far it brushed his knees.

By Wednesday evening, I'd had enough. I couldn't abide the idea of spending any more time in my matchbox-sized room, nor bear the prospect of sitting in the bar listening to the others drone on. As soon as dinner was over, I said, 'Excuse me, I'm going out. I'll see you all tomorrow.'

'Where are you going?' asked the small blonde, following me to the doorway.

'No idea, anywhere.'

'Mind if I come?'

'Course not.' I looked back to see the group's eyes trained on us. From their expressions, several around the table expected to be invited to join the excursion.

'See you all tomorrow,' I shouted into the room, waving. I turned to the blonde. 'Ready?'

I knew one of the women on the course was called Teresa, the other Rachel, but now to my embarrassment, I couldn't remember which was which.

We braved the horizontal rain in the hotel car park and I flung open the door.

'Hop in, Teresa.'

'I'm Rachel.'

'Shit, sorry.'

'We're easily confused, what with her being a foot taller and dark haired.'

We drove through a torrential downpour, the windscreen wipers smearing and re-smearing the screen with every stroke. At last we saw a small thatched country pub at the other end of a narrow hedge-lined lane. We ran across the car park and collapsed in a fit of laughter in the pub's porch. Breathless, I threw open the pub door and we toppled down an unexpected step into the saloon bar, just managing to stop each other from falling over. The cheery hubbub died instantly and a dozen faces stared at us, though the noise grew again when, drinks in hand, we positioned ourselves in a quiet corner near the smouldering log fire.

'What do you make of our fellow participants?' I asked.

'Jerks,' was her succinct reply. I was surprised. She seemed to get on well with all of them. 'Half of them are besotted with themselves, the other half obsessed with Trust Law. I don't know which is worse. And then there's that awful Australian, Clive.'

'What about Andrew?' Andrew was the most self-opinionated of them, rarely letting you forget his double first in something useless from one of the crumbling piles.

She wrinkled her nose. Then without warning, she sucked in her cheeks, exposed her front teeth and swivelled her eyes in a passable impersonation of a rat, and a perfect imitation of Andrew.

'I say, everybody!' she exclaimed, catching his nasal intonation faultlessly.

'And Mike?'

'Walks as though he's clenching a ten pence piece between his buttocks.'

'Peter and Claude?'

'Teresa calls them the body-space invaders. I think Claude had too much to drink at the opening dinner. In the bar afterwards, he put his arm around my shoulder and said, "I'd like to make love to you." I whispered in his ear, "If you do" and his eyes widened so much I thought his forehead would split, "and I find out, I'll be most annoyed." I haven't heard a peep out of him since.'

'How about the others?'

She ran through all the others, mimicking their voices and mannerisms; she'd missed nothing.

'What's your impression of me?' My heart was pounding.

'You always seem to be in your room or asleep in class, so you're our koala. They sleep twenty-two hours a day, probably slightly less than you.'

'At least they're cuddly'.

'That,' she replied, 'is a myth. They only look cuddly. Anyway, I'll give it some more thought now I know you a little better.'

'Fancy another gin and tonic?' I asked, pointing at her empty glass.

'My shout.' She picked up our glasses. I looked at her fondly as she headed for the bar. I love women who stand their round.

Back at the hotel, she invited me to her room for a coffee, where I discovered she was learning Trust Law by heart and had already memorised long tracts.

I positioned myself on a small sofa in the corner. Minutes later I found Rachel planting herself next to me, kissing me full on the lips and wrapping herself round me. As we kissed and undressed, she began to recite, in snatches, what she'd learned. It may well be the only time that anyone has ever found Trust Law erotic, but it certainly inflamed me, and we made love, with her still reciting extracts, more and more urgently and loudly, up to the point when we both climaxed and she fell silent.

Then she started to giggle, her body convulsing. Soon we were laughing uncontrollably, the tears streaming down our cheeks. After a few moments, she collected herself and said, 'Ten out of ten; the only way to learn this subject. Let's revise again together tomorrow.'

That night I lay awake, my arm around Rachel. The storm had temporarily given way to a clear sky and, with a full moon peeping through the half-open curtain, I thought I could make out a smile on her lips as she lay curled up beside me, breathing rhythmically. Rachel was so attractive, so amusing, so intelligent, and yet here she was, in my arms, her firm warm body lodged against mine, our breath commingling, our heads sharing her pillow. I stroked her hair gently and, for a moment she stirred, before readjusting her position and submerging herself more deeply in sleep. I couldn't believe my luck. Surely, she would soon come to her senses? I didn't dare ask what she saw in me in case it broke the spell, consigning me once again to my own lonely cell. The only thing I could think of was that I wasn't like the others. I didn't have a flash car to boast about, I didn't own my own flat, I didn't talk about myself all the time, and she seemed to enjoy my jokes. It wasn't much to hang onto, but it was enough, for the moment at least.

The next day, she went early to the meeting room and rearranged the place names, putting mine next to hers.

Mike, realising what must have happened, tried to freeze me out. I didn't care because I was the one with Rachel. On Thursday evening, after dinner, we went out and found a different pub, and we spent the night locked in a tight embrace listening to the roaring wind hurling rain and hail at her small iron-framed window.

Thanks to Rachel's memorable recitations, I learned more about Trust Law in two days than ever before.

★

'Bottom of the class,' Mike growled as he threw my test papers on the table in front of me on the final afternoon. I picked them up gingerly, expecting to have done miserably and saw a score of 51% written in red ink. I couldn't believe I'd passed.

'Don't know how you did it,' he added. 'The ignorance you displayed this week was astounding.' The other course members chortled sycophantically.

'Revision,' I replied. 'That's my secret.' I shot a glance at Rachel, who suppressed a grin.

He screwed his face into a sneer and continued to hand out the marked-up test papers. No one else had got less than 70%. Rachel, of course, passed with a near perfect score.

★

The ends of courses are strange affairs with people usually affecting a bonhomie they may not have felt during the preceding five days. This one was different. The women were held back for a few minutes on some pretext by Mike. Apart from Frank Zappa, who patted me on the back, the men ignored me as they went through the motions – shaking hands, exchanging business cards and promising to meet up again at some unspecified place and time – before spilling out onto the dark grey granite steps of the hotel. I followed them out, feeling like an outcast. Then I watched them, like a swarm of bees, surround Rachel and Teresa as soon as they emerged. I breathed deeply. The air was sweet. I didn't care about any of them, apart from Rachel, of course. The sun had finally broken through from behind a mountainous bank of black clouds and, for the first time the wooded grounds looked inviting. Rachel and I hadn't spoken about what would happen after the course, and I was wondering how she'd play it. Even if she weren't in a relationship already, she must have a host of admirers.

The other participants gradually drifted off leaving only me and Rachel, her hair a golden halo in the sunshine.

'Well,' she said. 'Is that it? You've had your evil way with me, so it's goodbye, is it?'

'Er no.' I still wasn't used to her directness. 'I'd love to see you again, if you'd like to see me.'

She laughed. 'I wouldn't be standing here if I didn't. I'd be halfway to the station in a taxi.'

'In a taxi? Haven't you got a car?'

'No, and if I stand around here much longer, I'll be moved on by the hotel porters as a vagrant.'

'Oh, right. Would you like a lift with me?'

'Thought you'd never ask. Not that I'd want to put you to any trouble.'

*

I took Rachel back to her flat in Notting Hill Gate and let the engine idle, expecting to be invited in but not wanting to appear presumptuous.

She leant across and kissed me on the cheek.

'Thanks for the lift. I've got a heavy day tomorrow and must get an early night. Otherwise I'd offer you a coffee.'

'Tomorrow's Saturday.'

'Yes, a great chance to catch up.'

Bloody hell, I'm getting the brush off, I thought. All she wanted was a taxi service.

'So now you've had your wicked way with me, it's goodbye, is it?' I said. 'I'm history.'

'No, of course not. I do want to see you again. It's just that I've got a lot on, and I haven't had much sleep in the last couple of nights.' She flashed me a conspiratorial grin. 'How about next Friday?'

Friday, a whole week from now, seemed an eternity away.

'I suppose so.'

She must have noticed the disappointment in my face.

'I don't normally socialise in the week. I like to keep myself fresh for work.'

This was an idea that had never occurred to me and I wasn't sure whether she was stringing me along.

'How about Friday about eight thirty then?' I ventured, thinking we could pop out to the pub I'd seen at the end of her road, a 1950s' place covered in Virginia creeper and coaching lamps which was trying to look two hundred years old.

'Well...' she said, biting her bottom lip.

Perhaps the pub wasn't a good idea. If I didn't invite a girl to the pub, I would usually take her to the cinema or, if she seemed very special, to a little but basic trattoria I frequented for its large portions of pasta and its inexpensive wine. I had the uneasy feeling that Rachel might not be impressed with any of these options, so I cast about for other ideas. None came.

'What would you like to do?' I asked.

'You choose. Theatre, concerts, opera? Whatever you fancy.'

I coughed to mask a gasp. That sounded like an expensive evening, especially with dinner first. I wondered whether to suggest meeting her at whatever venue we agreed on to keep the cost down, but abandoned the idea for fear of appearing miserly.

'I'll get some tickets. Let's go for dinner first.'

'That would be lovely.' Rachel's tone of voice was that of one accustomed to being indulged.

I jumped out of the car and opened her door with a flourish, followed by a bow. Then I spread an imaginary cloak over a puddle she had to step over.

'You are a fool,' she said. I kissed her on the lips.

'I'll look forward to Friday.' I got back in and drove off with as much of a roar as my car could muster while Rachel stood at the door of the house and gave me a brief, brisk wave.

At least I had a few days to acquire a *Time Out*, read up on what was on, and buy tickets. I finally managed to obtain some returns for a performance of *Tosca* at the London Coliseum, thinking the opera would impress her.

The week dragged slowly by. I borrowed a book on opera from the library. It was full of pictures of famous singers from the distant past and reproductions of posters of historic performances. I doubted whether I could steer the conversation around to Enrico Caruso or Dame Nellie Melba, and if I did so, whether I'd be able to sustain it for more than a couple of minutes.

*

We met outside the restaurant I'd booked in St Martin's Lane. Though I watched closely for signs of coolness, Rachel seemed warm and friendly.

'Good week?' I asked.

'Work, work and more work. Got lots done though.'

'Sounds terrible,' I said. 'Didn't you have *any* fun?'

'Some of the work was pretty interesting. Apart from that, nothing.' She attached herself to my arm as we walked into the restaurant. 'So, let's make up for it now.'

'You must like Puccini?' she said as we seated ourselves and took the menus from the waiter.

'Mmm,' I replied in what I hoped sounded like an affirmative way.

'Which is your favourite Puccini opera?'

'Well—'

'Have you seen *Tosca* before?'

'Er, no.'

'*Madam Butterfly*?'

'No.'

'*La Boheme*?'

'Not exactly.'

Rachel looked at me closely, a half-smile playing around her lips.

'Have you seen *any* of his operas?'

'Not really.'

'Have you ever listened to *any* of his music?" By now she was smiling broadly. It was quite possible that the school music teacher had included some of Puccini's works in the collection of classical masterpieces he'd inflicted on us during our 'appreciation' lessons every Thursday afternoon, but I couldn't be sure.

'May have done.' I had a sinking feeling, the sort you get when you stare at an exam paper and realise you can't answer any of the questions. Surely, once she realised I was culturally illiterate, she'd blow me out?

'You may have done?'

'Er, well, I mean, I'm not sure.'

She reached out a hand and placed it on my arm.

'In that case, you're very sweet to bring me to one. I'll have to educate you. The thing you have to remember about Puccini,' she said, as I gazed at her face. I loved her animated expression and the small laughter lines which appeared and disappeared around her mouth as she spoke. The tip of her nose was so delicate and finely shaped, I felt like leaning across and kissing it.

'...And so, sometimes you can even get to hear the original version of *Madam Butterfly*,' I heard her say as I emerged from my thoughts and found her staring at me.

'I don't think you've heard a word I've said.' She gave my arm a squeeze. 'This is going to be tougher than I thought.'

I'd never been to an opera before and was surprised at how normal the audience looked, like any cross-section of the metropolitan population. Though I quite enjoyed the performance, more for the spectacle than the music, I couldn't wait for it to end. I kept imagining being in bed with Rachel, the thought blotting almost everything else from my mind.

At last it was over, and we walked back to my car, arm in arm.

'That was a wonderful evening. Thank you.' She kissed me on the cheek. 'Come back to my place and I'll introduce you to Linda and Jean.'

I must have frowned. Linda and Jean, whoever they were, were the last people I wanted to meet. Rachel misread my expression.

'They're my flatmates. Identical twins, both

solicitors working for the same firm. They're a hoot.'

When we got back to the flat, Linda and Jean, solid women with their shirtsleeves rolled up to reveal broad forearms, were about to start a game of Monopoly. I stood watching them set up the board as Rachel brewed coffee in the kitchen. I couldn't wait for her to bring it out so I could observe the niceties, gulp it down and manoeuver her towards the bedroom.

'Want to play?' either Linda or Jean said. Dressed identically, I couldn't tell them apart.

'Great idea,' Rachel shouted from the kitchen. She emerged holding four mugs. 'Coffee's up.' She looked at me. 'You don't mind, do you? It'll be fun.'

I shook my head. This was no time to appear a bad sport.

I placed my cup carefully beside me and promptly knocked it over with my elbow. Coffee spilled everywhere, all over the board, the piles of bank notes, the stack of properties and dripped slowly off the edge of the table onto the cream carpet.

'Don't worry,' Rachel shouted as she raced to the kitchen, returning with a couple of cloths and a bucket and mop. The twins rolled their eyes and set to work wiping while Rachel wielded the mop. I sat on the edge of my seat, feeling useless. After ten minutes, they finished and we selected our metal tokens. Rachel took the top hat, one twin the battleship and the other the boot. I rummaged through the remainder and selected the iron, thinking it would show me in a non-sexist light.

The game took almost three hours, for most of which it seemed the result would be a stalemate, that is until Rachel and The Battleship did a deal in which Rachel acquired Park Lane in return for Coventry Street and £100. Soon houses and then hotels sprouted on her dark blue set while the three of us spent our time trying to leapfrog that corner of the board. Inevitably each of us, in turn, failed, and Rachel was left with a pile of coffee-stained properties in front of her and a stack of slightly soggy cash at her elbow.

'The set's ruined,' The Boot lamented.

'Well done, Monopoly Queen,' I said to Rachel, hoping my magnanimity would prove endearing.

'No one landed on my properties, not even him,' complained The Battleship. I'd definitely been the game's unluckiest player, arriving regularly on the income tax square and frequently being sent to jail.

'Popping to the loo,' Rachel said and left the room.

'Rachel always wins at board games,' The Boot said.

'Ruthless and lucky,' The Battleship added. 'Quite a combination.'

'Lucky at Monopoly, unlucky in love.' The Boot cast a meaningful look in my direction.

'You've never seen my abacus,' I retorted, with a light-hearted laugh. Two square-jawed faces stared at me. We lapsed into silence.

'Er, I suppose you've met quite a few of Rachel's admirers,' I hazarded, not expecting a serious answer.

The twins exchanged glances.

'Rachel only likes really challenging people,' The Boot said.

'Or nature's pushovers. They offer no threat,' The Battleship added.

'Really?' I said. 'How strange.'

'Which category do you think you fall into?' The Boot asked, her tone of voice leaving me in no doubt as to her own views. I resolved not to be brow-beaten.

'She certainly revelled in drubbing you two.'

'Getting her own back for the thrashing we gave her and Louise at bridge the other day. She can't get over the fact we're virtually telepathic.'

'Bit like the Krays then?'

The twins, sitting on the sofa, arched their backs like a pair of cobras, and I understood how a small animal, which has been chosen as dish of the day, must feel.

'You know, Ronnie and Reggie were meant to be—' I trailed off weakly.

'Think it's time to go to bed,' The Boot said. The Battleship agreed.

'Good night,' they chorused.

'Nice to meet you. See you again soon,' I said.

They looked doubtful about both statements.

I hung around while the twins used the bathroom.

Rachel, now pottering in the kitchen, had given no indication she was going to invite me to stay. She emerged yawning and stretching.

'Oh, I'm so tired.' She yawned again. That's it, I thought. The sign for me to leave. The twins had been right. At least I'd depart with dignity. I looked at my watch.

'Suppose I'd better be going now.'

Rachel's eyes widened.

'Don't you want to stay?'

'Thought you were tired.'

'Not too tired.' She came and stood close to me, the fragrance of her recently shampooed hair filling my nostrils. We kissed.

'Sure you want to?' she asked, breaking off for a moment. I buried myself in her neck and breathed in her sweet and gentle aroma.

'Well?' She glanced at my crotch. 'You look like you'd prefer to stay.'

I nodded vigorously and she took me by the hand and led me to the bedroom.

I wondered whether our lovemaking would be accompanied by a recitation of tracts from Trust Law. However, Rachel remained quiet, except for the odd gasp, until shortly before the moment of climax when I heard her start to hum *Vissi d'arte*, her rendition building to a crescendo at the exact moment of orgasm.

Chapter 12
NEIL, 1980

The almost horizontal rain, driven by a gusting wind, drenched everyone in the cinema queue in Leicester Square.

'I'm not sure I even want to see it. I'm soaked. Shall we go home?' Rachel brushed the water off her Barbour. It had been my idea to go and see *Seems Like Old Times*, largely because I fancied Goldie Hawn, though that wasn't what I'd told Rachel. The queue shuffled along a little as another couple abandoned it. The doors weren't due to open for another fifteen minutes.

'Won't you miss the Sisters Kray?' I asked. Rachel usually objected when I used that term.

'Not in the least.' She waved a dismissive hand. 'In fact, since I started beating them at bridge we've barely been on speaking terms. Come on let's go.'

I looked up into the sky. Somewhere between

the towering black clouds I was sure I could glimpse a chink of brighter weather. I really wanted to see Goldie Hawn.

'I think it's a clearing shower. Let's give it another few minutes.'

Rachel shook her head and a cascade of droplets spun from her hood. She looked up.

'It'll still be raining when the film ends.'

A fork of lightning ripped through the gloom and illuminated the sky, followed by a loud peal of thunder. As though infused by the electric storm's energy, the wind hurled a fierce barrage of rain in our faces.

'I'm leaving.' Rachel stepped out of the queue, hunched her shoulders and made for the kerb.

'They told me they were telepathic,' I said, following. A passing car splattered my trousers with muddy brown water from a flooded gutter.

'Who?' Rachel shouted as another peal of thunder broke.

'The Krays.' I shook my leg and gesticulated at the driver.

'Huh! They had a system and I cracked it. Now I can trounce them at will.'

She stuck out her hand and a taxi miraculously appeared. We sat in a deepening pool of water on the back seat as the taxi threaded its way through the dense traffic of Coventry Street.

'Bet they were pissed off. I can imagine their faces.

You'd better be careful you don't end up in a concrete pillar on some motorway.'

'Enough about them!' Rachel exclaimed. 'You haven't answered my question. Do you want us to move in together or not?'

'Yes, but—'

'But what? I suppose you're one of those commitment-averse men.'

As the taxi inched forward, the driver muttered something through the half-open window separating us, but neither of us caught it. As far as one could see, the rain had brought all traffic to a standstill and, sure enough, having nosed up to the back of a white van we, in turn, stopped. Now the only thing moving was the meter, which clocked up additional cost relentlessly. I felt my inside pocket for my wallet, worried that if we didn't start moving soon I wouldn't be able to afford the fare. Rachel nudged me. She was obviously expecting a response.

'It's not that. It's—'

Another flash of lightning was followed almost immediately by tumultuous thunder.

'The storm must be directly overhead,' Rachel said, her features as dark as the weather. The taxi, buffeted by a gust of wind, rocked.

'Feels like it's in the taxi,' I said. She didn't smile.

I swallowed hard. I didn't want her to think I was insecure, but the simple fact was I still didn't know what she saw in me. She was more intelligent and energetic, and I'd never deluded myself that I was good looking. I remember around the age of seven my mother saying to her friend Janet that Janet's son was going to grow up to be very handsome. I'd torn myself away from my game of Dinky cars to ask, 'Will I be handsome too, Mummy?' only to be told, after a pause, that I'd be 'fun to be with.'

'Rachel, I'd love us to move in together. There's nothing I'd like more.' I swallowed hard again and tried to keep my voice even. 'But are you absolutely sure you want to live with me?'

At last the taxi started moving, albeit slowly.

'That's why I suggested it, you chump.' She squeezed my upper arm. 'We'll have a great time together. You're such fun to be with.' My heart sank. The 'fun to be with prize' was what schools probably awarded to no-hoper children to console them.

'That's settled then,' she said. 'We'll start looking for a place. How about Richmond? I've always fancied Richmond.'

I looked through the taxi's windows, but they were so smeared with water now I couldn't see much. I rolled the window down and then back up again. It had stopped raining.

'Richmond sounds fine,' I said, and Rachel kissed me. A milky ray of sunshine broke through the separating clouds.

'I'll contact some agents first thing tomorrow.' She

reached for her purse as the taxi built up speed. 'This is on me.'

Although the Kray sisters' words echoed in my ears, I brushed aside my suspicions that Rachel was ticking the 'obtain partner' box on her own mental CV, and doing so by signing up someone undemanding who wouldn't compete with her or distract her from her career. After all, Rachel was an extremely attractive woman, and if she wanted to live with me, why should I object?

The wet pavements glistened in the bright sunshine as we stepped out of the taxi outside Rachel's flat. Shouting out 'hello' as we entered the hall, she dashed into her bedroom to change. I heard some rumbling noises, like the grunting of bison across the North American plains, and locked myself in the bathroom, a small pool of water rapidly forming on the cork-tile floor around the bottom of my waterlogged trousers. As I combed my hair I scrutinised my face in the mirror. She must see something in me. Perhaps I wasn't so bad looking. Although my hairline might be receding a bit, surely that and my thickening waist were only signs of burgeoning maturity, of worldly experience, of gravitas? On the work front I'd recently been promoted to Manager and a team of accountants and trainees was at my beck and call, clients treated my audits with respect, sometimes even bordering on trepidation, and on the social front I was going to move in with a most desirable woman, and at her suggestion. Surely, I'd arrived?

A loud knocking on the door startled me from my thoughts.

'Are you ever coming out of there?' It was the rasping voice of one of the Krays.

I opened the door slowly. Wearing a shiny black shirt, tight black trousers and Doc Martens, she stood blocking my way, her arms akimbo.

'God, you look like a drowned rat. What sewer have you just crawled out of?' She shuddered. 'Ugh, you're still dripping.'

'Ever thought of moonlighting as a nightclub bouncer? You look just the part,' I said as I squeezed past her muscular frame and into the sitting-room.

Rachel emerged barefoot and wearing a voluminous white cotton dress. Apart from slightly damp hair, she could have stepped from the pages of a fashion magazine. She went into the kitchen to make some drinks.

'You'll make the sofa wet. You better sit here,' the other Kray twin said, pulling up an upright wooden chair. 'Every time you're here you wreak havoc.'

'Won't be for much longer,' I said.

'Why, has Rachel told you to sling your hook?'

'Not before time,' added her sister from the doorway.

'No, we'll be moving in together soon.'

I wish I'd had a camera handy to catch the way

their jaws dropped. Rachel would probably be cross I'd broken the news. It was worth it though.

★

I quite enjoyed sensing the misery rising from Neil's hunched shoulders like mist off a marsh. He'd been to a better school and he'd gone to university. If that wasn't enough to make me envious, he'd pulled the desirable Samantha and started a business which was going to make lots of money. Then he'd lost the girl and now he'd all but lost the business.

'We couldn't match their rates. They were so aggressive. I don't know how they could do it and make money. We couldn't.'

'How have you survived so far?'

'Bank loans, and then more bank loans. Now I can't even pay the interest.'

In the gloom of the East End pub his face appeared gaunt and his jacket hung limply from his shoulders. He sipped the beer I'd bought him. Normally he would have swigged it.

'No sign, then bang, they were all over us. From nowhere. We can't keep going much longer. John stopped advertising a while back and we've lost most of our other advertisers. Worse still, hotels say they don't want more than one free newspaper anyway.'

I clucked sympathetically to mask my feelings of smug self-satisfaction.

Work was going well and Rachel and I had moved in together.

'Want another?' Neil said, dragging himself to his feet. I was torn. Should I let him persevere with the charade of offering even though he couldn't afford it, or should I take the magnanimous option and buy the drinks myself, thus reinforcing my superior financial status? I chose the latter and, brushing his token protests aside, shortly afterwards, with a flourish, placed the two pints on the table.

'Thanks, mate. Cheers!'

We clinked glasses and each took a mouthful. He sighed.

'I'll never meet a bird like Samantha again. Nobody matches up. I would have married her, you know. Apparently, she and John split up almost straightaway. How could he do it to me?'

'Didn't you ask him?'

Neil sighed. 'He said she'd seduced him and then dumped him. Not sure I believe him though. She wasn't like that. She was quite shy underneath that glamorous exterior.'

I thought it prudent not to mention my chance encounter with Samantha at Jemima's.

'Yeah, it's strange,' he continued. 'Almost as though he did it to spite me. But why? He was helping me on the business front and every time we met he seemed very friendly.'

I shook my head and shrugged. I'd no wish to

discuss Beart. In any case, anyone not blinded by lust could see that Samantha was in a different league from Neil.

I invited Neil to join Rachel and me for dinner one night; I ached to show her off to everyone I knew. He declined, and I sympathised. Spending time with couples, especially if they're still all over each other, is never much fun when you're single.

*

My next encounter with Neil, several months later, came as a surprise. I'd visited my parents for the first time in nearly four years. Rachel was spending a few days with her uncle in Bridlington, and I hadn't been invited. The ostensible reason for my visit was to tell my parents that Rachel and I were living together. I'd dropped her name into telephone conversations with my mother a few times, keeping my references casual as though she were something between a good friend and a non-serious girlfriend. However, my real agenda was to visit Mrs Beart. After all these years, I still felt guilty about my less than gentlemanly conduct and, having at last plucked up the courage, wanted to make amends, although I wasn't entirely sure how.

I waited till my mother was on her own in the kitchen.

'A storm's brewing,' she said as I perched on a stool. 'The weather forecast is terrible.'

‘Mum, Rachel and I are living together.’

She continued to bustle about, clattering saucepans and peering at the boiling vegetables for a couple of minutes before she looked at me.

‘Is she from a nice family?’ She opened the grill and pulled out the pork chops, already leathery and blackening around the edges. This meal was not going to put my father in a good mood.

‘She’s a vicar’s daughter.’

My mother’s face brightened. ‘How lovely, dear.’ She slopped some cabbage onto each plate and I wondered whether McDonalds had opened in Feston yet. My mother carried two plates into the dining-room where my father was already sitting at his place, a napkin tucked into his collar. She plonked one in front of him and sat down. He eyed it suspiciously and, without saying anything, poured himself a large whisky from the bottle at his elbow. We ate the meal in silence, broken only by the odd request to pass the apple sauce or the salt. Outside the wind had started to howl.

‘This could bring some trees down,’ my father said as though he found the thought comforting.

I left most of my food.

‘I hope you’re not sickening for something, dear,’ my mother said. ‘Perhaps it’s the weather.’

‘The boy doesn’t appreciate good home-cooked food,’ my father said. ‘I suppose you spend all your time in Wimpys eating all that hamburger muck.’

‘On the contrary, I never set foot in one of those places. I am partial to the odd Big Mac though.’

He knocked back his drink and poured himself another. My mother removed the dirty plates and brought out some tinned fruit salad awash with condensed milk. When my mother got up to clear away, I decided it was time to tell my father. His face was bright red and his eyes bloodshot. He listened in silence, staring at the half-empty whisky bottle.

‘Can’t be up to much or she wouldn’t be associating with you.’

I took a deep breath and pointed out she’d been to Cambridge.

‘They let anyone female in these days just to get the numbers up.’

‘Hardly, Dad—’

‘Which college?’

I knew he thought only two were any good, Trinity because Prince Charles had been there, and King’s because of the Christmas Eve carol service.

‘Girton,’ I replied. My father’s face became a gargoyle’s mask.

‘The place that’s full of blue-stocking dykes?’

‘It’s co-ed now, Dad.’

‘Men at Girton! What’s the world coming to?’

‘Lots of colleges are co-ed. It’s called equality. The days when one half of the population dominated the other because of its chromosomes are long gone. We compete on merit now.’

'Ridiculous nonsense. Like that Thatcher woman becoming Prime Minister.'

We lapsed into a tense silence which lasted until I excused myself to help with the washing-up.

The wind during supper was the vanguard of a storm of hurricane-like proportions, which raged all night and drove a cargo vessel ashore at Feston. The next day, when the wind dropped, the promenade was full of people gawping at the wreckage. The beach was littered with debris and large wooden crates carrying various types of electrical goods, and had been closed to the public. While a portly constable sat in the comfort of a nearby patrol car, a young police cadet was left with the task of preventing the crowd from spilling down and scavenging. I didn't give him a second glance, until I realised my mother was talking to him, the young man was Neil, and he was waving us through as though we were dignitaries.

'Why the fuck are you dressed like that?' I asked him.

'Meet me for a beer later and I'll tell you.' He opened the cordon for us. 'The Dolphin at eight?'

I nodded, impressed by this brazen display of police corruption, and we went onto the beach to take a closer look at the stranded vessel and its cargo.

⋆

That afternoon I passed by Mrs Beart's ground floor flat. The windows looked different although I couldn't exactly say why. A woman appeared in the small front garden, armed with a pair of secateurs. She saw me staring.

'Can I help you?' Her firm voice had a forbidding tone.

'Yes, er, I mean possibly… is Mrs Beart in?'

She looked at me as though I'd uttered some profanity.

'Mrs Beart doesn't live here anymore. She hasn't for months.'

'Do you have a forwarding address?'

The scowl on her face deepened.

'I believe she's taken up residence in London somewhere.'

*

The Dolphin was crowded that evening, and we were lucky to get a table.

Neil bought the first round and threw in a bag of crisps to show he wasn't broke.

'I'd never seen you as a rozzer, Neil,' I said. 'What made you accept the Queen's shilling or whatever it is you plods do? Especially after all the scorn you've heaped on them in the past.'

He flinched slightly.

'After the business folded I had a mountain of

debt. Then I saw an advert promising accelerated promotion for graduates, so I applied. I start at Hendon soon.' His chest puffed up slightly.

'To guard well-heeled bookies from aggrieved punters?'

'Hardly. The dog track disappeared years ago. No, it's the police training college I'm going to. I'm doing an initial six months' course.'

The idea that the police were trained intensively came as a surprise. I'd assumed a couple of hours' schooling in controlling traffic and half an hour running through the arrest procedure would have sufficed.

'If you do well, there's nothing to stop a graduate from becoming chief constable by the age of forty-five.'

While there was little I'd have liked less than to parade around in uniform and interact with undesirables, possibly even risking physical violence, Neil was looking so much more like his old self that I didn't want to deflate him.

'And in the meantime, I'm assigned here so I can live at home while I pay off some of my debts.'

'Don't worry mate. Once you graduate, a couple of hefty bribes will clear them completely.'

'It's slander like that which gives the force a bad name,' he said. 'I've met some really decent blokes since I joined. I'd trust them with my life.'

'You may have to one day, mate. I hope they live up to your faith in them.'

I sensed Neil's annoyance. Tough! He deserved a bit of ragging after this volte-face. In his youth, he'd been the most strident critic of the police I'd ever met.

'We policemen stick by each other. It's like an unwritten code. Support your fellow officers at all times.'

'Thought that was only when you're fitting someone up for a crime they didn't commit.'

'It's your round,' Neil said, pushing his empty glass towards me, 'and if you don't get them in smartish, I'll bloody well nick you. Oh, and by the way, get me some salted peanuts.'

'Well in keeping with the finest traditions of British law enforcement, Neil.'

As I stood up, I chanced to catch sight of a familiar figure out of the corner of my eye. It was Ronald Carrot-Top. Later, on my way back from the gents I took a slight detour so I'd pass close to him. He was locked in an animated conversation with a brunette with lots of hair piled up on her head and a very tight skirt stretched thinly over her ample bottom.

'Hello Ronald.'

He looked at me without any sign of recognition. I prompted him and he said, in a vague, uninterested way, 'All right?' and resumed his conversation with his lady friend without waiting for an answer.

'Still friends with Mrs Beart, are you?' I asked.

'Who?'

'You know, petite lady, dark hair, slim build, violet eyes.'

'Never heard of her.'

He was either a supremely gifted actor or telling the truth.

'See anything of Erica these days?' I asked.

His brow furrowed and he drew breath as though about to say something.

'Who's Erica?' the brunette asked. He took a few seconds to answer.

'The wife,' he muttered, his eyes fixed on the floor.

The woman took half a step back.

'Congratulations! I hadn't heard.' I seized his hand and pumped it up and down. 'How is she?'

'Up the duff.' He wrenched his hand out of mine and glared at me.

'Your first?' I asked, estimating how long it would take me to reach the door.

His shoulders sagged and his face seemed to crumple. 'Number three.'

'Great stuff! Well done!' I said in a patronising voice as the brunette receded rapidly into the background. 'Please give her my best wishes, and you take care.' I patted him on the shoulder in an avuncular manner.

He stared at the pub's door closing behind the brunette and then, with a start, gave the appearance of waking from a dream and squared up to me.

'Now I remember you. You're that fat little turd who was always hanging around. What's your fucking game, crashing in on other people's conversations, you wanker?'

I held my hands up.

'Just saying hello, Ronald. Old times' sake and all that. No harm meant.' I backed off quickly and made my way back to Neil.

'See that one over there, the one with the red hair?'

Neil nodded.

'Recognise him?'

Neil shook his head. He'd obviously forgotten our schoolboy encounters with Ronald and his gang.

'He's a bad'un, a dealer. You want to keep a close eye on him.'

Neil seemed to be soaking in the details of Ronald's appearance. He hadn't even asked what he dealt in or how I knew. Those criminals were going to run rings around him.

Chapter 13
SETTLING DOWN, 1981-82

After a while, Rachel and I had sufficient savings to do what every other young couple seemed to be doing, and took out a mortgage on a flat. Ours was in Teddington, even though most of our friends chided us for being suburban. We commuted into Waterloo together and then went our separate ways before meeting up again in the evening for the journey home or, on Thursdays, to attend a wine appreciation club. I loved the routine and the feeling of security it gave me.

Rachel went on a course in Leadership Essentials, but only after I'd exacted a promise from her that she'd always revise on her own. After a dull day in the office I felt at a loose end and decided not to return to the empty flat. Instead I headed for Val Polly's wine bar in Covent Garden, a favourite haunt of some of the younger audit team members. I negotiated my way through the smog and mass of bodies to squeeze into a seat by the bar, and ordered a glass of over-priced house red. After a while there was a tap on my shoulder. It was John Beart, his pronounced canine teeth lending his half-smile a feline and sinister air.

'Why don't you come and join us?' He nodded towards a table where a balding and corpulent young man in a loud blazer was slumped. I looked John up and down. He was immaculate in a chalk-stripe suit with light blue shirt and maroon tie; I was sure, had I asked, he'd have taken great pleasure in telling me the name of his Savile Row tailor.

While I felt shabby in my creased suit, his companion, Martin, who I discovered was his Finance Director, looked even scruffier, his chocolate and pink striped blazer bearing witness to the remnants of at least one meal.

I took my wine with me. John waved it away. 'Absolute gut rot, have some of this instead.' He pointed to a bottle of Krug cooling in an ice bucket and made his way to the bar to get an extra glass.

'The Aussies stuffed up good and proper,' Martin said. 'Quite a collapse after their first innings.'

Though I'd barely followed the third test, I'd heard one brief item on the news a little while before.

'Thought Dyson might do us some damage after his first-innings century,' I said, not knowing what had happened after that.

'Not so hot in the second though, was he?' Martin

chortled. 'Can't wait to see those little Ocker faces when we win the Ashes.'

'What are you doing now?' John asked, handing me a glass of champagne.

'Still at AP. What are you up to?'

He raised an eyebrow.

'Would've thought that a capable fellow like you would've gone to one of the big four by now."

'Happy where I am,' I replied, feeling defensive. 'Besides, I'll make partner soon.'

'Congratulations,' John said, and he sounded genuinely pleased. He exchanged glances with Martin. 'We were just saying we need some new auditors. Perhaps your lot might fit the bill. You might even be our audit partner.'

'Don't know about that. Your Board has to appoint the auditors and my firm would have to decide which partner to put in charge.'

John smiled enigmatically.

'These things can be arranged.' He gave me his card. 'Tell me when you've been promoted. Accountancy firms just love it when someone brings in new business. You'll be their blue-eyed boy. Could earn you a big fat bonus.'

He recharged the glasses and raised his in a toast. 'To an enduring and profitable partnership.'

★

It seemed that every other weekend some friends or other of ours were getting married. I was best man at Richard's wedding and, despite almost paralysing nerves, managed to stumble through my speech, even raising a few laughs.

Just as the flow of weddings seemed to be drying up, a cousin of Rachel's married an Honourable. Rachel's parents hardly acknowledged me and, while Rachel was placed amongst titled dignitaries on the top table, I found myself in the furthest corner, surrounded by distant and batty old relatives.

'Who did you say you are, dear?' an ageing second cousin on my right asked me every five minutes, while the old boy with mutton-chop whiskers on my left, I never did discover who he was, kept up a rambling monologue on what was wrong with modern Britain. The afternoon seemed endless, and even a lot of alcohol failed to deaden the pain.

'Wasn't that a wonderful wedding?' Rachel seized my arm as we walked to the tube station. 'A beautiful bride in a fairy-tale dress, lovely venue, delicious food, plenty to drink, great speeches; ten out of ten. That's how I'd like my wedding to be.'

'Shame about the groom,' I said. 'He's probably two out of ten, and that's being generous.' I'd met him socially a few times and had always found him an arrogant prig. I'd overheard him at the reception, surrounded by his Old Etonian chums, sneering at what they referred to as the penny-pinching attitude of the bride's middle-class family. While I'd hated every dragging moment, I'd considered the hospitality generous.

'Oh, Toby's all right underneath his Lord Snooty impression. It's just bombast. He's quite sweet really.'

I shook my head. There was no point debating this. She'd always been dazzled by the aristocracy, even those of dubious provenance like Toby, whose grandfather's unabashed toadying to Anthony Eden during the Suez crisis had earned him his viscountcy.

★

We'd spent Christmas apart as Rachel felt obliged to visit her family. At New Year we were reunited, and inevitably found ourselves at a party, this time held in the suburban wilderness south of London and given by someone in Rachel's office. I was driving and had very little to drink. Rachel had tucked in to a rather sinister bowl of punch and, on the way home, settled into the passenger seat in a contented stupor. Drizzle fell continuously and, as the windscreen wipers splish-splashed rhythmically, a pleasant calm descended on the car. It was broken when Rachel erupted suddenly from her reverie and asked, 'Why don't *we* get married?'

'Us?' I reached for the car radio and started to twiddle with the dial. 'Bugger, I don't seem to be able to get Capital. It's usually good at this time of night.'

‘Yes. Us.’ Her voice sounded determined and I wondered how long she’d been thinking about it.

‘What’s wrong with living together?’

‘Well, for a start, we can’t spend the night with each other when we’re with my parents. It would be so much more convenient to avoid all that embarrassing tip-toeing about at the dead of night.’

‘We hardly ever spend nights with your parents and we never visit mine—’

She swatted my objection aside. ‘And then there are the children.’

‘What children? I wasn’t aware we had any children.’

‘I’d like to have children one day.’

Thoughts of sleepless nights, dirty nappies and a house littered with baby toys consumed me, and I shuddered.

‘You’ve had too much to drink,’ I said, perhaps a little unwisely. Drunks never like to be told they’re drunk.

‘I’m completely sober.’ She sat bolt upright in her seat. ‘Do you want to marry me or don’t you? Why do men never want to commit?’ She looked away and sat in silence as I considered my options. While I regarded the whole wedding business as an expensive farce, I certainly didn’t want to lose her.

We passed an all-night kebab shop as a crowd of middle-aged men fell out of the pub next door and started to form a queue. It was like a vision of Saturday Evenings Future if I remained single.

‘All right, Rachel,’ I said, ‘let’s get married. But on one condition.’

She eyed me suspiciously.

‘What’s that?’

‘We don’t invite bloody Toby.’

‘You are a fool,’ she said as she stretched across from her seat and gave me a big wet kiss on my cheek. ‘I do love you, you know.’ Her hand reached out and fondled my crotch, like a film star stroking her miniature pooch.

Perhaps marriage won’t be so bad, I thought to myself. Maybe it is time to settle down.

‘Toby or no Toby, I want it done properly you know,’ she said. ‘You’ll have to ask Daddy’s permission, and then it’s the full bended-knee-job and a massive rock.’ She paused for a moment. ‘I want to choose the ring though; your taste is terrible, and besides you’d probably come away with the cheapest one in the shop.’

Chapter 14
PROMOTION AGAIN, 1983

'Do you think they'll make us partners?' Richard said as we ate our sandwiches in the scrubby little patch of green which passed for a park near the office.

'They have to,' I replied. 'They're taking on more and more junior people. From what I heard, they can't recruit any seniors because we don't pay enough. It's a simple case of supply and demand.' I threw some crumbs on the ground and they were immediately covered by a swirling mass of pigeons.

'Thought Braithwaite said you weren't ready,' Richard said.

'That was six months ago, and you look at the wankers they've promoted to manager since then. Some of us managers have to become partners.' All around me pigeons perched expectantly, waiting to compete for the next bonanza.

'I hope you're right. Those skinflints will do anything to save money. It would suit them fine to have all cheap Indians and no properly rewarded chiefs.'

A week or so later, I got a call from Braithwaite's secretary.

'He wants to see you. Now.'

Braithwaite sat hunched over his desk. Apart from a curt 'Enter', when I knocked, he ignored me completely, leaving me standing while he finished reading the document in front of him. I looked around. A half-smoked cigar smouldered in an overflowing ashtray while a bluebottle hurled itself repeatedly against the window, through which I could see a crane perched motionlessly over the site next door, and beyond that the concrete skeleton of a skyscraper under construction.

'I've decided to take a risk,' he said, his eyes still fixed on the document. 'I'm going to promote you to salaried partner. There are those who say you're not ready.' He looked up and stared at me. 'It's up to you to prove them wrong. Roger will tell you your new salary.' He looked down. The interview was clearly at an end.

'Thank you, Mr Braithwaite,' I murmured. When I got into the corridor, I executed a quick dance. I'd done it. I'd caught up with Rachel, at least in job title.

*

'Congratulations,' Rachel said as she lifted her glass to toast my success as we sat with Richard in a corner of The Magpie. 'It means you'll have to work much harder now though. No more skiving off.'

'I hope it's not going to affect our midweek golf matches,' Richard said. 'I rely on the money I take off you to keep the family budget afloat.'

'You'll soon be getting your own call from old Braithers,' I said. 'I'm sure that as partners you and I will need to spend even more time together at off-site meetings.'

'This is a great opportunity. Please don't stuff it up,' Rachel said.

'You don't seem to be putting too much effort in yourself these days, Rachel,' I replied, savouring this unprecedented opportunity to criticise her work ethic.

'Will do once I get the wedding sorted.' Rachel was heavily involved in making plans and fighting the many battles associated with an expensive event for which someone else was paying. She was in opposition to her mother and, seemingly, the rest of the family, on every possible point. I had no say in the proceedings. Mine was a walk-on part, necessary only for completeness on the great day itself. Until then, thank God, I was insignificant.

*

The wedding was held in the old Norman church in her parents' village. Linda and Jean were ushers.

When Richard and I shuffled nervously into the church, one of them beckoned me over.

'You know that bit when the priest asks if anyone knows of any lawful impediment?'

I cleared my throat. 'Yes.'

'We haven't forgotten.'

'Forgotten what?' I croaked.

'Never mix it with lawyers,' the other one said.

They grinned and winked at each other before going back to handing out orders of service, leaving me with a cold sense of foreboding.

'What was that all about?' Richard asked. 'And who are they?'

'They're history, thank God,' I replied. Whatever else married life brought, the Krays would not be part of it.

Rachel's father wanted to be able to enjoy the proceedings as a parent, so a pasty-faced curate with a lisp conducted the service. My heart skipped several beats when the just cause or impediment question was asked and a loud cough and throat-clearing noise erupted at the back of the church. After a nerve-racking pause no objection materialised, but my hand was still shaking so much I dropped the ring while trying to slide it onto Rachel's finger. Rachel lifted her veil and gave me a reassuring smile before we kissed. I was a fool to have worried about the Krays; Rachel was more than a match for them.

Much of the rest of the day became a blur except

for Richard's entertaining if slanderous best man's speech, and Rachel's father's caricatured impression of me which had all the guests laughing except for my mother, who spent her time crying into a lace handkerchief. My father guffawed rather too loudly at the slurs on my character while he put away as much champagne as he could. I'd worried he'd place a dampener on proceedings. In fact, throughout the afternoon every time I encountered him he was telling slightly risqué jokes or clapping members of the bride's family on the shoulder. He even spent time talking to Linda and Jean, and I was pleased to see all three of them burst out laughing until I remembered that the subject they all thought most risible was me.

As Rachel and I were about to leave the reception my father materialised and clasped me by the elbow.

'Glad to see you're making something of your life at last. It's taken you rather longer than most people.' I winced as he slung his left arm around my shoulders. 'I think you're getting there at last, my boy. Now you've got a secure job and a pretty wife you can settle down and give us grandchildren we can be proud of.'

I looked down at his puffy red face, and couldn't think of a suitable reply. He proffered his hand and, reluctantly, I took it.

'Good luck, my boy.' He gripped my hand tightly and, for a moment I thought I detected a slight moistness in his eyes. I averted my gaze; I couldn't bear the sight of him becoming sentimental after everything he'd done to oppress us all.

My mother hugged me, brushing her wet cheek against my waistcoat and whispered in my ear, 'I know Rachel's very pretty and intelligent. I do hope she's nice enough for you though. She's very ambitious, isn't she?'

'That's the way with modern career women, Mum,' I replied. 'We new men are used to coping.'

'I hope so, dear. I do hope so.'

The crowd of well-wishers engulfed us, and I found myself being propelled by the Krays towards a chauffeur-driven vintage Daimler trailing a tin can and a pair of kippers from its exhaust. We waved at our guests as we pulled away en-route to a local hotel for the night, and I reached out and took Rachel's hand in mine.

'Happy?' I asked.

She looked at me very seriously. 'So-so. Seven out of ten.' She proceeded to run through all aspects of the day, critiquing and scoring each. The church service had been a six as the curate had stumbled his way through his part and the readings had been delivered with little feeling by her relatives, the quality of the food had been an eight but its service, which had been slow, only merited a five. The speeches had been awarded a nine, particularly her father's, the wine a six, the champagne an eight, the venue a seven and the guests had only earned a five for their lacklustre singing at the church and their muted responses at the reception.

'And how would you score it?' she asked.

Even then I couldn't remember that much about it. As I'd been dreading the day, I took that as a good sign.

'Oh, ten out of ten for me.'

Although I hadn't paid much attention to History lessons at school, Disraeli's confession to laying it on with a trowel when flattering Queen Victoria had always stuck in my mind. It seemed like sound advice.

'How could marrying you warrant anything less? Yes, absolutely, ten out of ten.'

Rachel kissed me.

'You're sweet,' she said. 'It's what I like most about you. You've no edges.'

★

For our honeymoon, we drove around Tuscany for a fortnight. Rachel had organised everything, taking us from one idyllic hotel to another, and the places we stayed could all have been used as settings for up-market holiday brochures.

Rachel was in an uncharacteristically carefree mood, and even I was surprised by the spontaneity and passion of our lovemaking; in the woods, in the car and on the beach as well as in our bedroom. I found myself wondering whether we could create a life for ourselves in Italy and formulated a plan to set up a business to export garden plants to the UK market. I would suggest it to Rachel on our last night.

*

We were dining at a hill top restaurant with views over rolling Tuscan hills. In the distance was a dark clump of woods. On the slopes below us were the orderly ranks of a vineyard, and a jumble of gnarled and twisted olive trees. The cooling evening air was scented with pine. I held Rachel's hand, looked into her eyes, and outlined my idea. At first, she looked bemused, then amused and finally irritated.

'And I thought you were being romantic.'

'Sorry. Er, what about it though?'

'Out of the question. This is a great place for a holiday, ten out of ten. I don't want to live here though. I've got a job and a career. I know it'll be frantic when I get back to the office, a real adrenaline rush; that's what I love. I couldn't waste my life becoming a lotus-eater.'

'We wouldn't be. We'd be working, and we'd be doing it for ourselves. It could be very profitable. There's a longer growing season and the plants mature more quickly out here. I could easily establish links with UK garden centres and start exporting. Think of the quality of life, the food, the wine, the sunshine. It would be fantastic, a dream existence.'

She silenced me with a single look. You couldn't argue with Rachel once she'd made up her mind.

When we came home we opened the wedding presents and among them found a small, ornately-fashioned gold and silver chess set in a mahogany box, on which our names were inscribed in gold lettering. We'd been so intent on tearing the wrapping paper off, we'd no idea who'd sent it. When I retrieved the paper, I found a card inside from John Beart, though I couldn't think how he'd found out we were getting married.

'What a generous gift.' Rachel seemed impressed, more because the gold and silver were real, (so the maker's card inside was at pains to point out), than because of the intricacy of the craftsmanship.

'Rather over the top, don't you think?' I said, appalled at its extravagance. I couldn't think what you'd do with a chess set like that. It was so ostentatious you couldn't leave it on display. The insurance alone would probably cost a fortune. As far as I was concerned we should sell it. Failing that, the best place for it would be in the vaults at the bank.

'Oh, I don't think so,' Rachel said. 'It doesn't really go with what we've got, but as we upgrade everything else, it could fit in nicely.'

I looked around at our few possessions. I'd grown fond of them and the idea of throwing them all out and buying in more fashionable furniture and fittings gave me a vague sense of unease.

'We must invite him over for dinner,' she continued, weighing the pieces in her hand.

‘I don’t know how to contact him. Anyway, I don’t like him very much.’

Rachel looked at me disbelievingly. ‘Don’t be feeble. He obviously thinks highly of you. Just look at this amazing gift he’s given us.’

I told her about his proposition.

‘We must definitely have him over then. He’s right. Bringing a new client in will set the seal on your partnership.’ She burrowed in the pile of papers again, and found the external wrapping.

‘Look, here’s his address. It’s on this other card.’ She put it carefully in the cupboard drawer. ‘Let’s make sure we don’t lose this. It could be the making of you.’

*

The role of partner wasn’t particularly onerous. Others did the real work and I could adopt a hands-off approach, liaising with the client’s finance director and controller at the beginning of the audit and then reviewing the work done and signing it off at the end. In the interim, there was a certain amount of schmoozing the clients.

The recently recruited accountants, all so anxious to take on extra work and shoulder additional responsibilities, seemed a different breed from my generation. It was all a little frightening and I reckoned it best to keep out of the way of all these highly motivated, extremely competent people.

Our social life was now very enjoyable. We ate in fashionable restaurants, took various interesting European city breaks, and booked holidays wherever the fancy took us, business schedules permitting. I started to appreciate going to the theatre and to concerts and was even becoming quite knowledgeable about opera. We moved from Teddington and bought a sizeable terraced house in Richmond which, at Rachel's insistence, we re-decorated completely. My only regret was that the garden was very small and dark, and it was difficult to grow anything of interest there. Filling the house with stubby yuccas, angular dracaenas and spiky urn plants somehow didn't compensate.

Rachel was now the target for approaches by head hunters attempting to recruit her as finance director of organisations of increasing size and importance. Although she rejected them, she only did so after skilfully manipulating her own firm into repeatedly improving her compensation package. Recognising how little I contributed at work, I already felt guilty at being paid so handsomely, so it didn't matter I wasn't ever approached. In fact, it was a relief. I couldn't believe how well everything was turning out. It seemed my father had been right. Accountancy, as a profession, did have prospects.

Occasionally we'd visit Rachel's family for the weekend, and despite a polite welcome, her parents' lack of interest in me was still apparent. The elegant eighteenth century, wisteria-clad vicarage, which smelled of old leather furniture downstairs and of antique dust and mildew upstairs, needed repainting outside and redecoration inside.

Of Rachel's sisters, only the youngest, Suzie, a tall, slender girl in her late teens whose straw blonde locks fell around her shoulders, still lived at home. She seemed to be in permanent motion as she shimmied barefoot around the house and garden, her long thin feet like luminous white levers protruding from her flowing ankle-length skirts. Sometimes she was dressed in a paint-stained smock. Whatever her attire, she smelled of marijuana and wore a permanently abstracted expression. Occasionally I'd catch a glimpse of her at her easel at the bottom of the garden. More often she would seclude herself in her bedroom, with a large 'painting in progress: do not disturb' sign on the door. She ignored everyone, including me, despite my attempts to ingratiate myself.

Rachel would become angry by just looking at her, berating her for her idleness, her lack of motivation and her unwillingness to do anything as mundane as laying the table or washing up. Suzie would merely smile and glide past to only she knew where.

'The girl's as high as a kite,' Rachel said to me one day. 'I don't know where she gets the stuff, or the money. She was thrown out of school for smoking dope and she's still permanently stoned. Years of exorbitant school fees and all she managed to do is scrape two

O-levels, and they were in Art and Religious Studies. Can you believe it? Now my parents are talking about sending her to a finishing school near Reading. Good money after bad.'

'Isn't that a bit harsh?'

'Harsh?' Rachel exploded. 'I still haven't forgiven her for being so out of her mind on acid she missed our wedding. Absolutely inexcusable.'

Though I nodded, I couldn't bring myself to join in. It rankled with Rachel that she and two of her sisters had attended the then newly formed and chaotic local comprehensive, whose results at the time were appalling. Rachel, the oldest, had of course shone academically. The next two sisters had done equally well; one was now a doctor and the other a research scientist. In contrast, Suzie, benefiting from an aunt's legacy, had been sent to an exclusive boarding school where she made little impression until her expulsion. Despite Rachel's continual criticisms I sympathised with Suzie. I'd spent my own youth drifting and knew what it felt like. Now she seemed to have found something which she loved – the paintings I saw were certainly accomplished – and she couldn't care less about anyone else, least of all her big sister. I admired that.

★

It was a hot afternoon, the still air heavy with the spicy fragrance of tall pink and white Dianthus flowers, the silence broken only by the resonance of assiduous bees and the humming of hover flies.

'What are you planning to do?' I had found Suzie in the vegetable garden, sitting sketching lettuces. She was wearing what appeared to be a dull brown sack and, for once, baseball shoes. Her hair was pulled up into a loose and straggling bun.

'What, when I'm grown up, you mean? You're not talking to a child, you prick,' she replied, her pencil hand still skimming across her pad.

'I meant when you leave finishing school.' I leant across and looked over her shoulder. The lettuces were rapidly taking shape.

She looked up at me with contempt in her eyes.

'I'm fucking well not going to finishing school. I'm going to art school even if I have to fuck the entire faculty to get a place.'

I brushed a persistent bluebottle away from my face with a wave of my hand.

'What about your parents?'

'I'm not into incest. They can go fuck themselves.'

When I told Rachel of Suzie's determination to study art, omitting reference to how she was proposing to bring it about, she said, 'Daddy will make her go to finishing school, despite all her wheedling. Mummy's adamant this time.'

Later that week I was sitting in the drawing-room reading the newspaper while digesting a traditional English breakfast of enormous proportions when I heard a car pulling up on the gravel drive. I ignored it and was surprised when Edwina, Rachel's mother announced that a visitor was waiting for me in the study. I couldn't think of anyone who knew I was here. Curious, I eased myself out of the old leather chair, a thin strand of horsehair stuffing adhering to my arm, and went to investigate.

John Beart, standing with his back to the mullioned window, extended his hand.

'I hope you don't mind me barging in like this. I was just passing.'

'Just passing? This place is in the back of beyond. How did you know I was here?'

'I gave your parents a ring. They seem to be in pretty good shape from the sound of it.'

I had a distant recollection of sharing my plans with my mother.

'Anyway, I don't want to disturb your weekend too much. I dropped in to see whether you'd be interested in taking my business to your firm. I don't think you gave me an answer when we spoke last.'

I was about to respond when the door opened and Rachel entered, as though by accident. Still in her sweat-stained singlet and shorts, she'd just returned from one of her regular early morning runs. Without hesitating, John introduced himself and she said, 'I've heard so much about you. You gave us that lovely chess set. You must come for dinner.'

‘Love to,’ John replied. ‘But look, I’ve got a little place about ten miles from here. Why don’t you have dinner with me there the day after tomorrow? We can talk about my proposition. Seven thirty for eight?’

Before I could respond, Rachel accepted and John shook us both briskly by the hand, though I did notice him surreptitiously wipe his on his trousers after disengaging from Rachel’s sweaty palm.

‘Who on earth was that?’ Edwina asked as his Aston Martin crunched slowly down the long gravel drive. ‘Very polite, but with the eyes of a crocodile.’

‘That’s a bit tough on crocodiles.’ I laughed loudly at my own joke. Rachel merely looked thoughtful.

Rachel and her mother, deep in conversation, left the study. Through the window I saw Suzie, who was standing by the gate, flag John’s car down, speak to him through its open window and get in. They drove off together.

★

The next day Suzie was waiting for me in the library after breakfast, and asked me to give her a lift to the station.

‘I don’t want my things to get wet,’ she explained. ‘It’s absolutely pissing down.’

Dressed neatly in a light grey suit and with her hair scraped into a pony tail, she held a bulging folder under her arm. Despite the deluge outside, she wasn’t wearing a coat or carrying an umbrella.

I was surprised she'd singled me out for this task.

'Where are you going?'

'London. I'm meeting the principal of Tooting Art College. And can you pick me up this evening?'

'I suppose so.'

'Let this be our little secret, OK?' She reached out and gave my crotch a painful squeeze which made me wince. 'Unless you want me to tell my parents you've been putting the moves on me.'

I couldn't let the little minx get away with that.

'And I might tell them where you've been getting all your gear.'

'You have no fucking idea,' she said, then tailed off, staring at me. Although she thought I was bluffing, she wasn't sure and seemed reluctant to take the risk.

'In any case, there's no need for threats, Suzie. I'll do it as a favour.'

'You're not getting anything off me,' she replied. 'Not just for a lift.'

'I said it was a favour and that's what it is. Anyway, won't your parents wonder where you are?'

'No one ever knows where the fuck I am. I make sure of that.'

We got into my car, which was parked in a secluded spot at the side of the house, and nosed slowly and quietly down the drive.

'Where did you go with John yesterday?' I must have caught her off-guard because she faltered for a second.

'What the fuck's it got to do with you?'

'Fair comment,' I replied. 'It's worth remembering though that people may know more about you than you think.'

We arrived at the station and I let the engine idle while she collected her things together before getting out.

'Thanks,' she said, leaning across and kissing me full on the lips. My heart missed a beat and then started to pound. She leaned back and squinted at me, probably amused at my startled expression.

'Be careful. You never know who's watching.' She got out. The car door was still open and commuters were milling all around us. 'Six thirty. Don't forget, lover,' she said loudly, slamming the door.

I was waiting in my car outside the station that evening when Suzie filtered through the crowds standing by the doors. She slung her folder into the back and slid into the front seat.

'How did it go?'

'Fucking lousy, he's gay. Third one in a row. There must be some fucking art schools run by straight men. Or lesbians.'

A few months later, Rachel told me Suzie had got a place at art school.

'I don't know how she managed it. She didn't meet any of the entry criteria.'

Chapter 15
SEEDS ARE SOWN, 1983

It was the day we were due to dine with John and, after a substantial lunch at the Vicarage, I was on the point of opening the newspaper when Rachel announced we were going for a walk.

'Not now,' I moaned. 'I might go for a run tomorrow.'

'Lying toad!' She gripped my arm and pulled me to my feet. 'The only running you do is to fat. You're coming with me.' She dragged me to the coat cupboard and forced me into wet-weather gear.

We covered about eight miles along boggy footpaths and across sodden fields, ducking into the woods whenever the persistent drizzle became heavier. My walking boots were clogged with mud, my trousers sodden and my upper body clammy with sweat. Rachel, on the other hand, seemed to gain strength from the adverse conditions, striding through the deep puddles as though they didn't exist. She even laughed loudly when she slid down a muddy bank, coating her body and splattering her face. Her persistent cheerfulness was the most dispiriting aspect of the whole soggy episode.

Using exhaustion as an excuse, I proposed we should give dinner at John's a miss in favour of a quiet evening's recuperation. Rachel would have none of it.

'I'm looking forward to getting to know him. I've heard whispers he's one of the coming men, one of the movers and shakers.'

I shuddered at the term. The City seemed to be fuelled by jargon.

'In my view, he's rather flaky,' I said, secretly proud to have mastered some of it myself.

'You haven't known him properly since prep school. People change, you know.'

'He's all show. You'll see,' I said, bravely hoping he would be exposed as a poseur that evening but dreading he wouldn't.

★

John's place was considerably larger than the Vicarage, and of a very different configuration. At the centre was a modernised and extended farmhouse, around which several barns had been converted into luxurious amenities: a sauna, a squash court, a fully equipped gym, a well-stocked library. Terracotta-tiled walkways connected the different buildings, giving the property the feel of an exclusive holiday resort. A silver Aston Martin DBS, a bright yellow Lotus Eclat and a dark grey Range Rover Classic were parked carelessly outside. I nosed my Ford Escort in between the Range Rover and Aston Martin, taking care to ensure the rust patch behind the wheel arch faced away from the house.

The dark oak door was opened by a tall, slim woman in her very early twenties. In the background, I could hear the strains of *King of Pain*.

'Hello, I'm Sonja.' She had a faint accent which I found difficult to place. 'Do come in and make yourselves comfortable. John's on the phone. New York.'

We handed over our bottle of medium priced Rioja, and accepted glasses of champagne. *King of Pain* gave way to *Wrapped Around Your Finger* with its subtle keyboard playing.

'You obviously like The Police,' I remarked. Sonja murmured that the album was John's and she preferred Afrika Bambaataa and the Soulsonic Force. Not recognising the name, I shook my head and Sonja smiled in the way a teenager might at an ignorant parent.

'Hip hop,' she said. 'I'm trying to convert John. I think he's gradually warming to *Planet Rock*, though with him it's difficult to tell.'

A sleek young cat wrapped itself around our

ankles. Rachel stooped to stroke it and it purred loudly. I stepped back, a sneeze forming in my nose.

'Meet Oscar,' Sonja said. 'John rescued him from a building site. Now they're inseparable. '

'A bit like Blofeld and his cat,' I said. Sonja and Rachel ignored me.

'What do you both do?' Sonja asked.

'We're accountants,' Rachel said, and I'm sure I saw Sonja's eyes glaze over. 'What do you do?'

'I'm writing up my PhD in psycholinguistics. I'm almost there, only about 5,000 words to go.'

'What's psycholinguistics?' I asked.

'Representation of language in the mind, Chomsky and all that.' Sonja replied.

'Fascinating field,' Rachel said. 'In your view, is human ability to use language qualitatively different from any sort of animal ability?'

I stretched out on the sofa and peered at Rachel through narrowed eyes, wondering how she knew so much. Half-listening, I only caught some of Sonja's reply, '– well I certainly believe an innate mechanism is involved in language acquisition—' before my mind drifted off completely and I became oblivious to the rest. My eyes scanned the room. Dominating the mantel-piece was a large framed photograph of a teenage John, arm in arm with his youthful looking mother, gazing into each other's eyes like newlyweds. It was only when the door opened and John padded in that I came to.

He seemed to grow in stature every time I saw him. Dressed very casually in a cream sweater and faded blue jeans, he kissed Rachel on both cheeks, shook my hand, asked Rachel some polite questions, cracked some jokes, and topped up our drinks. Even though there were only four of us in the room, I felt I'd shrunk into inconspicuousness.

Oscar wrapped himself around John's legs and John picked him up and kissed him.

I'd been expecting Sonja to scurry out to the kitchen and was surprised when John said, 'Do excuse me. I must check how the main dish is doing and put the spinach on. You both like Beef Wellington?' He put Oscar down on the thick Persian rug, where he started kneading the pile with his claws and purring.

'Bless,' said Sonja as John closed the door. Oscar immediately headed in my direction and I stood up.

'What's the matter?' Sonja asked.

'Bit allergic,' I replied as Oscar pursued me purposefully round the sofa, looking for an opportunity to launch himself at me.

'Don't be pathetic,' Rachel said. 'It's only a cat.' She leant down and stroked Oscar, who jumped onto her, purring and flicking his tail under her nose before settling down into a tight ball on her lap.

Sonja, more out of a sense of politeness than interest, I suspect, started asking me about my work. After a couple of minutes Rachel dismissed Oscar, stood up and brushed his fur off her dress.

'I'll go and see whether John needs any help in the kitchen.'

We didn't see her again until shortly before the food was served.

My hopes that the dinner would be uneatable were dashed. Mushrooms a la Grecque cooked in olive oil and lemon juice were served cold as an appetizer. The succulent meat in the Beef Wellington was just the right shade of pink and the puff pastry golden and crisp. The pavlova which followed was even better than the one Edwina, no mean cook herself, had produced a month or two before. I was dumfounded. My culinary skills barely extended beyond heating up pre-prepared meals.

'Where did you learn to cook like that, John?' Rachel asked.

'From my mother. I didn't have any real friends when I was little.' He shot a look at me. 'So I didn't go out much. Cooking made us very close.'

'How is your mother?' I asked after a moment's hesitation.

'She's fine now. Living in a lovely cottage in Kew. Why don't you drop in on her?'

I stared at his face, but it betrayed nothing.

'Yes, I'd like to do that,' I said at last.

After dinner, John and I repaired to the library, with its shelves full of leather-bound books, while Sonja gave Rachel a tour of the house. John handed me a glass of 25-year-old Talisker, much finer than any single malt at the Vicarage, and put on Judie Tzuke's *Sportscar* album.

'Such a beautiful voice. Do you know this record?' he asked, as a contented Oscar settled on his lap.

'Not heard it before.'

'*Welcome to the Cruise* was a brilliant album too. I'll play it after this one.'

We lapsed into silence as we listened to the music, at times energising, at others soothing. John seemed to be in a trance, which suited me, so I sipped my whisky quietly, allowing its peppery, warming flavours to permeate my palate.

Just as Rachel and Sonja came in chattering and laughing, John suddenly sat up, tipped Oscar off his lap, and stared at me, as a mongoose might at a snake.

'I've spoken to Braithwaite. He's delighted you've persuaded me to bring the business to you lot, and he's only too pleased to reassure me that you'll be the partner, or at least one of the partners, assigned to the audit.'

'You did what?' My mind reeled and I felt hot and dizzy. I tried to get a grip on my crumbling sense of reality, and the only way I could do so was to concentrate on cold facts till I'd had time to think.

'Where did you see him?'

'At Boodle's.'

My brain was beginning to catch up with what had happened, and my suppressed resentment started building towards explosive levels. John had gone behind my back and spoken to my senior partner. It was a *fait accompli* which trampled me.

'Look John, very kind of you, but—'

Rachel cut in, giving me a very sharp look.

'I think what he's trying to say is, "Thank you". I wish I could attract a company as big as yours to my practice. It would set me up for the future beautifully.' Rachel directed a radiant smile at John, who gave a self-deprecating shrug of the shoulders and smiled back. I glanced at Sonja to see what she made of this newly formed mutual admiration society only to find her engrossed in reading the lyrics on the back of the *Sportscar* album.

John's broad smile was replaced by a look of intense concentration.

'You're not planning to stay as an accountant, are you Rachel? Britain's economy is finally beginning to take off. We've swallowed Maggie's bitter medicine. Now things are on the up and there's tremendous potential for talented people like you. Of course, you could continue to lead a comfortable existence poring over the books and counting the stock of people who are making it all happen. If you really don't mind missing out on the excitement and are prepared to settle for the safe, the dull and the vicarious, that is.'

Rachel, a thoughtful look on her face, didn't respond and I had the feeling a seed had been sown. I looked at my watch.

'Past midnight. Think it's time we were going.'

'God, is that the time?' John said. 'I'm due to talk to Boston in half an hour.'

Rachel was very quiet as we drove back to the vicarage.

'What are you thinking?' I asked.

'I'm going to contact the head hunters tomorrow. John's right. I need to be where the action is, not spectating from the sidelines.'

'Auditing is hardly on the sidelines. Without us to provide the framework and police it, business would be chaotic and anarchy would reign.'

'Yes, but we're more like referees. I want to be one of the players; in fact, I want to be a top goal scorer.'

I glanced at her as I drove us through the dark lanes. Even in the dim glow from the dashboard, I could see that her eyes were glinting and her body was tense with excitement.

'John is quite a man,' she said in a soft voice.

I peered at her through the half-light.

'You don't fancy him, do you?'

She hesitated for a second.

'No, but he has got…' she paused, searching for the right word, 'chutzpah.'

'And an ego the size of a helium balloon,' I added, though I don't think she registered what I'd said.

'Those blue eyes of his are quite, quite…' again she paused, 'mesmerising.'

'Are you sure you don't fancy him? You spent enough time in the kitchen together.'

'Of course not. Nice eyes, and very easy to talk to, but he's not really my type. He's a bit too opinionated, too sure of himself, too certain he's right.'

'And what is your type?' I said fishing for a compliment. Rachel didn't answer. From the faraway expression in her eyes, I could see her mind was elsewhere.

Chapter 16
THE BEART ENTERPRISES ACCOUNT, 1983

Very little goes unrecorded in offices. Senior people delude themselves that their movements go unnoticed. In fact, every action is noted, every mood interpreted and reinterpreted, and the subsequent assessment relayed to others in the organisation by a process akin to osmosis. I was told by various confidential sources, not unrelated to some of the senior partners' secretaries, that Harry Burrows, one of the most senior partners at AP for longer than he cared to remember, had been sitting with his feet up on his desk, smoking a Havana cigar and gazing out of the window, when the summons came from his brother-in-law, Brian Braithwaite to join him for a chat. My sources told me they heard him express considerable surprise when told that the young fellow, that new partner whose promotion he'd questioned, had brought in the biggest piece of auditing business AP had ever handled, and Harry was invited to act as an overseeing partner to make sure nothing went wrong. Braithwaite was the prime mover in the growth strategy and saw the acquisition of Beart Enterprises as a client as a major step in achieving his ambition. Burrows was, apparently, not keen to take on this role. Only a year from retirement, he was renowned for his predilection for the good life and his aversion to shouldering more responsibility. However, when Braithwaite insisted, he consoled himself that with another partner heavily involved and a full team on the account, he probably wouldn't have to do much more than eat a few lunches and ask some probing questions, both of which activities he'd transformed into an art. In the firm for over forty years, he'd come to be regarded as an institution. Few criticised his lifestyle or his lack of work ethic. For many, he represented, in a romanticised form, what the profession had been years ago, before the seismic changes it was currently undergoing. He was a 'gentleman', in cricketing terms, while now the 'professionals' had taken over.

I didn't relish the prospect of working with him. In my limited experience, he could be extremely acerbic and, even if he eschewed hard work, his formidable intellect was never in doubt.

I awaited his call with trepidation. When it finally came, I rubbed a tissue over my shoes, straightened my tie and set off, heart fluttering, down the long corridor which separated us.

'Come in, sit down my boy.' A smile winged its way across his face. 'Congratulations on landing the Beart Enterprises business. I hear from Brian that you'd been working on it for some time before he decided to come across. Quite an achievement, my boy, quite an achievement; tell me, how did you manage it?' His eyes were fixed on me and the evanescent smile had been replaced by a twist of the lips which might equally have been a facial quirk or a sneer.

I shifted uncomfortably in my hard, leather-backed chair and cleared my throat, acutely conscious I didn't know what John had said to Braithwaite, and what he, in turn, had passed onto Burrows. Modesty seemed the safest policy.

'It was nothing really, just persistence.'

To avoid eye contact, I stared at the large crystal paperweight on his desk.

'You're too self-effacing, my boy. There must be more to it than that. I hear you were at school together. You must have been good friends.'

I wondered what the best response would be. If I agreed, it might diminish my achievement. If I said we weren't, it might make me seem less well-connected. I opted for honesty.

'Not really. We only coincided at prep school for a couple of years and he was two years below me. We didn't have much to do with each other, though I did get him into trouble for starting an insurance business. Now, of course, I realise he was only developing his entrepreneurial skills and what I should've done was invest all my pocket money in him there and then.'

Burrows chuckled, the rolls of fat around his neck wobbling.

'You're lucky he didn't bear a grudge. Wasn't there anything else?'

'I did a brief piece of consultancy for him once, in one of his early acquisitions. Since then we've only met socially.'

'Well, you've certainly made an impression on him. He speaks very highly of you. Says you're the reason he's come to us.'

I decided the most prudent approach would be to ingratiate myself.

'I'm really looking forward to working with you, Harry. I'm sure I'll learn a lot.'

His twisted lips softened into their normal thin slivers and I had the uncomfortable feeling he was still summing me up. Then the corners of his mouth flicked up into what I took to be another fleeting smile.

'We need to establish a few principles. First, I'm about a year from retirement, I've been the firm's golden boy for longer than I care to remember and I have no intention of letting anything or anyone stuff that up. This piece of business must go well, and if it doesn't, it's your neck that's on the block. Understood?'

I nodded.

'That means,' he continued, 'you keep close to it, and tell me early on if there is anything, absolutely anything, to be concerned about. We don't want to piss Beart off. This isn't one of those jobs where you can lounge about on Mount Olympus and let the audit team to do all the work.'

'You can rely on me, Harry,' I said, although I'd no intention of adopting the role he'd outlined. 'I'll make sure you hear of any potential issues very early.'

His brow furrowed.

'Not that anything will go wrong, Harry. I'll see to that, I promise.'

He looked out of the window at two pigeons, one fluffed up and striding back and forth cooing, the other sitting impassively.

'You have the reputation of being somewhat, how shall I put it, laid back.'

I would have liked to say that he, as the master of that style, should know. Instead I leaned forward.

'I think it's important to delegate to allow staff to develop, always within clear boundaries, of course, and subject to close scrutiny, particularly in the higher-risk areas. Perhaps this approach has led to some people misinterpreting my working style.'

'Perhaps.' The two pigeons now sat rubbing against each other on the window ledge, while the silence we sat in for twenty or thirty seconds seemed like an eternity. 'Misinterpretation or not, so long as you're clear what's needed, and are committed to delivering, then we'll say no more about it.'

'I absolutely am. I'll stay as close to this job as those two pigeons are to each other.'

Burrows' eyes narrowed.

'Those are just the preliminaries. One of those two pigeons is about to fuck the other one.'

He stared at me intently and I looked out of the window to avoid his penetrating grey eyes. One pigeon mounted the other amidst a frantic fluttering of wings.

'Just make sure you don't fuck this up, or my parting act with AP will be to fuck you up good and proper.'

I glanced at what was taking place on the roof opposite. The two pigeons were sitting side by side as though nothing had happened. While I didn't feel that I could ignore Burrows' warnings entirely, I had no intention of managing the audit closely myself. The technical aspects of auditing had never been my strong point, and I'd no wish to expose my professional weaknesses to my very able subordinates. In a well-oiled bureaucracy, there was only one possible course of action. I returned to my office and summoned Martha, the manager assigned to the audit.

'Martha,' I said as soon as she was seated. 'I've been to a great deal of trouble to bring Beart Enterprises to this firm, and I've no intention of letting it go wrong. This must go well. I want you to give me daily reports on any potential issues. This is a very important audit, and your career will depend on its success.'

Martha, obviously shaken by such a blunt message, gazed at me nervously. Only recently promoted, her own rise from qualified to supervisor to manager had been almost as swift as mine to partner. She lacked experience, although she made up for it in diligence.

'Of course,' she said. 'I'll make sure everything goes smoothly.'

She closed the door behind her and I allowed myself the luxury of leaning back in my swivel chair and putting my feet on the desk. No doubt Martha would shortly be summoning the audit supervisor to her office and relaying my message to him. I could now relax, secure in the effectiveness of delegation.

Chapter 17
SURREY, 1985

At about the time I was promoted to partner, Rachel finally succumbed to the entreaties of Showell Deeley, a FTSE100 global distribution organisation, and accepted the role of finance director at a significantly enhanced salary. John had tried twice to lure her to Beart Enterprises, taking her first to Paris for dinner at Maxim's and then to the newly opened Union Square Café in New York and offering her an initial salary package which would have gratified at least half the CEOs in the FTSE 100. Both times she'd refused.

'There's something a little sinister about John,' she'd said to me as we sat drinking Campari and tonic on the terrace of The London Apprentice shortly after her return from New York. 'Something vaguely menacing. It's not that he isn't perfectly pleasant. When he turns it on, he can be charm personified, still—'

'What do you mean, menacing?' The ice in my glass chinked as I placed it on the wooden table. What was left of the river at low tide crawled sluggishly through the dark mud flats, and the stagnant smell clung to my nostrils. We'd chosen the wrong evening to visit a riverside pub.

She thought for a moment. 'Like a great white shark, circling through the water till it picks up the smell of blood.'

I was relieved she shared my discomfort. I'd no wish to have any more to do with him than necessary, and always felt on edge in his presence. It wasn't something I could describe, but it was deep-seated in me.

A few seagulls had clustered around something grey and shapeless deposited by the retreating water, their screams piercing the air until one of them fought off the others, grasped whatever it was and, with a strenuous beating of its wings, took off, pursued by its rivals.

'So, you don't think him charismatic?' I was reluctant to let the matter drop until she said something unequivocally critical.

'Oh God, he's charismatic all right. The way he looks at you, with those enormous eyes probing your mind and digging into your soul. And that smile of his, it's almost as though you're the only person he's ever been interested in.' She took a sip from her glass. 'Yes, I could certainly imagine people following him slavishly.'

'But not you?' Far from being reassured by Rachel's answer, I was now trying to conceal an increasing disquiet.

'No. I'm too hard-bitten to fall for his charms.'

Rachel shivered as a sudden breeze made the small golden hairs on her slender arms stand up.

'Would you like to borrow my jacket?' I started to ease myself out of it.

'No thanks. Let's go and have dinner. I fancy an Indian, How about The Rawalpindi?

We stood up, and I put my arm around her. She nuzzled under my jacket and I murmured softly in her ear.

'Even that trip over on Concorde didn't win you over?'

'Far from it. Much too flash.'

I swallowed the comment welling up in me so as not to puncture the mood on one of the rare evenings Rachel and I had spent together recently. If anyone liked the good things in life, if was Rachel.

'Just as well for me, Mr Down-to-Earth,' I said, kissing her sun-warmed hair.

'That's how I like 'em,' she said, turning her face up to mine for a kiss. 'Now let's go and eat. I could murder a Chicken Jalfrezi.'

*

Rachel's new job meant she was away on business

for about half the year, and working long hours in central London for the remainder. If she did manage to take time off on a Saturday, she spent it shopping for clothes and shoes and handbags, many of which she would use only a few times before donating them to the charity shop. It was her shoes which caused me the greatest frustration. The height of the heels made her resort to taxis for even the shortest journeys.

'They're not fit for purpose,' I would moan.

'It's essential to wear fashionable clothes,' she would reply. 'Especially shoes. You just don't understand.'

I spent my time pottering about on the golf course and, through complete boredom, was even reduced to doing work at home, so much so that Richard, who'd been made a partner shortly after me, accused me of being a workaholic.

Then, one day, I saw the house – and I mean *the* house – and fell in love with it. Even though our place in Richmond was pleasant, the streets around it were narrow and parking was difficult. In the summer, when the windows were open, the sound of the neighbours' televisions, arguments, and lovemaking would drift in.

I'd noticed the 'For Sale' sign on my way to West Hurtle golf course. Double-fronted, red-brick and of the Arts and Crafts era, Thorpe Barton was tucked away in a quiet road in East Tattingfold, not far from Dorking. It looked noble but forlorn and neglected, an impoverished aristocrat in frayed finery. It begged me to stop and implored me to step inside its lush, overgrown garden. Secluded within a grand porch was a bottle-green door, its brass knocker and letter box tarnished and its paint peeling badly. I stopped the car, relishing the semi-circular gravel drive with an old wooden gate at either end. For some inexplicable reason, ever since I was a boy I'd coveted a house with a drive like that.

Thorpe Barton would require serious renovation and any sensible person would have walked away, but I stood enraptured. I yearned to rescue it and give it the love it deserved. In any case, I reasoned, the poor condition would probably be reflected in the price, and even if it weren't, I could negotiate. With the way that house prices in the South East were increasing, any money we spent would be an investment.

Such was my infatuation with this building I forgot that Richard was waiting for me at the golf club and drove straight to the estate agent's office, where I found a stocky young man lolling back in his chair to expose an expanse of flabby stomach. He leaped to his feet and greeted me effusively.

'I'm Alan Daniels.' He extended a damp hand. I mentioned the property I'd seen.

'Lovely place, in great demand, lots of interest, fantastic scope for refurbishment, and priced very competitively too.'

'How much?'

When he told me, I staggered back a step.

'How long has it been on the market?'

He paused.

'Not that long.'

'How long?'

Sighing heavily, he pulled a file from the cabinet.

'Four months.'

In such a hot housing market, it was inconceivable anything other than a complete dump would still be for sale after four weeks, let alone four months.

'Sounds like they've overpriced it. Could we go and see it?'

'Sure.' He drew on his cigar. 'When would you like me to make an appointment?'

'How about now?'

He looked around the room, as though seeking a means of escape.

'I'll have to phone the owner to check it's convenient.'

The telephone conversation was brief. 'It's OK,' he said. 'We can go now.'

Getting out of his car, he leaned towards me conspiratorially and I smelt stale cigar smoke and yesterday's curry on his breath.

'Funny woman, Mrs Martell. Doesn't really want to sell; divorce settlement, you see. She has to move when the youngest reaches eighteen, and that's happened. She lives here with her three daughters, when they're not at university, and her mother, who's, how can I put it, not the easiest person.'

The front door creaked open slowly revealing an old lady in black with a face the colour and consistency of a roasted sweet chestnut.

'Good morning, Mrs Simpson. How are we today?'

Mrs Simpson treated his question with disdain.

'My daughter's in the garden. Come in and I'll call her.'

The beautifully proportioned hall, its original black and white tiles still intact, smelled of mushrooms. The paintwork was flaking and the skirting boards cracked. I shivered; the house felt damp.

When Mrs Martell finally arrived, she ignored our attempts to shake her hand, giving only a cursory nod.

'Do you mind if I show this gentleman around? Could we start—'

'I'll come with you,' Mrs Martell interposed.

We trailed after her into the sitting-room.

'It needs a lot of work. Already reflected in the price, of course,' she said. 'And there's the aircraft noise. That can be a nuisance.'

'Doubt it compares with Richmond,' I responded. 'We're right under the flight path.'

She gestured at a hole in the skirting board.

'Problems with mice, quite a lot of rats too.'

We wandered around the rest of the house

looking at rotten window frames, flaking plaster and plumbing which should have been in a museum. We ended up in the hall, where, compared with the rest of the house, the air now smelled relatively pure. While it was clear the property was in a terrible state of repair, it was nothing that couldn't be put right. It needed love, and I was going to give it love by the spadeful.

'When was it built?' I asked Mrs Martell.

'1905,' she replied, gazing up at a yellow stain on the ceiling and refusing to meet my eye.

'How long have you been here?'

'Twenty-two years.' Her eyes finally met mine. 'We bought it from a divorcing couple. They were only here a year or two. They'd bought it from another couple who'd split up. Not putting you off, am I? We've been very happy here, at least since he left.' She nodded in the direction of the sitting-room, as though Mr Martell were ensconced there.

'No, you've been very helpful. Of course, I'll need a full structural survey if I decide to go ahead.'

Before getting back in the car, I stopped to look up at the house. Nothing Mrs Martell had said had diminished my feelings for it.

'Vastly over-priced,' I told Daniels. 'It's virtually a slum. If something isn't done soon the council will probably pull it down. Who else is interested?'

He shrugged his shoulders. Perhaps the temptation of not having to take people around it again and face the Martell-Simpson ordeal made him open up.

'Just one, a developer. He'll only buy it if he can get the ones on either side.'

'You mean he'll pull it down and put up a ticky-tacky development?'

'That's the idea. I don't think it'll work because the people on either side are retirees and don't want to move.'

'Will she take an offer?'

'She'd hold out for the full asking price. Her ex-husband might be more accommodating. He's got a young family with Mrs Martell mark two and needs the money. I don't think Mrs M mark one has much of a leg to stand on. There's a clause in the divorce settlement which settles the minimum price. It's the average of three different valuations. We're one of the valuers, the other two are also local firms. I can't disclose anything officially of course, though I think it might be worth chancing an offer.'

I viewed the house again the next day. During the previous evening I'd started doubting my judgment, and wanted to be certain of my feelings for it. By the end of the second visit I was sure. I was particularly excited by the south-facing garden, with its dilapidated greenhouse and its ramshackle gazebo, imagining what I could create out of it. Thorpe Barton was the house for me. Now all I had to do was persuade Rachel.

★

'Look, I'm comfortable living here. I've got everything sorted. We don't need to do anything. If we buy this new place we'll take on a large mortgage, we'll have to pay a fortune to do it up and it'll be a massive amount of hassle.' Rachel didn't look up from the documents she was reading. She turned the page and scrutinised a dense column of figures. A few moments passed. The chimes of a passing ice cream van grew and then faded into the distance. I wasn't prepared to drop the idea as easily as that, even though I was risking the mood of one of the few Saturdays that Rachel and I had spent together in the last three months.

'With our combined salaries, we can easily afford it and still lead a pleasant life. And don't worry about getting it all done. I'll take care of everything.'

Rachel looked up at me as I paced around the room, my hands clasped together in front of me.

'When are you going to have time? I certainly couldn't have done it while I was an audit partner.'

'I'll manage. It's not too busy at work right now and, besides, I can always delegate.'

She folded the document and put it to one side, fixing me with her full stare.

'There are some things you can't delegate. A partner is more than a full-time job if you do it properly.'

'It's a question of priorities. We have to allow staff to develop; empowerment and all that.' I was becoming adept at management jargon and, having realised it sounded definitive without actually saying anything, was using it increasingly.

Rachel sighed.

'It's bad enough living where we do. Now you want us to move even further out. All our friends live near the centre: Kensington, Wandsworth, Pimlico. We'll be the only ones out in the sticks.'

'Ah, that's just a phase. They'll all be moving out when they start families.'

She didn't reply. She hadn't mentioned the topic of our having a family for some time and her interest in friends' children, of whom she was godmother to several, didn't extend beyond buying them a birthday present.

'We are going to start a family soon....aren't we?'

While I wasn't particularly anxious to start a family, it suited my argument to bring it up.

Rachel muttered something and went back to her work.

*

I went to see Thorpe Barton another three times, and loved it more with each visit. Once you got past the initial impression of damp and decay, a deeper, more permanent redolence of solid craftsmanship permeated the house. Like a wolf returning to its lair, I felt at home. I started to think about the possibilities. I could see it as it was going to be, and the vision filled me with energy.

Rachel only viewed it once and was so jet lagged at the time she probably didn't know whether she was in Surrey or the VIP lounge at JFK Airport.

'It's all right, I suppose,' she said.

'All right?' I replied. 'It's a gem, or at least it could be with a bit of time and effort invested in it. It's beautifully proportioned, and it's even got some of its original brick fireplaces and wooden fittings. Besides, I'd give my right arm to have a garden with that potential.'

'I suppose so,' she yawned. 'It could be a lovely house if it weren't in the wrong place and if it weren't so big. What do we want with seven bedrooms?'

'Perhaps we'll have a large family.' I was conscious that prediction would be unlikely to come true, bearing in mind the infrequency of our sex life. On the other hand, Rachel was renowned for her efficiency, and I wouldn't put it past her, if she wanted a large family, to wait for the last ticking of the biological clock before popping into a clinic to have five embryos implanted simultaneously.

'Why do you want this house so much?' she asked, rubbing her eyes.

'It'll be my project, something I can create. You love your work, but I don't have anything. Let me do it for us, for our family.' I kept playing the family card as I thought the nest building aspect might just appeal to some maternal instinct buried deeply in her.

'Let's talk about it tomorrow.' Rachel sighed.

'You'll be at work.' Even though the next day was Sunday, I knew she'd been summoned to a meeting at his house by her Chief Executive; something to do with a possible takeover target.

'Oh yes. I'd forgotten. Well, we can talk about it next week.'

'You're in Amsterdam all next week, leaving early Monday and arriving home late on Friday. Other people are interested in this house, and if we don't act now, we'll lose it.'

Rachel shifted uncomfortably in her seat. Commuting wouldn't be an issue for her; her firm paid for a chauffeur to take her to and from the office. Although she would probably rather have lived somewhere more fashionable, the location was pleasant enough, the house could be beautiful, it was potentially a sound investment and she was hardly ever there anyway.

'I'll agree on three conditions.' She exhaled deeply. 'One, you organise the sale of our house in Richmond; two, we buy a small flat in the city so I don't have to put up with the mess; three, you do everything, and I mean everything. Agreed?'

'Agreed.' I suppressed a triumphant punch in the air and kissed her. In the past, she hadn't even trusted me to buy my own clothes. This was either a massive vote of confidence in me or a sign of her dissociation from day-to-day life.

We found a buyer for our house in Richmond so quickly it made us wonder whether we'd undervalued it, Rachel went ahead and bought a small, completely refurbished one bedroom flat in Smithfield and I started to negotiate to buy Thorpe Barton. To condition their thinking, I submitted a low offer, which was rejected by both Mrs Martell and her husband, before increasing it by five per cent, still a long way off the asking price.

Then the next part of my strategy came into play. Richard, having forgiven me for not turning up at the golf club, went to view Thorpe Barton and put in an offer lower than mine, taking every opportunity to talk disparagingly of its faults and saying only a madman would offer more. I waited for this information to be relayed to Mr Martell before increasing my offer slightly and, after a few days' deliberation, it was accepted.

When the surveyor visited the house, his report was full of dire warnings. Neglected for years, the whole of Thorpe Barton needed renovation, or at least serious attention.

I photocopied the report and asked the estate agent to send a copy to Mr Martell, while I took the original around to Mrs Martell and reduced my offer by ten per cent.

'If you don't spend a substantial sum in the very near future, your house will become uninhabitable.' I handed a copy of the report, marked up in yellow highlighter to her.

'Most of this is cosmetic,' she countered.

'Cosmetic?' I forced a laugh. 'Only if you think dry rot, wet rot, beetle infestations, a leaking roof, a boiler that's on its last legs, faulty electrics, rotten window frames and leaky plumbing are cosmetic. This house could kill you and your family.' It was a risk talking to a virtual stranger like this, and I'd laid it on a bit thick, perhaps a little too thick. I watched her face closely. The way she swallowed hard, almost gulped, told me I'd made an impact and I breathed a sigh of relief.

A few days later, my reduced offer was accepted. The Martells moved out, unscrewing everything that unscrewed and leaving their detritus everywhere. I was glad Rachel wasn't there to witness the disheartening sight of Thorpe Barton, now stripped of its furniture and carpets. There were more problems and faults than I'd imagined or the surveyor identified, and my description of the state of the property to Mrs Martell had been an understatement. I spent my first night there listening to the scrabbling of an army of vermin in the loft above me, and concluded that my first appointment would be with a pest control firm. Then, still half asleep, I got up to relieve myself in the middle of the night, and was jolted awake by an electric shock from a light switch which left my whole hand tingling. If I didn't make the electrician my first priority, I might not live to call in the rodent people.

Over the next year, I confronted the challenges of renovation. A profound sense of accomplishment suffused my entire being as the house was moulded according to my wishes and the project moved to completion.

★

It was three months since Rachel had seen Thorpe Barton. We were leading separate lives; she, self-contained in her apartment, I in the slowly receding mess. I'd seen her for dinner three times in that period – all strange evenings, with both of us skirting around the topic that concerned me most, the state of our relationship, and talking about almost anything else instead. At the end of each of these dinners, I would see her home, receive a perfunctory kiss and then be sent on my way.

The decorators had put the finishing touches to the rag-rolling in the sitting-room, leaving only the hall to decorate. I phoned her, imploring her to come down and see the work.

'It looks fantastic. You'll love it, I promise.'

'I'm a bit busy right now.' Her voice was drained of energy.

'We haven't seen each other for ages.' I hated myself for sounding like a wheedling little boy.

'Why don't you come up here instead? I'll take you out to dinner.'

I couldn't make out her exact tone. Remote? Listless? Disengaged? Was this the end of our relationship? We certainly didn't seem to have much in common.

'All right. I'll see you about seven.'

The restaurant was 'typically Rachel'. The main dining-room was a sizeable conservatory, wreathed in Purple Bell Vine, its dark green foliage studded with purple-red pendent flowers with black centres. The furniture was angular bamboo and the cuisine a melange of disparate ingredients – pease pudding laced with cumin seeds and lemon grass was the first to catch my eye on the menu – in minute, intricately arranged portions. In the corner, a male TV actor from one of the soaps was dining with a heavily made-up brunette sporting a deep, sun-baked cleavage, who presented the breakfast news. The editor of a tabloid sat in another corner, surrounded by a simpering coterie of indeterminate sex.

'It's the ambience,' Rachel said, gazing around as though in wonder. 'It's so airy and leafy, you feel as though you're out in the country, even though we're in Kensington.'

'Come to our house and you will be out in the country.'

'As if!' she sniffed histrionically. 'Outer suburbs, more like.'

'Well it's a bloody sight closer to the country than this poncey restaurant.'

I regretted the words as soon as I'd uttered them. She looked at me coldly, one thin eyebrow arched.

'Don't you at least like the food?'

'Ghastly.' I decided not to back down. 'This place is phoney, from the menu to the people eating in it. The only thing that's real is the bill. I'd rather have a Big Mac any day.'

'I'm sorry you don't like my choice of restaurant. Perhaps we should pay and leave before it offends you further.' She waved a gold card at a waiter. Having gathered her things together and retrieved her coat, she stalked ahead of me onto the pavement.

'I'll take a taxi. There's no need to see me home.' She extended a cheek for me to kiss and then, seeing a cab on the other side of the road, summoned it.

'Is that it?' I wasn't sure whether I was referring to the evening or our marriage.

She didn't look at me. As she opened the taxi's door, she said over her shoulder, 'That's rather up to you.' The evening was over already so it seemed clear what she was referring to.

Weeks passed and I didn't bother to contact her. I was still irate at the off-hand way in which I'd been treated. I presumed that my comments about the restaurant were still rankling, though from time to time the thought occurred to me that I was flattering myself and she'd probably been so immersed in work she hadn't given me a second thought.

I had, some months before, booked us on a summer holiday in Turkey and now needed to discuss arrangements with her. I was engrossed in reading some draft reports one sultry afternoon, the sun streaming through my office window, when the phone rang.

'It's Wendy,' the voice said. Wendy was Rachel's secretary. 'Rachel asked me to phone you. She's on an aeroplane to Sydney; she'll call you when she can. She's asked me to pass on a message. She won't be able to come to Turkey after all because it looks as though she'll be in Australia for some time. If you incur a loss cashing in the tickets, SD will reimburse you.'

I gulped, struggling for air.

'Are you still there?' Wendy asked. I forced a cough to give me time to compose myself.

'Frog in my throat.' I drew a deep breath. 'Thanks for letting me know.' Replacing the receiver, I stood up, took careful aim and, with a deft kick, sent my wastepaper basket hurtling against the wall, its contents spilling across the floor. I slumped back onto my chair, my head in my hands. I still couldn't believe Rachel hadn't spoken to me herself.

There's only one turkey around here, I thought, and that's our marriage.

When Rachel did call, the line was poor and her voice kept breaking up.

'I'm sorry,' she said, just audible amidst the crackling, 'that's the way it is. I have to do my job and, after all, it's only a holiday.'

It might only have been a holiday to her. To me it could have been the opportunity to rebuild our failing marriage. In a bout of self-pity, I went to the pub where it took two hours to deaden, albeit temporarily, my pain.

The next day, with my head throbbing, I carefully constructed a letter, hoping I'd do better this time than I had when writing to Mrs Beart.

"Dear Rachel,

Welcome home. Even though we hardly see anything of each other these days, I've missed you while you've been out of the country. Usually it's a comfort to know you aren't that far away, at least geographically.

I know things haven't been going well between us for some time. I'm not trying to blame you, just to lay it out clearly, and I'm sure you're as concerned as I am.

We had a great relationship till life got in the way. I really think we ought to spend some time together, deciding what we both want. We owe it to each other.

Please let's go away for a weekend, with the

understanding we'll return home more certain about our future together.
Although it may not always show, I still love you, and hope you feel the same about me.
I'll phone you."

I struggled how to finish it, eventually settling on "*With much love, as ever*" and despatched the letter.

The day she got back, Rachel phoned me. Adrenaline pumped through my body at the sound of her voice and my hands trembled.

'I'm sorry. I've been very stressed by problems at SD. I agree we need a new start. Let's go away for that weekend and work things out.'

I let out a deep sigh and my shoulders, previously up around my ears, gradually sank back to their normal position.

'You mean it?'

'Were you expecting a different answer?'

'No, I'm delighted. When will you be free?'

'Next weekend? Let's not wait.'

'OK, I'll find us a nice place in the country.'

'Mind you do. I've had to endure some of the so-called deals you've come up with in the past. Let's do this properly.'

I felt buoyed up by the conversation. I'd thought our marriage was in injury time. Perhaps it wasn't entirely hopeless to believe we could rebuild our relationship, just as I'd renovated our property. I'd dedicate all my restoration work to her. Thorpe Barton would be a shrine to our union.

*

Tilston Grange in Suffolk, a cream-coloured Palladian mansion with tall pediments, airy porticos and acres of parkland, looked like the opulent setting for a Merchant and Ivory adaptation of a Jane Austen novel. The clean symmetry of its marble interior matched that of its exterior, and I was pleased to hear Rachel's gratified murmurings as we entered the hall. The mouldings featured masks and shells and its wall paintings portrayed scenes from *The Odyssey*, the one closest to the desk depicting Penelope weaving to put off her suitors.

With the memory of Rachel's words echoing in my ears, I'd spared no expense and had booked the best suite. A chilled bottle of Dom Perignon awaited us.

'I want you to promise one thing,' I said, as I held the cork and gently twisted the bottle. 'You won't think about or talk about work until we leave on Sunday evening.'

Rachel looked strangely uncertain.

'There are two things I have to tell you first.'

I froze, the cork half out of the bottle.

'The first is that John Beart has made me a very attractive offer to join his organisation as CEO.'

'What did you say?'

'I turned him down. Can't say I wasn't tempted. He was very flattering about what I could bring to his company. He said there was real chemistry between us.'

'Is there?'

'Well, I'm warming to him. I always knew he had a rare talent. It was that manner of his, his air of superiority that put me off. I think I misjudged him. Now he strikes me as a sincere person. In fact, the dinner was great fun.'

'You had dinner with him?'

'Yes, he took me to this delightful little Italian place just off the Fulham Road. I must take you there. You'd really like it. It's not at all what you would call poncey, and the food's divine.'

My mood darkened as I imagined them sitting side by side, chatting easily as they twirled spaghetti round their forks and sipped Chianti. I knew I couldn't afford to ruin the weekend, so, with a supreme effort of self-control, I merely nodded.

'Then why didn't you accept?'

'That brings me to the second thing. I'd just been offered and accepted the role of CEO by SD. I couldn't let them down.'

'Congratulations,' I said, trying to process the information. I was relieved Rachel wouldn't be working for Beart. As for her new role, she could hardly be any busier, so it couldn't have much impact on me. Perhaps she might be able to delegate more and we could get our relationship back on the rails. 'So, we've got a great reason to celebrate.'

'Thanks for taking it so well. I thought you might worry we'd see even less of each other.'

'If it's what you want, you must do it.' The words sounded hollow, though I don't think Rachel noticed, because she came to me, put her arms around me and kissed me on the lips, our first full-blooded kiss in months. I barely noticed the cork unleashing itself from the bottle and the spurt of champagne that followed.

When we went to dinner, arm in arm, I was suffused with a deep sense of post-coital satisfaction. It was as though Rachel's passion, held like water behind a dam, had finally burst through as an exhilarating cascade of sexual gratification. Now Rachel glowed in her backless black satin dress, and I was sure everyone would smell her pheromones wafting tantalisingly around the dining-room.

I'd booked a table in the corner, shielded from the view of other diners by the spreading fronds of a potted palm eight inches taller than the waiter. The food was beautifully prepared and, to my delight, the portions substantial.

Even though I was eating fish, I ordered a bottle of Brouilly from the famous Pisse Vieille vineyard, challenging Rachel to tell me what aromas she could detect. She cupped the glass in her hand for a few moments, swilled it around, inspected it and raised it to her nostrils.

'Blueberries,' she said, 'or possibly cherries.' She inhaled again. 'Perhaps a hint of raspberries and currants.'

'Sounds like a whole fruit stall. You've only left out the bananas.'

I lifted my glass to my nose, closed my eyes and puckered my eyebrows, as though in deep thought.

'Mmm, ye-es, I get the che-e-rries,' I sniffed the bouquet again theatrically. 'Perhaps with a hint of an old woman's ne-ether garments.'

'To you, lowering the tone has become an art form, hasn't it?' Rachel's look was reproving.

'We complement each other,' I replied. 'Yin and Yang, Norman and Saxon, Dalglish and Rush.'

Rachel stared at me blankly. She'd never taken much interest in football.

'So, what are we going to do?' I asked. 'Do we still have a future together?'

'Do you want us to?' she said, her eyebrows raised slightly and eyes wide open.

'Of course,' I replied, stretching out my hand and placing it lightly on her forearm. 'Do you?'

She hesitated for a fraction of a second, glancing down at the embroidered white table-cloth.

'Yes, I do.' Her unblinking eyes met mine and she smiled.

I could feel tears welling-up. I looked at Rachel's face, calm and collected as ever and thought, 'I mustn't be the one to blub. Only women cry.'

'We have to sort out our living arrangements,' I said, hoarsely, gazing over her shoulder at one of the palm's fronds and noticing, for the first time, that it had started to turn yellow, probably through over-watering.

'Yes,' Rachel said.

I dragged my eyes away from the mistreated palm and fixed them on Rachel. She was looking exquisite.

'We can't plan to stay together and then live apart indefinitely. It won't work.'

'Let's see how it goes,' Rachel said. 'I might be able to spend weekends and Monday nights in Surrey and live in the flat the rest of the time.'

'If you like, I could follow the complementary pattern, now I've finished the renovation work.'

Rachel's warm hand enclosed mine gently.

The rest of the weekend passed as quickly as the countryside through the window of a bullet train. All too soon, it was Sunday evening. We kissed affectionately and Rachel took a cab back to her flat. It must have cost a fortune.

*

As soon as I put my key in the lock, I sensed something was wrong.

Then the smell hit me and I nearly retched. In the hall, curled up like thick black sea cucumbers, lay a pile of faeces. I staggered from room to room. Every cupboard had been emptied and its contents strewn around. The dining table and chairs lay broken and the three-piece suite had been slashed, its stuffing spilling out like entrails. Worst was the red daubing on the dining-room wall:

'YOU'RE NEXT!!'

Despite my hand shaking uncontrollably, I noted down what had been taken: my grandmother's silver urn, a couple of pairs of cufflinks, a television set, my best suit, some prints and maps, a portrait by a minor Victorian artist, a few other odds and ends. Lots had been left which could have been sold illegally quite easily. I called the police. They were useless, saying if I wanted to buy the stuff back, I should go down to the Brighton Lanes over the next couple of weekends.

'What about the threat in red paint?' I asked.

'Probably a prank. Your house was most likely done over by drugged up teenagers looking to finance their next high.'

Though it only took a few weeks to clean up and redecorate, the house felt desecrated.

Understandably, Rachel was worried about living there, even though I had a new door and window locks fitted and installed a burglar alarm, because she said the house's seclusion, such an attraction in the bright sunlight of day, became threatening at night. All the progress we'd made at Tilston Grange seemed to have dissipated. While I went to stay at her apartment two or three nights a week, her new role proved just as time-consuming as her old, and

I'd be vaguely conscious of her crawling into bed after midnight and dragging herself up at five every morning. I might as well have been a pillow for all the attention I received.

After a few dispiriting weeks, I moved back to Surrey full-time, intent on exorcising the ghosts left by our intruders. I gave a drinks party for our neighbours and, even though nothing explicit was said, sensed their surprise when I admitted that my wife was living in London. Although most of my neighbours were considerably older, one was married to a much younger wife, Amelia, who followed me into the kitchen when I went to replenish the snacks.

'It must get lonely rattling around in a great big house all on your own.' She took a packet of salted cashew nuts from my hand, tore it open with her teeth and poured the contents into a bowl.

'Suppose so,' I replied. 'My job's pretty demanding, so I'm not here much. How about you? Are you working?'

'I used to be a primary school teacher. Now I just look after him.' She nodded in the direction of the other room. 'And the children and the house.'

'I thought you said they were at boarding school.' I searched the fridge for more olives and pulled out an empty jar I must have absentmindedly put back.

'They're here in the holidays, except when they go to activity camps.'

I arranged some cheese straws carefully on a plate.

'Do you play squash?' Amelia asked.

I shook my head. 'Bit energetic; I do stretch to a round of golf. Do you play?'

'Old man's game. I prefer racquet sports.'

Amelia walked into the drawing-room in front of me, and a subtle vapour trail of perfume teased my nostrils as she glided across the hall. Although she was physically attractive, the last thing I wanted was an extra marital relationship when my own marriage was struggling to survive.

At eight thirty, as though prompted by a message only I couldn't hear, my guests rose, thanked me for my hospitality and departed. As she walked past me I was conscious of Amelia's gentle touch on my arm.

★

I enrolled in the East Tattingfold Society and the local history group, and found all the other members to be at least twenty years older. I joined the golf club and spent mind-numbing evenings in the clubhouse being regaled with tales of yore by the biggest bores I'd ever encountered. Nothing seemed to break life's all-embracing monotony.

Work was no more interesting, despite my career being on an upward trajectory. Burrows had retired and Braithwaite decided that, with resources already stretched, I no longer needed supervision. Beart Enterprises was growing fast, both organically and through takeovers. The income to my firm increased massively and we hired more staff.

Braithwaite patted me on the shoulder one Friday evening as we coincided in the lobby.

'Well done, my boy. We couldn't have expanded like this if you hadn't brought us Beart. He's a goldmine and having him on our books has done us no harm in the eyes of potential clients.'

*

It was about then I received a call from my mother.

'Your father has had a heart attack. He's in Abbotsford Hospital. A lot of damage. They're not sure he's going to make it. He's asking for you.'

'Are you all right, Mum?'

'I'm fine. Your brother's here.'

Taking the first train, I arrived at my father's bedside to find my mother and Philip and his wife, Angela. My mother stood up and hugged me. Philip gave me a curt nod and Angela smiled.

'Long time no see, Phil,' I said quietly. 'Surprised to see you here.'

He leant towards me and whispered.

'Want to make sure it isn't a false alarm.'

My father's face was ashen and his eyes filmy. Numerous tubes went into and out of him, while wires on his chest were linked up to a bank of flashing and beeping computer screens. His breathing was irregular and every now and then he would give a slight cough.

'We must go and get some food,' my brother announced. 'Haven't eaten since breakfast.' He and Angela disappeared.

My father made a noise, a cross between a groan and a cough. My mother leant over him and he whispered something.

'He's right here.' She beckoned me over and I crouched down, my ear close to his mouth.

'Proud of you,' he croaked. 'Don't fuck it up like your useless brother.'

Gazing at me through watery eyes, he stretched out his hand. He didn't have the strength to hold it up, and it flopped onto the bed in front of me. I was on the point of placing my hand on his when I checked myself. Why should I make it easy for the old bastard? He'd never made it easy for us.

He exhaled sharply, then shuddered twice, his body convulsing. His last breath left him and the inert calm of the dead descended on him as the bank of computers emitted a long, monotone beep and green lights flashed. My initial reaction was relief, followed by the feeling I should do something.

'We'd better get someone,' I said, looking at the door. My mother grasped my sleeve.

'Leave him in peace. It's better this way. We'll tell them in a few minutes.'

I sank into the chair and we sat holding hands. I looked at my mother, expecting tears. She remained erect, an impassive expression on her face. A few minutes passed.

'Now you can tell them.'

I went to get help. A young female doctor and two nurses came and tried to resuscitate him. After about five minutes' feverish activity, they declared it too late.

'I'm sorry,' the doctor said, bowing her head.

'You did your best, dear,' my mother replied. 'No one can ask more.'

'Do you want us to leave you with him for a while?' the doctor asked.

'No thanks, dear; I've said my farewells.'

'What about your other son?'

'Philip? He said his farewells, such as they were, years ago.'

The medical team left and a couple of porters came in to wheel my father's bed away. My mother didn't glance at him once while he was being trundled out into the corridor.

My mother was collecting her things together.

'Are Philip and Angela staying with you tonight, Mum?'

'Good Lord, no. They've got to get back to the children in Milton Keynes. I'll be perfectly all right on my own. I've got the remains of Sunday's leg of lamb to eat cold. Why, do you want to stay?'

On the spur of the moment I accepted.

That evening, my mother poured herself a large gin and tonic as she laid the cold meat and salad out on plates, and started to tell me stories of her youth, laughing loudly at her reminiscences in a way I'd never seen before. I realised how little we'd spoken when my father was around, his looming presence an oppressive thundercloud over everything that went on in the family.

'What will you do now, Mum?'

'I think I'll go on holiday.' She produced a clutch of travel brochures from her handbag. 'I popped out to pick these up while your father was unconscious. Shall we have a look at them while we eat? I've always fancied going to Pompeii. Your father wouldn't hear of it, of course.'

She buried her head in the glossy pages, occasionally reading out details of one which caught her eye.

'Will you be all right on your own, Mum?'

'I've been on my own for years. Besides, I'm not going to stint myself. I'll go on a guided tour with everything laid on. You never know, I might make some new friends.'

Chapter 18
ANOTHER REUNION, 1986

It must have been late October because it was dark when I got home. I always resented the onset of winter, the loss of the long summer evenings and the ridiculous reversion to Greenwich Mean Time to pander to those Scottish farmers.

The trees around Thorpe Barton shrouded it almost completely, cutting out the dim orange glow from the street lamp. I had still not repaired the external lights, another casualty of the break-in, so I was inching carefully across the inky porch with my key extended when I heard a soft cough in my ear. I spun round, the key clattering onto the tiles.

'Didn't mean to alarm you,' said a confident voice I couldn't immediately place.

'Who on earth—?'

'I was passing and wondered whether we could have a chat.'

I could just make out the dark outline of Beart standing in the gloom.

'What the fuck are you doing here? You gave me the shock of my life, looming out of the pitch black like that.'

I fumbled around on the floor, retrieved my keys and opened the door. Beart walked in ahead of me, uninvited.

I switched on the hall lights.

'Nice place.' He strolled into the sitting-room, and stretched out, legs crossed, in an armchair. I eased my tie and hung my jacket up in the hall before following him.

'Drink?' I asked.

'Got any scotch?'

I took out the 10-year-old Macallan I kept for special occasions and poured him a slug. I always preferred a cup of tea when I got home, so I put the kettle on.

'Where were you going when you happened to pass by?' I shouted from the kitchen though I knew he wouldn't answer my question. He appeared at the door, glass in hand.

'I want Rachel to join me as my Chief Executive. You know the investment fund. Well I've got major expansion plans for it, and I need someone who's financially savvy to run it.' He leant against the doorpost. 'I thought you might put in a word for me.'

'I see,' I said as we went back into the sitting-room.

He knocked back the substantial measure I'd

poured him, went over to the drinks' cabinet and helped himself to another, twice the size.

'Will you?' he asked.

'What's it got to do with me?' I sipped my tea, feeling like a maiden aunt confronted by a niece's ardent suitor. 'Rachel makes her own decisions.'

'When will she be back?' He placed the half-full glass directly on my polished wooden table, inches away from the coaster.

'Not tonight,' I replied, determined not to give anything away. 'In any case, why don't you put your case directly to her? Why come through me?'

'Oh, I've tried, believe me. Repeatedly,' he drawled. 'We had lunch at The Ivy a week ago, and before that at the Savoy Grill, and before that at a few other places. She's very obstinate, and I don't know why. Do you?'

I was surprised he'd entertained Rachel so frequently, though I wasn't going to show it.

'Rachel's got a mind of her own. Once she's made it up, she's very difficult to shift.'

'That's why I like her, and that's why I want her to work for me. I'm tired of yes-men.' He picked up and drained his glass. 'Anyway, how's the audit going? I hear you're now The Man at AP, and hailed as one of the coming men in accountancy.'

'The audit's going OK so far.' I didn't need to be reminded I owed my success to him.

'By the way,' I said, 'I presume that if Rachel did

come and work for you, I'd have to step down from my role in the audit. Conflict of interest and all that.'

He smiled. 'There are ways and means. It wouldn't be an insurmountable problem.'

'I'm not so sure. As we're married, I don't see how I could claim to be objective.'

'Well, when you get the chance, tell Rachel how much I'd like to work with her. The job will be exciting and the package incomparable. If she does well, she'll be the hottest property in the City.' He got up and sauntered to the door. 'Thanks for the scotch, most pleasant. That's a good distillery. I have a bottle of 1926 Macallan. I'm keeping it for when I have something really worth celebrating.' He turned to me as he grasped the door-handle.

'A couple of your neighbours, I believe, are friends of mine; Simon and Amelia. Lovely people.'

He let himself out and I finished my tea. I didn't believe he really thought I had any influence over Rachel. So why had he come? And as for my continuing as audit partner if she did go and work for him, well that was just nonsense.

I phoned Rachel who, predictably, was still in the office.

'An admirer has just been round here. He fancies your brains and insists you go and work for him.'

'Who's that?' she asked irritably. Rachel never liked to be disturbed, and was rarely in the mood for light-hearted banter.

'John Beart.'

'Again! He's been inundating me with job offers, invitations to dinner, weekends in the south of France, you name it.'

'Are you tempted yet?'

'He made me a very attractive proposition. I told him I couldn't leave SD because I'd promised the Board I'd stay for at least three years to turn the business round.'

I was consoled by her response. 'Of course, if you did go to work for him I'd have to stand down from the audit.'

'Right.' I could tell by her voice that Rachel, her mind elsewhere, had returned to her computer screen, and was waiting for me to say goodbye.

'One other thing.'

'Yes,' she said absently.

'When will I see you?'

'Oh, not now! Can't you tell I'm busy? Let's talk later in the week. Perhaps we can have dinner.'

'OK. I'll call in a couple of days. Bye for now.'

'Bye.'

As the line went dead, I leaped to my feet, slammed my cup onto the table, and paced the room, swearing and cursing. Then I kicked the sofa. Rachel treated me like a troublesome sales representative.

The front door bell rang. I collected my thoughts and went to answer it.

Amelia stood there, wrapped in a dark coat, the hood casting a deep shadow over her face.

'I baked a ginger cake this afternoon and wondered whether you'd like some.'

'Oh, how sweet of you.'

'You don't exactly make it easy for visitors, do you? I nearly broke my neck on the step, and it's taken me five minutes to find your bell in the dark.'

'I'm so sorry. You'd better come in and recover. Drink?'

She looked at her watch.

'Better not.'

'Sure?'

'Oh, all right, just a quick one.' She pushed her hood back and stepped over the threshold. 'Simon likes dinner on the table when he walks through the door.'

'Lucky man,' I said, feeling a sharp pang of regret at the absence of such comfortable domesticity in my life.

I poured two gin and tonics.

'You know John Beart, I hear,' I said.

'Such a darling man. Simon does quite a lot of business with him, and we've socialised a bit. How do you know him?'

'We were at school together. I also work for his auditors.'

'What a coincidence. Simon's one of the major institutional investors in his fund. John's such fun, isn't he? Hardly what you'd expect of a big City financier. He's got a wicked, irreverent side, though you have to get to know him really well to see it.' She paused. 'I'm sorry, banging on about him when he's one of your oldest friends.'

'He's not really a friend. More an acquaintance. I generally only see him at work. Do carry on; it's interesting hearing another side of him.'

She looked at her watch again. 'Actually, I must be going. Thanks for the drink.' She drained her glass.

'And thanks for the cake,' I replied. She left quickly, not turning back at the gate to wave.

*

A few weeks later I went down with my annual cold. It happens every year at about the same time and it's always a stonker, more like 'flu really, and it lays me low for a few days. It was on the second day of the infection, when my eyes were burning in their sockets and my whole body racked with shivers that, out of the window, I happened to notice Beart's distinctive Maserati Quattroporte outside Simon and Amelia's house. Though I would have liked to linger and observe what happened, I felt too feverish and, with a feeble shrug of the shoulders, made my way back to bed.

When, still rubber-legged and unworldly, I dragged myself back to work, I was told that Martha, the sharp-suited audit manager on the Beart account, wanted to see me.

She bustled into my office, a stack of plastic folders in her hands.

'There are some issues on which we need to take a view.' She ran through several technical points where she thought the Investment Fund was not in compliance with audit standards.

'Should we qualify their accounts?' she asked.

'Martha,' I replied, 'Do you remember what I said? It's our biggest client, its fees pay your salary and mine and those of a large number of other AP staff. We could go in, guns blazing, and risk losing them, or we could take a more measured approach and have a quiet word. Having reflected on it, what do you think we should do?'

'They're quite significant irregularities...'

'Yes, and it's a big business, still finding its way. I think we need to make allowances. Leave it to me.'

Martha bristled.

'Do I have to?'

'Yes, you do.'

She grabbed her papers and swept out of the room, muttering.

⋆

Later that afternoon I phoned Martin, who'd moved over from the Corporate Office in Beart Enterprises to be Finance Director of the Investment Fund, and ran through our concerns with him.

'Glad you brought this to my attention.' I could hear him drawing on a cigar at the other end of the line. 'Rest assured, I'll sort it out.'

'I'm reassured to hear it. We won't be qualifying your accounts, this time at least. Of course, some muted references will appear in our audit report.'

'Much appreciated, old chap. I'll look forward to thanking you more formally at the end of audit dinner. We're booking somewhere rather special. Well, cheerio then, and thanks again.'

CHAPTER 19
THE NEIGHBOURS, 1986

'The new job is fantastic.' Rachel took a sip of her wine. 'You have so much more freedom as CEO.' The wine bar was crowded and, casting a quick glance around her, she leaned forward. 'We're looking at some take-over targets. One of them much larger than SD. Even so, the investment bankers think we can pull it off with a rights issue.'

'I'm sure they do, so they can earn a fat fee.'

Someone passing nudged my elbow and I slopped my red wine, staining my white shirt. I dabbed ineffectually at it with a tissue.

'You're such a cynic. They've done an in-depth analysis. All the pros and cons, all the synergies. It's incredibly exciting. The biggest ever rights issue in UK history. Just imagine.' She sat back in her seat, glowing.

I shifted in my chair to avoid the cigarette smoke swirling across from a neighbouring table.

'So, no chance of your decamping to join Beart's Investment Fund then?'

I topped up our glasses, emptying the bottle. I already felt lightheaded. I should have eaten some lunch.

'None. I'm in my element. Why would I want to move?'

'More money, higher public profile, the chance of working with one of the most talked about men in the City—'

'None of them interests me. I have a vision for growing my business beyond all recognition, and as for working with John Beart, he's the one who appears in the newspaper articles and colour supplements. I'd forever be in his shadow, like the Duke of Edinburgh.'

'I hope you'd be more tactful and less racist.'

The wine bar was crammed with City types and the smoke was becoming unbearable.

'Want to move on somewhere?' I asked. 'Perhaps get something to eat?'

Rachel nodded and drained her glass.

'What about you? Still happy out there in darkest Surrey?'

'It's pretty dull,' I confessed. 'Everyone's so much older, apart from Amelia, of course.'

'Who's Amelia?' Rachel had all but lost interest in me sexually. Even so, another woman's name was still enough to elicit a slight spark of interest.

'Amelia Ellice, married to Simon Ellice. They

live opposite. He's one of John's biggest institutional investors, apparently.'

Rachel's face took on an enigmatic expression.

'I met them at some do organised by an investment bank. He's a lot older than her, right? Balding, portly and she has long auburn hair; quite pretty if you like skinny women.'

'Yes, that's them.'

Rachel's sphinx-like expression was still in place.

'Why the suppressed smile?' I asked. 'What's so amusing?'

'Nothing, really. There were some rumours about him. He was what they used to call a "confirmed bachelor." Then, suddenly, he married and had a couple of children.'

'He's got two daughters at boarding school.'

'Boarding school already? They can't be more than ten. Anyway, what's your interest in the lovely Amelia? I hope you're not thinking of having an affair.'

'Would you care if I did?'

'I'd never sleep with you again.'

'You never sleep with me now.'

'Don't exaggerate. I know it's not very often .... anyway, I'm very busy. If you'd wanted someone to be at your beck and call whenever you fancy a bit, you should have married one of the secretaries. They'd probably have been all too happy to throw everything up to cook your meals and minister to your other needs.'

'You sound really sexist, Rachel. Just because someone's a secretary doesn't mean she doesn't have career ambitions. In any case, I'm not thinking of having an affair with Amelia. I think she may be doing a bit on the sly with Beart.'

I recounted my sighting of Beart's car. As I did so, I wondered whether what I was saying was true. I'd been feverish and could have been mistaken.

'Sounds like John, from what I hear,' she replied. 'He has quite a reputation as a ladies' man.'

We finished the meal and, unusually, Rachel invited me back to the apartment. I don't know whether it was jealousy of Amelia or the desire to prove that our sex life wasn't completely moribund, but we did make love, in a cool and passionless way, before Rachel's eyes closed and she began to snore lightly.

I lay awake wondering why we were married. Although we got on well enough as friends, most of the time we lived separate lives. Perhaps, as neither of us seemed to have a strong inclination to be with anyone else, and there was no financial imperative, there was no reason not to remain married. Still, it seemed a curiously negative logic for staying together.

*

Sipping an espresso, I gazed through the dining-room window at the persistent rain making a marsh of the lawn. Then, unshaven and wearing a threadbare dressing-gown over my pyjamas, I slumped onto the sofa, picked up *The Sunday Times* and lobbed the review – I'd stopped bothering with culture – into the wastepaper basket. In about an hour I'd stroll down to the pub and have a couple of pints. I might even treat myself to one of their roast dinners. Then, suitably anaesthetised, I could while away Sunday afternoon with a siesta.

A loud, urgent knock on the front door made me jump. I walked slowly into the hall, pulling my dressing-gown cord tight. Through the glass, I could see four shapes, one large, three small.

Opening the door, I found Amelia, her two daughters, and a giant teddy bear dressed in a tartan overcoat. Behind them were two bulging suitcases. I scanned their expectant faces. One of the daughters was sniffling quietly, while Amelia's eyes were puffy and red. The other daughter was hugging the bear, which returned my stare glassily.

'Well, hullo,' I said, not quite knowing what tone to adopt.

'Do you mind if we come in?' Amelia glanced over her shoulder.

'Sure.' I held the door open and stepped outside to pick up the suitcases.

'Go into the drawing-room, darlings,' Amelia said, and they trailed off. When they'd gone, she whispered, 'Simon's thrown us out, the bastard.'

'God, that's terrible. Legally he can't do that, can he? I'm sure you have a right to be in the house, particularly if you have the children.'

She stifled a sob and I resisted the temptation to put my arm around her.

'He was in such a rage, throwing things, threatening me…we just couldn't stay there.'

'So you came here?'

'I wondered if you might put us up for a few days, until we sort ourselves out.' She looked around the sparsely furnished hall. 'I know it's a lot to ask.' A tear rolled slowly down her cheek. 'We wouldn't be any trouble and I'd pay rent, of course.'

I shook my head at the suggestion.

'When do the girls go back to school?'

'They're meant to go next week. They're so upset I'm not sure they should. It was all his idea to send them to boarding school anyway.' She stood rigidly in front of me while a shiver seemed to run the length of her body, starting at her head and ending at her feet.

'I'd like to help. I don't want to end up in the middle of a matrimonial war though. Does Simon know you're here?'

Amelia shrugged.

'He might have spotted us crossing the road.'

'What if he comes over and tries to muscle his way in?'

She looked disappointed I'd even asked the question.

'Sorry to impose on you. I'm not thinking straight. If I can use the phone to call a taxi, we'll leave you in peace.'

'Where will you go?'

She shrugged her shoulders again. 'We'll find somewhere. There's probably a B&B not too far away.' She stepped away from me and called the girls.

'Look,' I said and she turned back. 'You can stay for a day or two. Make yourselves at home. I'll take care of Simon if he tries to throw his weight about.'

Relief swept across her face, and she hugged me, kissing me on both cheeks.

'You're such a darling. We're so grateful, aren't we girls?'

I consoled myself that Simon looked too badly out of shape to present much of a physical threat.

Before I knew it, Amelia was upstairs assigning bedrooms to her daughters and rummaging in the airing cupboard for bed linen. I brushed past the bear which was guarding the foot of the stairs and went to shower and dress. It struck me they might be hungry and there wasn't much food in the house.

'Want to come to the pub for lunch?' I bellowed. Amelia's head emerged from one of the bedrooms. 'My treat, of course,' I added quickly.

'Can Bruno come?' Annabel's disembodied voice piped up.

We marched into the pub, Bruno on my shoulders like a mahout on an elephant, and I asked for a table for five. Annabel had been insistent he have his own seat, so when we were offered bread rolls, I wrapped a napkin round his neck and placed one on a side plate in front of him.

By the time we returned to the house the girls' tears were long forgotten. I found an old pack of cards and, with much hilarity, taught them to play Cheat. Amelia won comfortably every time.

The next few days were odd, but pleasantly so. It was strange coming home to delicious cooking aromas, to have someone there to ask after my day, and to listen to the two girls explaining in quirky detail what they'd been doing. By Thursday I was becoming accustomed to it, and liked it.

On Thursday evening, after dinner, Amelia drew a deep breath.

'We'll be going tomorrow. I'll wash the sheets and vacuum before we leave. Thank you. It's been so kind of you. I hope we haven't been too much of an imposition.'

I felt a pang of regret. I would miss the companionship, the smells, even the sisterly squabbles between the girls. At last the house was feeling like a home.

'Why not stay a little longer? Anyway, where will you go?'

'I've found us a couple of rooms in Sedley and I'll look for work as a supply teacher, if they'll take me back after all these years.'

'Well, it's up to you. I'd like you to stay.'

'Sounds like that old cliché about a man's stomach has come up trumps again.' She laughed and I joined in.

'Your cooking's great. What I really like, though, is your all being here.'

'That's very kind of you. We'll see. I'll decide tomorrow.'

That night, for the first time, she came to my room and slipped into my bed. There are two ways to a man's heart, and she was taking both. It was a delight to awake the next morning and find her cuddled up close to me.

'Are you still planning on moving out?' I said, breathing in the fragrance of her sleep-soft body. 'You'd be more than welcome to stay.' I ran my hand lightly down the silky skin of her stomach.

She wriggled, invitingly.

'Our landlord seems nice. Perhaps we could stay a little longer, after all.'

She kissed me, our tongues met and she slid on top of me.

Several weeks passed in what seemed like domestic bliss. Even the rain stopped and the world was bathed in sunshine, encouraging us to take long rambles in the Surrey Hills, where the girls picked wild flowers and Amelia and I walked arm in arm, soaking in the surrounding beauty.

★

My mother phoned me one evening. In my happiness, I'd forgotten to call her.

'How was the holiday, Mum?'

'That was ages ago. Thanks for asking.'

'Did you meet anyone nice?'

'None of your business, dear, but I did. In fact, I'm phoning to let you know I've accepted an offer on the house and I'm moving to Halifax with Reginald.'

'Reginald? Who the bloody hell is Reginald?'

'Please don't swear dear; I had enough of that from your father. Reginald was on the holiday with me, and we're going to live together. He's a very lovely man who's been let down badly in life. We've got a good deal in common.'

'Mum, these holiday romances never work. You hardly know the chap. Why not wait—?'

'I'll drop you a card to tell you my new address.'

'Hang on, Mum. Who is Reginald, what does he do, how old is he? Please tell me something about him.'

My mother's voice was both calm and dispassionate.

'He's an undertaker who's going through a very messy divorce, and he's forty-two.'

'Mum, he's more than twenty years younger than you. He's probably just interested in you for Dad's money.'

'It's my money now. Anyway, it's nice to have someone interested, whatever the reason. No one's paid the slightest attention to me for years. I've been the cleaner, the cook and the bottle-washer, that's all. Now I'm going to have some fun before it's too late. I think I'll take some of this HRT stuff. Ellen says it's marvellous.'

My stomach clenched.

'Surely you're not sleeping with him?'

There was a pause.

'I really think that's my business, don't you? I'll be in touch. Goodbye dear.'

There was a click and the line went dead.

Chapter 20
MARTHA, 1986

The air in AP's suite at the Beart Enterprises' offices was cool and fresh, yet I couldn't wait to exchange it for the dense fug of a nearby pub. It was two minutes till 5.30PM, the earliest I, as partner, could reasonably slope off. As I stuffed the last of my papers into my briefcase, the door swung open and Beart ambled in, wearing a canary-coloured shirt, a magenta tie and matching braces. I tried to suppress my shudder at this latest affront to taste. I'd never liked yellow and pink together, and had always avoided this combination when planting seedlings.

'Hi, how's it going?' He was as nonchalant as ever. He nodded in the direction of the outer office, which was still buzzing with activity. 'Looks like you chaps are earning your monstrous fees for a change.'

I forced a smile. 'You're looking very bright today. Many a canary would be most jealous.'

'Yes, these colours go well together, don't they? I'm thinking of incorporating them in our logo. Should brighten the City up a bit, don't you think?'

My face must have betrayed me because he laughed. 'In any event, it would cut down on the number of corporate gifts doshed out to all and sundry.'

He must have spotted me glancing at my watch as he shut the door.

'I won't waste much more of your time. There's a bit of a ticklish matter, and I'm not sure how to broach it.'

I was intrigued. I didn't know Beart contained a single grain of sensitivity.

'Go on, John, I'm sure you'll find a way.'

'It's about Martha Grant.'

'Yes?'

'I won't beat about the bush. She's upsetting a lot of my people. She's got the tact of a rhino on heat, and about as much common sense. It would be better for all concerned if you found her something else to do, well away from our audit.'

He stared at me. Though I knew I had to rebut his suggestion, my brain, submerged by the icy waters of his deep violet eyes, refused to respond.

'OK?' he added, in a tone which suggested the matter was closed, and stepped towards the door.

'Hang on a moment, John.' He swung round with an enquiring look on his face. 'It's most improper for a client to suggest such an action without going through the agreed formal procedures.'

'Bugger the formal procedures. I don't want her bugging the daylights out of my people and making their lives a misery. Do I make myself clear?' Without waiting for an answer, he swivelled on his heel and strode out of the room, the door clicking shut behind him.

I went straight to the pub and sank several pints. As well as irritating me deeply, John's demand had put me in a very difficult position. Walking to the station, I rehearsed telling him no one could dictate who AP deployed as auditors on his account. However, after a night of tossing and turning in a sweat-soaked bed, my resolve weakened. I imagined becoming the partner who lost the Beart account, and the acrimony I would face from my own workforce as I informed them of the resulting redundancies.

The next day, I told Richard what had happened.

'Martha's a good audit manager,' Richard said, folding his arms. 'Basically sound, even if a little headstrong and prone to rubbing people up the wrong way. We're not going to cave in to Beart's demands, are we? Next he'll be writing our audit report for us.'

I bought time by taking a sip from my caffe macchiato. He was, of course, right, though I didn't want to admit it. I put the cup down slowly, and locked eyes with him.

'Not an easy one,' I said.

'No,' he replied.

'What would you do? Over half our revenues and two thirds of our profits are generated by Beart's business.'

He nodded slowly and we sat in silence for a few moments.

'What will you do with Martha?' he asked. 'You have to make sure she doesn't lose out because Beart's taken a dislike to her.'

'Swap her with Alana on the Dickinson account.'

'Mmmm.' Richard stroked his chin.

'Come on Richard, be realistic. What else can I do?'

'OK,' Richard sighed. He knew Beart Enterprises was a juggernaut. 'Make sure you handle it carefully. We don't want Martha going around telling everyone Beart's calling the shots.'

★

'You've got to be having me on!' Martha expostulated. 'I'm onto some real funny shenanigans, I'm convinced of it, and you want to reassign me. What's going on?'

'I have to prioritise work according to AP's business requirements, and right now we need you on the Dickinson account.'

'Bollocks you do,' she replied, slamming her fist on the desk. 'You want a quiet life. Either that or you're too frightened to do your job properly.'

‘Nonsense—’ I started to say, but she was already on her feet and surging towards the door.

‘I quit,’ she shouted over her shoulder, ‘and I’m taking you for constructive dismissal. This is going to be all over the papers.’

Chapter 21
DIVORCE, 1986

I shouldn't have been surprised when I was cited as co-respondent on the divorce petition, although it seemed a little unfair as Amelia and I had started our relationship after Simon had thrown her out.

I suppose Simon must have told Rachel somehow, because I received an urgent summons to meet Rachel at eight o'clock the following evening at a restaurant in Chelsea.

I felt sheepish as I waited for her at the reserved table, small trickles of sweat soaking into the back of my shirt. Rachel was unusually late, and I was drinking my second large scotch when I heard her voice and saw her at the entrance handing her briefcase to the head waiter.

We kissed perfunctorily when she swept up to the table. She put something the size of a brick down beside her, and it took me a few moments to recognise it as one of the new mobile phones which were rapidly becoming an essential part of the well-groomed yuppie's wardrobe.

'So, I hear you've got a bird after all,' she said, placing her hand on the phone as though expecting a call any minute.

Though I didn't like the disparaging term, I let it pass. I coughed.

'I've started, I'm in a— '

'Yes, I know. It's a pity I had to hear it from someone else. Are you sleeping with her?'

'Yes.'

'Then you know it's all over between us. We can never sleep together again.'

Her illogicality irked me. 'So, if you divorce me, you'll only go out with virgins. Is that what you mean? If it is, you'll probably have to limit yourself to 12-year-olds or complete wallies.'

'That may be so. I certainly won't be sleeping with you again, whatever happens.'

The food came and we ate in silence. I put my knife and fork together and waited for her to finish. I looked at my plate and had no recollection of what I'd just eaten. I looked at Rachel's glazed expression and wondered where her mind was. It certainly wasn't here with me. Her body jolted slightly and she stared at me.

'I've been to see my solicitor. You'll be receiving the petition shortly.'

‘I’ll add it to my collection.’ I forced a laugh. Rachel didn’t smile.

We pecked each other’s cheeks as we said good night, and I had the strong sensation of an era passing.

★

On the train home, I mused on my lack of emotion. I still felt nothing, despite the length of time Rachel and I had been together. Perhaps it was because we’d drifted apart gradually over so many years, like two continents inching almost imperceptibly away from each other and opening a massive rift between them.

When I got in, a gentle aroma pricked my nostrils. I guessed they’d had spaghetti bolognese for supper. I took off my tie, made myself a cup of instant coffee and opened a couple of envelopes before wandering slowly upstairs. Amelia was in my bed, warm and soft with sleep, hints of garlic on her breath. She raised her arms and I burrowed my nose into her supple neck, breathing in the smell of her warm skin. Within a few minutes we were making love, and Rachel faded from my mind.

★

Life seemed simpler and more straightforward now that our relationship was in the open. Amelia and I got on well. Her daughters, Chloe and Annabel, had taken to me, and to the casual observer we would have appeared a happy family unit.

Domesticity suited me and I found myself looking forward to coming home. The only problem in our firmament was Amelia's reluctance to talk about her past. She skated over her years with Simon with a few derogatory words and acknowledged no other lovers. I didn't have the courage to confront her over the time Beart's car had been parked outside her house. When I did ask her how she'd got to know him and how well she'd known him, she added little to the very first description she'd given me. 'Such a darling,' she would say, 'such fun underneath that austere exterior' or 'secretly he's quite a rebel.' When I probed for evidence to support her statements, none was forthcoming.

Every so often, she would decamp for the weekend, taking the girls with her. She would never tell me where she'd been, except to say, 'with friends.' Whenever I pressed her for an answer, she lapsed into a sulky mood which lasted for days, and only came to an end when I swallowed hard and apologised. Because of the oppressive atmosphere I was brought up in, I've always hated moodiness and rows and would go to almost any lengths to avoid them.

Despite this, the few months that followed were happy ones. Unfortunately, this halcyon period had to come to an end, and it did so with the sale of Thorpe Barton as part of the divorce settlement. I tried to buy

Rachel out and keep it, but couldn't get a big enough mortgage.

Feeling tearful and sick at what I was having to do, I invited the estate agents round and selected the one I thought respected the property most. It didn't take long to find a buyer and the price we achieved reflected a healthy profit on our purchase price and all subsequent outgoings. It was only after we'd exchanged contracts that I found out that the purchaser was a front man for a developer, and the house, along with the one next door, would be demolished to make way for eight town houses.

I was alone in the house when the phone rang. Someone started shouting as soon as I picked the receiver up. I held it a foot away from my ear, recognising the voice as Allan's, a retired insurance broker who lived next door but one.

'You people make me sick, despoiling the neighbourhood for a quick profit. You should be ashamed of yourself—'

I put the receiver down on the telephone table, the rant continuing as I left the room and shut the door. Planting myself on the dining-room floor, I cradled my rapidly emptying bottle of Macallan. Dusk was falling and the room was gradually merging into the darkness. I placed my palm flat against the wall, which was as cold as a body in a morgue.

'I'm so sorry, so very sorry.' I paused, half-expecting Thorpe Barton to reply, as hot tears pricked my eyes. 'I've let you down, I've betrayed you, and now you're going to be destroyed, all because of me.' The house's silent stillness was the most eloquent and dignified condemnation of my self-absorbed negligence.

I told Amelia I planned to rent for a short period as I didn't want to be rushed into buying a property I didn't care for. I would, however, make sure there was room for her, Chloe and Annabel and after that, perhaps they would care to move into my new house. I stretched my hand out towards her, hungry for the reassurance of her warm palm in mine. Amelia didn't take it, and after an uncomfortable few seconds I withdrew it.

'What's the matter?'

'I don't want to impose on you anymore. My divorce settlement has come through. I've got enough to buy a place of my own and I don't ever want to be dependent on someone else again. With the property market as it is, I'd be crazy not to buy now.'

'Perhaps we could pool our resources and buy a place together?'

She looked at me like a big sister consoling a younger brother who's broken a favourite toy.

'The last few months have been great, and you've been wonderful. While I love you dearly, I'm not sure I want to settle down with you.'

'You're not sure. So there's still a chance?'

'No. My mind's made up.'

'Oh. You are sure.'

'I hope we can stay friends. You're really very special, and very important to me.'

'Is there someone else?' My voice was thick with emotion.

'No, of course not!' She hugged me and kissed me on the lips. 'It's just that I'm not ready to settle down with someone again. I need some space.'

'You needed some space when you tipped up uninvited on my front doorstep – space in my house and then space in my bed. What's changed?'

She looked away.

'It's been great, but— '

'Where will you live?' I asked interrupting her. I couldn't bear to hear what might follow the 'but'.

I was shocked when she told me she'd been looking for some time, and had made an offer on a Victorian cottage nearby.

'Will we still see each other?' I asked.

'I hope we'll always be friends. I'm very fond of you, you know.'

'This is so sudden, so unexpected. Can't we give our relationship another go? We all seem to get on so well together.'

'I'll always be grateful for what you did for the girls and for me.'

'Surely there was more to it than that. I thought we had something good going on between us. I didn't realise I was just doing you a favour.'

Her expression blended the sympathy and determination of a pedigree dog breeder who knows her favourite bitch must be put down and is resolved to see it through. I shook my head in disbelief. How could I have misjudged the relationship so badly?

'I'm sorry,' she said, looking at the ground.

'Not half as sorry as I am.' I left the room and dragged myself upstairs, my self-pity a dead weight round my shoulders. I slumped onto the bed where I lay face down with my hands over my head. I don't know how long I was there but it was dark outside when I opened my eyes. I half-hoped Amelia would come and say she'd changed her mind. She remained downstairs, the faint sounds of her chattering with the girls as though nothing abnormal had happened a bitter confirmation of the demise of our relationship.

During the next few days, dejection seeped through me, permeating every fibre of my being. My mind was enveloped by darkness. Nothing seemed worthwhile. I slept only fitfully. I couldn't eat. Even taking a shower and shaving were too much of an effort. Amelia moved back to her own bedroom and there were no more nocturnal visits. We barely spoke again. I did everything I could to avoid her. Even though I found it difficult summoning the energy to crawl out of bed every day, I left the house very early, went through the motions at work and came home very late, usually quite drunk. On returning late one evening, I found Raffy, Annabel's soft orange giraffe on the kitchen table. Its floppy neck was twisted so its large brown eyes were staring at me, and I broke down.

The next morning Richard stopped me in the street outside our offices.

'I was about to give you a few bob for a cup of tea before I realised it was you. You look ghastly. What the hell's the matter?'

'Nothing.' I tried to edge past him, but he held me by the arm.

'Come with me.'

He led me to a small café around the corner and ordered two coffees and a round of buttered toast.

'You look as though you haven't eaten for a week.' He pushed the toast towards me and sniffed the air. 'Or taken a shower. Come on, what's the problem?'

I didn't need further prompting to unburden myself. He listened carefully, nodding occasionally and asking a few questions.

'I'm so sorry,' he said when I finished. 'Everything seemed to be working out so well. I know it's not much comfort now, but you *will* get over her.'

'Plenty more fish in the sea, pebbles on the beach, that sort of thing you mean? What do you know about it? You found your pebble and have clung on like a limpet ever since.'

He put his arm around my shoulder.

'Fair comment. Only trying to console you. Anyway, come to dinner. After an evening with my wife and kids your life won't seem so bad, but please do have a shower first.' The prospect of experiencing their easy-going domesticity left a bitter taste in my mouth so I declined the invitation, though I did take his advice and slunk home to shower, shave and change my clothes.

Amelia and the girls moved out a couple of weeks later and I was left to pack up the house alone. I didn't have the energy, and eventually Richard got my secretary to organise a removal firm to do everything.

The contents were put into storage and I checked into a drab concrete and glass hotel overlooking the Cromwell Road. Finding the right house no longer seemed important, and I resolved to buy a flat convenient for work.

Tears ran down my cheeks as I walked round the empty Thorpe Barton for the last time. It had been a shrine to my relationship with Rachel, and then, for a short period, a home. Now it was a mausoleum for my unfulfilled dreams. Soon it would be rubble. As I slammed its front door behind me, Thorpe Barton seemed to encapsulate my every failure.

★

With the passage of time I gradually returned to a more balanced mental state, resuming my duties at work and socialising, on a small scale, outside it. At last I screwed up my courage and contacted Rachel. To her credit, she didn't bear a grudge. As far as I could ascertain, she was spending her time concentrating on her job and wasn't involved in any other relationships. We started to meet for a drink or a meal occasionally. When we were together we'd talk about mutual friends, acquaintances, work, the economy, politics, even sport. Anything in fact, so long as it wasn't about our marriage or its demise. She didn't express any regrets about what had occurred. It was almost as though our wedding had never happened.

★

To distract myself from the emptiness of my life, I spent much more time at work. The Beart Enterprises account continued to grow rapidly, driven by the success of the Investment Fund, which was delivering spectacular results. As time passed, I found myself gradually climbing the partner ranks, moving from salaried to equity partner and then becoming one of the senior partners. I loaded myself with more work and volunteered for everything irrespective of what it was, living entirely in the present.

I didn't allow myself time to look back on all my mistakes nor forward to a lonely future.

★

Unexpectedly a postcard arrived from Marbella. It was from my mother.

'Hello dear,
I hope you are very well. Reginald and I got married yesterday and we're planning to stay here. There's a lively British community, and we even have an English butcher from Hackney and a plumber from Bolton. There are so many of us, we don't need to speak any Spanish. I've bought a lovely villa called Nuestro Abrigo and we're very happy. I hope Rachel and you will come and visit us.
Love, Mum x'

I felt a guilty pang; I'd forgotten to tell her about the break-up of my marriage, let alone my abortive relationship with Amelia.

Chapter 22
THE TAKEOVER, 1990

I was in my office, leafing through some paperwork one Sunday afternoon. I'd been contemplating playing golf until the almost horizontal rain dissuaded me and, in any case, the office on a Sunday was convivial. The puritan atmosphere pervading the place from Monday to Friday gave way at weekends to one that was informal and relaxed. Lots of people abandoned their loved ones to come and do some work, either out of zeal, or in a surprisingly large number of cases, out of preference. Whatever their motivation, they seemed intent on making the most of it with take-aways, often accompanied by bottles of beer and wine brought in from the local Asian shop.

As I took a swig from my bottle of Duvel, the phone rang. It was Rachel.

'I need to talk to you.'

'I'm listening.'

'In person; what are you doing this evening?'

★

The nondescript trattoria in which we met was festooned with photographs of Venetian canals, and staffed by burly waiters with straggly moustaches and East End accents.

Apart from a cursory peck on the cheek, Rachel didn't waste time on pleasantries.

'This is absolutely top secret. You must swear not to tell a soul.'

'Anything you say will go no further.'

'John Beart is launching a takeover bid for my company.' She paused to gauge my reaction. I dutifully inhaled sharply, although, having worked closely with his organisation for some time, nothing he did surprised me.

She took a deep draught of her wine. 'It makes no sense. There's no fit between us and his other companies. I'm buggered if I can understand the logic. Got any ideas?'

'Perhaps he's awash with cash and wants to diversify.'

'No one diversifies these days. That's so 1970s. There must be a better reason. What the hell can it be?'

'How do you know about the bid if it hasn't been

launched? Surely that's privileged information?' I was secretly impressed Rachel had managed to hear anything in advance about Beart's plans. His security was normally impenetrable, hence his 'Dark Star' nickname.

'Confidential sources.' Rachel tapped her nose with her forefinger, and I imagined she felt pretty smug about how well-connected she was. 'Anyway, it's not much in advance. He'll announce his intentions tomorrow, and if we reject his proposal a hostile bid will follow shortly.'

'Time to brush up the CV. He's never been known to fail.'

Rachel's smile was rather wan.

'There's a first time for everything.'

Somehow her voice lacked the steely conviction I normally associated with her.

*

Rachel's intelligence was proved right. The following morning Beart phoned her. She recorded the conversation and played it back to me as we sat in another anonymous restaurant, this time an Indian near Waterloo. It went like this.

'Morning Rachel, it's John. How are you?'

'OK thanks, John. How are you?'

'Top of the world, absolutely top of the world, thanks. I thought it would only be polite to ring and let you know I'm going to buy your company.'

'Kind of you, John, although I struggle to see the shareholder value. We're in completely different businesses, there are no synergies, the City— '

'Yes, I know all that. Fortunately, I don't have to explain myself to anyone. We'll offer a good price for an amicable merger. If your board rejects that, then we'll go hostile. I've already had assurances from several of your major shareholders that they'd support the takeover. The choice is yours. Accept gracefully or be humiliated publicly. Oh, by the way, just in case you were wondering, there's a place for you in Beart Enterprises, which I think you'd find very interesting and, as I'm sure you're aware, would be a lot more lucrative than your current job. Well, must be going now; busy day and all that. You'll be hearing from us formally very shortly. Bye.'

She switched the machine off.

'The cheek of the man to phone me up and make it all sound like a *fait accompli*. And as for offering me a job to let the deal go through, that must break every City code there is.'

'He never had much time for codes. What are you going to do?'

'We're going to fight. The board's behind me. The take-over makes no sense.'

Our curries grew cold in their metal dishes as Rachel bombarded me with tales of the prowess of the investment bankers she'd retained to argue her case. Eventually I grew tired of waiting and spooned some food onto my plate.

'He'll find out he's got a fight on his hands, make no mistake of that,' Rachel said, and we raised our glasses of sharp and watery red wine to 'La Resistance'.

The takeover battle didn't materialise. Beart had been telling the truth when he boasted that the institutional investors would back him. A few soundings indicated resistance was futile and, after a brief period of negotiation, a merger was agreed.

*

I was at the Beart Enterprises head offices one evening when I chanced upon Beart sauntering down the empty corridor towards the auditors' office. He gave me a cheery wave.

'Mind if I come in?'

He didn't wait for my reply.

'Make yourself at home.' I gestured in the direction of a chair. He perched on the windowsill.

'How's the audit going?'

'Still on schedule. Why do you ask? I thought you left all that stuff to your minions so you could do the sexy take-overs.'

'You know Rachel's coming to work for me?'

Outwardly I remained calm and said nothing, though my heart missed several beats.

'Yes, she's going to be CEO of the Investment Fund. Should be quite a challenge for her. I hope it doesn't cause you a problem.'

'Me? Why should it cause me a problem?' I was stuttering despite my attempts at self-control.

'Conflict of interest, what with you two having been married and all that. Don't you remember? You were the person who alerted me to it in the first place.' He stared me coolly in the eye. 'Personally, I don't think it should be a show stopper for AP, seeing as that's all in the past now. Even so, no doubt you'll have to run it past your ethics committee.'

'No I don't think it should.' My mind was numb. I wondered whether it was jealousy about Rachel, or some deep-seated rivalry with Beart. I thought I'd got over both.

I couldn't get hold of Rachel when I phoned later that evening. I imagined life was hectic in a company merger, so I left a message and didn't try to contact her again for a while. Several days later she returned my call.

'I'd been meaning to phone you. I've got something to tell you.'

'You've accepted a job with Beart.'

'How did you know? It's not public yet.'

'Confidential sources,' I replied.

Chapter 23
NEIL AGAIN, 1994

Neil's hair was thinner and greyer, his face fatter and redder and his neck a lot thicker.

I greeted him in the time-honoured fashion.

'What's yours?'

'Bitter and a packet of salted.' He put his arm on my shoulder. 'Good to see you again. It's been too long. I should've been in touch sooner.'

'My fault,' I replied. 'I've been meaning to phone you for ages. You know how it is.' Two pints were slapped down in front of me, spilling a little from both. My money was taken and my change handed back without the barman saying anything, and I wondered what had happened to the fine old tradition of the friendly landlord and the warm welcome. We found a table, its surface awash with beer, and sat down. Looking around at the state of nearby tables it was obvious no one was going to wipe it, so I mopped it with a tissue which I then crammed into the already overflowing ashtray.

Neil lifted his glass to his lips.

'Cheers. Here's to you.'

'How's life, Neil?'

'I'm in B6 now. I love it.'

'What's B6?'

Neil spun a nut into the air and caught it in his mouth.

'You must be the only person in the country who hasn't heard of us. We're an Apollo squad bringing together all the police disciplines to combat the most sophisticated multi-disciplinary and global criminal gangs. And you?'

'Chugging along. Partner on the Beart Enterprises account.'

'Don't mention Beart to me.'

I was struck by the venom in Neil's tone.

'Whyever not? You used to be such mates.'

'That was before I found out it was Beart who closed my business down all those years ago. It's a perk of this job that you can do a little personal research. What's more, he sold his interests in the bandits that thrashed us as soon as my outfit folded.'

'Very strange,' I said. 'He never does anything without a reason, although it's often difficult working it out. He's definitely a one-off.'

Neil took a deep draught of his pint. 'Let's talk about something else. It's putting me off my beer.'

'Sorry mate. Do you reckon we'll make it into the Premier League next season?'

'I can't stand the Premier League. It's just the big boys trying to exclude the little clubs like ours, and snaffle all the loot. It'll be the end of football as you and I know it, and it's all down to greed.'

'Oh, come on, Neil. You can't blame them for wanting to make money. Their owners are only human.'

'Show me a human being, and I'll show you a crime waiting to happen.'

'That sounds a bit extreme mate; not everyone's corrupt. There are some good folk around. What about Mother Theresa?'

'Just because we haven't got the dirt on her doesn't mean there isn't any. I don't know anyone who isn't on the take in some way. Whether it's fiddling expenses, diddling the tax man, or setting up a multi-billion dollar ponzi scheme, it's all theft. It's only a matter of opportunity.'

'Does that mean you're corrupt too?'

'I'm pretty clean, probably cleaner than most around here.' He surveyed the people at surrounding tables. They looked a seedy bunch, most of them reading tabloids or racing papers or merely gazing into the middle distance. One well-dressed young couple was sitting in the corner holding hands and I wondered if they were so besotted with each other that they'd strayed into the wrong pub.

'Before you start feeling smug,' he continued, 'let

me remind you how, when we were lads, we both sneaked into Town's stadium through that hole in the fence, almost every other Saturday.'

'No doubt you boys in B6 will be putting a stop to major crimes like that.'

Neil stared silently into the depths of his beer before saying, in a voice which sounded very distant, 'I dream of the day when I discover what Beart's up to. There's something deeply rotten behind that flashy façade.'

We lapsed into silence again. Someone had put *Every Loser Wins* on the jukebox for the third time. I tried to block the sound out; I couldn't stand Nick Berry. Neil scratched his ear lobe.

'What's he up to?' he asked. I drew a deep breath before replying.

'Can't imagine Rachel working for a dodgy firm. My ex-wife has many faults; lack of integrity isn't one of them.'

'People often slip into dishonesty almost without noticing. They make one slightly iffy decision, then that goes wrong so they compound it with another; that doesn't work so they do something else that's close to the line, and then take an action that's just the other side of it. Before they know it, they're lying, sometimes even to themselves. If they're lucky, they get away with it and they cover their tracks. If they're unlucky ......well that's where we come in.'

'If it's a matter of luck, why do we need B6, and all those regulators to protect us?'

'To make you feel more secure. Believe me, there are lots of bad guys who get away with it all the time. You ought to know. You're an auditor. How many times have you caught a major malefactor? You might catch some junior buyer who's on the take in a small-scale way.' He sighed. 'Even that's unlikely. How many cases have there been of companies whose auditors signed off the accounts only for them to go belly up shortly afterwards? No, it's a jungle out there and the predators are winning. What B6 does is dependent on others' incompetence or bad luck.'

We went for a curry. Neil told me that after a series of disastrous relationships he'd given up with women. I told him I hadn't seen anyone since Amelia.

'Do you ever see Rachel these days?' he asked.

'Rarely, she's so busy with her job. We're still on good terms though.'

'Is she going out with anyone?'

'Not as far as I know. She wouldn't have time.'

A thoughtful look came over his face.

'I always liked Rachel. Nice woman.' Then his expression puckered into a sleazy grin. 'Quite fit too.'

I never liked it when Neil made lecherous comments. That Rachel was the object of them made me doubly uncomfortable.

'Easy, Neil. That's my ex you're talking about.'

‘So?’ He looked at me incredulously. ‘What does it matter to you? You dumped her for what’s-her-name.’

‘Well, in a manner of speaking, but—’

‘There you are then. Don’t be so precious.’

‘We may be divorced but I still respect her.’

‘Respect her? That’s why you went off and shagged someone else, is it? How mealy-mouthed. Give me old fashioned male chauvinism any day. It’s much more honest.’

I could see it was an argument I wasn’t going to win. I had to distract him.

‘What do you get up to these days? In your spare time, I mean.’

He emitted a sound somewhere between a sigh and groan.

‘I work, then I work some more and, just occasionally, I go for a drink with some of the lads.’

‘Any love interest?’

Shaking his head, he took a swig of his beer. ‘Only for this stuff.’

My own existence wasn’t very different. I stayed late at the office most evenings and went in at weekends. Sometimes I went for a drink with people at work. Occasionally I played golf or, if I found myself at home, would watch something trashy on television, a large scotch in my hand. My mirror presented me daily with inescapable evidence of middle age: skin creasing into wrinkles, gut expanding and scalp threadbare. The only compensation was a fattening bank balance.

‘There must be more to life than this, Neil.’

‘Must there? I know lots of folk for whom there’s a lot less. On the other hand, there are loads of supposedly honest so-called pillars of the establishment who are creaming it at our expense in ways most people can’t begin to imagine. I console myself that at least I’m doing my bit to bring some of those smug bastards to justice.’

Chapter 24
A PARTY AT JOHN'S, 1996

While I'd attended business dinners at Beart's Belgravia mansion many times, I had never before received a gold embossed cocktail party invitation. My first inclination was to decline. However, something, I couldn't say exactly what, intrigued me.

Arriving late, I heard the loud thrum of voices inside as I pushed my way through a group of smokers clustering on the front steps. A waitress showed me in and I was confronted by a room heaving with people shouting and gesticulating. They didn't look like City types. Some wore earrings and nose studs, others displayed tattoos. I was the only person wearing a suit and tie. John parted the crowd to greet me.

'You must come and meet Isaac. He's made the most fantastic film about Sonny Liston. It's going to be a box office sensation.' He led me in the direction of a small, balding man sporting a glittering gold earring on one of his fleshy earlobes.

Isaac's eyes glazed over as soon as we were introduced. He was much more interested in a very tall woman with bright red lipstick and a tight black miniskirt called Elsa, and I found myself pushed to the fringes of their conversation. Rather than find someone else to talk to, I clung on, interposing the odd question.

'I see you've met Isaac.' Rachel had approached from behind and took me gently by the elbow. 'He's such a darling, isn't he?' She pecked me on the cheek. Seizing the opportunity provided by this diversion to exclude me altogether, Isaac closed on the woman with red lipstick. Summing up the situation in a single glance, Rachel said, 'Let me introduce you to Alison and Mark.'

Alison and Mark had reason to be more welcoming; there's nothing more dispiriting for a married couple than to go to a party and end up talking to each other. Rachel drifted off.

'How do you know John?' I asked.

'We've only met him through Rachel,' Mark replied. 'I'm Rachel's personal fitness coach and Alison is her herbalist.'

'It's great they've got together, isn't it?' Alison said.

I was finding it difficult making out what people were saying against the background noise.

'Who've got together?' I asked, craning my neck.

‘Why, Rachel and John. They’re an item now. Didn’t you know?’

My legs wobbled and I reached for the wall to steady myself. I pulled out a tissue and blew my nose, hoping it would clear my head.

‘How do you know them?’ Mark asked. Now I knew he was a fitness coach, I could see the definition of his muscles under his tight shirt.

‘I’m Rachel’s ex-husband,’ I said in as flat a voice as I could manage. What I’d heard was only sinking in gradually. It made no sense. How could Rachel take up with Beart? I looked around the room and chanced to catch Rachel walking past him. He placed a proprietary hand on her waist and pulled her towards him for a fleeting kiss. The noise faded, I could no longer hear what Mark and Alison were saying; I felt as though, if I moved away from the wall, I’d topple over. After a few seconds, the sensation passed, and I heard Alison’s voice.

‘… so it makes sense for us to move to Clapham.’

I’d no idea what she was talking about, so I nodded vaguely. ‘Quite so. Please excuse me. I must find the loo.’

‘I wonder what she recites when they’re fucking?’ I muttered to myself, as I directed my stream at the plum coloured porcelain. ‘The latest Beart Enterprises’ results? Perhaps climaxing with quarterly EBITDA?’

On my way back, I lurked in the hall until Rachel came out of the kitchen carrying a tray of hors d'oeuvres in both hands. I grabbed her arm and the appetisers wobbled perilously.

'Why the fuck have you taken up with that bastard?'

She looked nonplussed for a couple of seconds. Then, balancing the tray in her other hand, she shook her sleeve free from my grasp.

'What's it to you? I don't think you have any right to complain if I go out with other people. I'm not the one who went off with someone else and broke our marriage up.'

'Beart, of all people—'

'Look, you have no idea what he's like. Your opinions are based on a load of hazy schoolboy memories and have never altered despite your success being pretty well down to him.'

'You weren't his greatest fan—'

'At least I'm big enough to admit I was wrong. Anyway, this isn't the place to discuss it.' She looked over her shoulder. 'And I don't think you're in the mood to talk about it in a civilised manner.'

I took a step back and muttered, 'Yes, I'm sorry,' and lifted a chicken vol-au-vent from the plate she was holding. Isaac and Elsa passed by arm in arm, engrossed in conversation. Rachel stared me in the eye.

'He's got a lot of good in him.'

'Sounds like faint praise.'

'Oh, come on—'

Rachel was interrupted by a tall Arab who, ignoring me, took her by the arm and led her off, whispering into her ear and making her nod and laugh. Waiting a few seconds, I followed in their wake, peeled off and squeezed into a corner of the much quieter study, which was occupied by three highly made-up women discussing their last trip to Milan. I hung around in there for ten minutes, idly scanning the leather-bound volumes which covered the walls while I collected my thoughts before venturing out again. Tentatively I opened the door. Alanis Morissette's *Ironic* was now blaring out from speakers fitted in all the reception rooms and the house was pulsating with energy; guests were swirling around the drawing-room, the dining-room, the hall and the kitchen. Several couples were dancing. Someone grabbed my waist from behind.

'Giles, I thought I'd see you here!' It was a woman's voice straining to be heard above the noise.

I turned to meet her deep-chestnut eyes. The smile faded from her face and she let her arms drop.

'Sorry, confused you with someone else.'

I looked around. Everyone who wasn't dancing was talking to someone. Only I was on my own. Completely drained, I decided to leave. I saw Rachel's back, approached her and, interposing myself between her and the Arab, pecked her on the cheek.

'I'd like to talk,' I said.

'I'll be in touch,' she replied, resuming her

conversation with the Arab. I didn't bother to say goodbye to Beart.

★

For several days, I waited in vain for her to contact me. Finally, I phoned her at her office and, with a lot of effort, persuaded her to agree to dinner at a Lebanese restaurant in Knightsbridge.

I'd almost given up when she did arrive, an hour and a quarter late. By then I'd drunk three large gin and tonics on an empty stomach and my early concern for her well-being had metamorphosed into a gnawing belligerence.

'I'm so glad you could make it,' I said, biting back the words 'at last.'

'Sorry. Everything's so hectic, big deal coming off, very hush-hush, can't say any more. That looks good,' she said eyeing my drink. She caught the attention of a hovering waiter.

'I'll have one of those.'

'How are you? Obviously still keeping busy.'

'Absolutely rushed off my feet, darling.' The 'darling' didn't ring true. It sounded like an affectation picked up from the showbiz set I'd seen at John's house. She'd never called me darling in all the years we'd been married.

'How's John?' I'd decided to start the conversation neutrally and build up to an interrogation. Rachel forestalled me.

‘Please don’t give me a hard time. I know what you’re going to say and I don’t want to hear it. You really don’t understand and, besides, I’m old enough to know my own mind. And I don’t want to spend the evening defending him.’

I could tell by the glint in Rachel’s eye that if I persisted, I’d be in for an argument.

‘OK,’ I sighed. ‘Let me say one thing and then I won’t mention it again. I hope you know who you’ve taken up with, because I don’t know anyone, even the people who are close to him, who say they really know Beart. He’s a mystery.’

Rachel looked at me dispassionately. ‘All right, you’ve said your piece, so I’ll respond and then we’ll move on. OK, so John’s a secretive person. What you aren’t aware of is all the good he does, all the charitable causes he supports and never speaks about. There’s a lot you don’t know about him. In any case, who’s to say that being mysterious is a bad thing?’

I leant forward, my heart beginning to thump.

‘Underneath all those good deeds and all that pastel leisurewear there’s something deeply untrustworthy.’ I could tell by the way in which her body stiffened and she leaned forward aggressively to mirror my posture that I’d gone too far. I sat back in my chair and waited for the onslaught.

‘You should be careful lecturing people when you don’t know the facts. John and I have things in common you know nothing about.’

'Such as?' I knew I was pushing it but I couldn't stop myself.

'None of your business,' she snapped. 'In any case, I won't take any lectures from you. How many successful relationships have you had?' She drew breath to complete the crushing demolition of my lack of social success. I read the signs and capitulated.

'OK, OK, let's drop the subject.'

I didn't see Rachel again for a long time, and when I did she was very cool towards me.

Chapter 25
A DEATH, 1998

'He's been found dead.' Alana, normally so calm and measured, rushed into my office. 'The police have sealed his flat.'

'Who?'

'Martin, Martin Vokes,'

My heart beat faster. Martin had been a lynchpin in Beart Enterprises. I sat forward, put my croissant down on a paper napkin and pointed to the seat in front of me. She perched on the edge of the chair, quivering.

'Hanged in his apartment.' She shuddered. 'They're suspicious. No clear motive. Why would he do it?'

Alana's eyes started to fill with tears, unnecessarily in my view. While we'd had a close business relationship with him, we'd never crossed the line and become friends. She looked at me expectantly.

Leaning back in my chair, I brushed some pastry flakes from my chalk-stripe trousers.

'People have lots of reasons for hanging themselves: unrequited love, money problems, drugs, a sexual thrill which goes wrong—'

'He's been a bit odd for a while. Last time I saw him, he reeked of alcohol and was very nervy, even a bit shifty.'

I affected a drawl.

'About what?'

'Everything.'

My heart started to race at the thought of Martin falsifying the accounts and then losing control and tumbling into a deep pit of despair.

'I want you to put a special investigative team onto Beart Enterprises. If anything doesn't smell right, tell me about it immediately. Oh, and you'd better look particularly closely at the irregularities you recommended and make sure they're not material.'

'You approved them.' Alana stood up. 'I only said they were of the same order as ones we'd signed off in the past.' She teetered to the door in three-inch stilettos, shutting it firmly behind her. The last piece of croissant had congealed in my mouth and I needed a swig of coffee to swallow it.

Later I received a call from Beart. He opened cordially before coming to the point.

'I assume you've heard about poor old Martin?'

I grunted.

'Poor chap, bit of a break down. Personal issues.

Andrew Goldstein will be standing in until we appoint a full-time replacement. Nothing for you chaps to worry about. Business must go on, as they say. Why don't you come over to dinner soon? Rachel says you haven't been in touch for ages. We'd both love to see you. I'll get Mary to contact your secretary and arrange a date.'

★

Rachel phoned me at my new flat. I'd been re-potting my house plants and smeared the ivory handset with compost answering.

'I've got something to tell you which you're not going to like.'

I wiped the phone with a tissue. The line was silent. Rachel seemed to be waiting for a response from me.

'You're going to marry Beart?'

I was delighted by her uncomfortable intake of breath.

'He proposed to me, and I've accepted. Thought I'd better tell you before you come to dinner in case it came as a surprise.'

'Hope he did the full works, down on one knee and all that.'

'Yes, all that and more. In a gondola on the Grand Canal.'

'Sounds very uncomfortable and quite risky. Those things are most unstable. It could have turned turtle and drowned you both before the gondolier had finished the first verse of *O Sole Mio*.'

'Don't be daft. It was perfectly safe and very romantic. You're not upset, are you?'

'What's there to be upset about?' I dug my fingernails into the palm of my left hand so hard I was surprised I didn't drawn blood. 'I suppose you know what you're doing.'

*

The police investigation into Martin's death proved inconclusive and the coroner entered an open verdict. Our scrutiny of the Beart Enterprises business revealed nothing untoward and I signed off the accounts without qualification. Martin's replacement arrived. Within a few weeks, it was as though Martin had never existed, leaving me wondering whether we were all as expendable and as forgettable.

My dinner at Beart's house was dominated by discussion of the impending nuptials. Five other people had been invited, two couples and an ungainly woman in PR who smelled of liniment. The whole experience seemed surreal. The two couples quizzed John and Rachel on the minutiae of their wedding plans while, at the other end of the table, the PR woman took me through a detailed comparison of Goodwood and Kempton Park. Now and then fragments of the main group's conversation would drift over to me, reminding me of the time Rachel had planned our wedding. I shifted and wriggled in my seat as the PR lady droned on. To make matters worse, despite one or two deft nudges from the toe of my shoe, one of Beart's seal point Siamese persisted in rubbing itself against my legs under the table. Already my eyes and nostrils were itching and would soon be swollen. I took a tissue out and blew my nose. My cat allergy was getting worse.

Towards the end of dinner, Rachel caught my eye and indicated she'd like to talk privately. We excused ourselves and went into the drawing-room.

'I'd like to have our marriage annulled.'

I cleared my throat, but Rachel continued regardless.

'John's a Catholic and we'd like to marry in church. He's got friends in high places and can fix it. All you have to do is sign a piece of paper.'

'Saying what?' I could feel the colour rise in my cheeks.

'That you were never serious about marriage and never wanted children.'

I rocked back on my heels. 'It wouldn't be true. Although it was you who insisted on getting hitched, I did my best to make a go of it. And as for children, the main reason we didn't have any was because you never sodding well had time for sex.'

'Hush,' Rachel said, and I realised I'd raised my voice. 'Please, it would mean a lot to John and me. You're not religious, so what would it matter to you?'

'I didn't realise he was a Cat.'

'He wants to please his mother, especially now she's not well. She's very religious. Like so many other things, he's always kept quiet about his own Catholicism and his contributions to the church.'

I thought of my sexual encounter with Mrs Beart all those years before. My abiding memory was of her slim body spread naked across the sofa, the soft light of gratification in her eyes. She hadn't seemed very religious then. If she was so devout, had she been using contraception? The thought intrigued me. I might have got her pregnant and unwittingly fathered a half-sibling for Beart.

'Well, what do you say?' Rachel tugged my arm. 'Will you do it for John and me?'

I frowned.

'Or at least for me, for old-times' sake?'

For the loathsome Beart? Never. For Rachel, of whom I was still very fond, just possibly. For the lovely Mrs Beart, for old-times' sake, well, why not? I could see her violet eyes, her dark hair cascading over her delicately sculpted white shoulders, I could almost taste the saltiness of her sensuous lips. Rachel tugged at my arm again, Mrs Beart's image evaporated and I found myself staring at an ornate gilt table lamp and wondering for a moment where I was.

Rachel looked up at me and smiled in what I assumed she thought was a beseeching manner.

'Well, will you?'

I nodded and she promptly produced a piece of paper from the drawer of an escritoire. Without bothering to read it, I signed with the pen she proffered.

She kissed me on the lips. 'You're such a lamb. Shall we go and join the others?'

Her nod to John and his acknowledgment of it as we re-entered, was almost imperceptible, but while I was resuming my place beside my PR friend, it replayed over and over in my mind's eye, and I felt used and soiled.

John rose from the table and rummaged in the distressed oak sideboard. He emerged holding a bottle.

'I'd like you all to try something rather special,' he said as he distributed thick, cut-glass whisky tumblers. 'I think you'll like it. It's a bottle of 1926 Macallan.'

Chapter 26
SUZIE, 1999

Rachel lifting her veil for me to kiss her, her graceful glide down the aisle, the smiles of the congregation, people shaking my hand and patting my back; these and a few other sepia-tinted slow-motion fragments of the day Rachel and I married flickered across my mind, though I wasn't sure whether they were real or imaginary. It was John and Rachel's wedding day. As the taxi crawled along the Brompton Road in the bright sunshine, I squinted through the window, trying to recall the obscure contours of my barely-remembered past.

Several cigarette smokers were lounging outside the whitish-grey neo-classical church. I joined them, lingering in the warmth until I saw Rachel's bridal car approaching, when I stepped into the cool interior. My eyes took a few moments to adjust to the relative darkness and I almost didn't recognise a shrivelled Mrs Beart, sitting hunched on a pew at the front of the packed church. It seemed inconceivable I'd ever desired her, I'd ever made love to her. Edwina, Rachel's mother, sat on the other side of the aisle with one of the aunts. From his absence, I presumed something must have happened to Rachel's father, although she'd never mentioned it.

The service seemed interminable. I looked around for faces I recognised and saw a few of Beart's colleagues, and some of the people I'd met at their house. I didn't like any of them. The reception at the Connaught promised to be a dull and tiring affair. Perhaps I could make my escape early I thought, as we filed, blinking, out of the church.

★

I think Rachel's mother and I found it equally odd I should be in the line of guests being welcomed to Rachel's wedding reception, though we pretended nothing was amiss and greeted each other in a friendly manner. My heart fluttered as I approached Mrs Beart. She gave me a warm smile.

'It's been so long, dear,' she said, emphasising the word 'dear'. It reminded me of my mother and seemed to accentuate the yawning difference in age between us. 'When was it, do you remember?'

'A long, long time ago.' I bent forward to kiss her cheek and the smell of decay was unmistakable. She gripped my arm tightly and I looked down at her scrawny, blue-veined hand.

'Lovely to see you here, dear. I've often thought of you.'

The pressure of the queue forced me to extricate my arm. I passed along to congratulate Rachel and John, before seizing and gulping a glass of champagne.

'You look like you needed that.' The voice was familiar. I looked round to see a tall girl smiling at me.

'Suzie, what are you doing here?' It was a stupid thing to say, even though Rachel and Suzie had barely been on speaking terms for years.

'I might ask you the same question. Isn't it odder for an ex-husband to be at a wedding than an estranged sister?'

'Suppose you're right. Sorry, wasn't thinking. What are you doing now?'

'I'm an artist.'

I cast my mind back. 'That makes sense. I remember you painting. What do you paint now?'

She looked at me with an expression I couldn't make out.

'Pet portraits.'

I laughed, thinking she was joking. I stopped when it became obvious she wasn't.

'You haven't changed much,' she said. 'You always were a supercilious shit.' She started to turn away and I grabbed her sleeve.

'Look, I'm sorry. It's been a bit stressful, Rachel re-marrying and all that.'

‘Why? You’re not still in love with her, are you?’ I could see contempt in her turned-down mouth. ‘I would have thought you’d have been pleased to be shot of her. What’s it to you if she’s collared some other sucker?’

Normally I would have defended Rachel but, that afternoon, I found Suzie’s irreverence refreshing.

‘You’re right. What’s it to me? Let’s have another drink.’

‘So, give me the dirt on Rachel, all her faults, everything that drove you mad.’

‘There wasn’t any dirt.’ I wondered whether my answer would terminate a conversation I wanted to continue. Suzie stared at me intently.

‘Pretend you’re David Attenborough and describe Rachel in her native habitat. I can’t imagine her functioning as a normal person.’

I stared out of the window. It all seemed an eternity ago. Then I drew a deep breath and put on my hushed David Attenborough voice.

‘This little creature is the Greater Crested Rachel. It flutters from its nest early every morning and runs around a lot to keep fit. It flies to a big aviary where it sits in front of a screen for fourteen hours, before flitting back to its own bird-box to warm up worms in a microwave. Then it hops back into its nest, taking a work file for company.’

I glanced at Suzie. Her eyes sparkled with merriment.

'Doesn't the Greater Crested Rachel ever do anything fun; go to concerts, or sit by the river on a sunny summer's evening watching the water flow by?'

I dropped my Attenborough impersonation.

'No time for idle pleasures. Sometimes a dinner out, usually to a new restaurant she wanted to try.'

'With nice fat files to pleasure her every night, how did you get a look in?'

I leaned towards her and lowered my voice.

'I didn't really. She didn't seem very interested and we ended up living apart. After that, it was only a matter of time.'

'Priceless, absolutely priceless.' Her voice was clearly audible above the loud hubbub. 'All those brains, qualifications and what-not and she became one of the living dead. A real corporate man. No wonder your marriage failed. Tell me more.'

'I think we'll be going in to eat soon.' Despite my qualms, talking to Suzie felt very satisfying.

'I'm enjoying this. I'm going to make sure you sit next to me.'

'There's a seating plan and name tags. I'm sitting with the gaga great-aunts and third cousins once-removed and you're probably at the centre of things.'

'Just watch me.' She disappeared into the melee, reappearing beaming a few minutes later.

'I put us both on a nice table by the window.' She took my arm. 'It must be time to go in; shall we take our seats?'

As we passed, I peered at the seating plan and saw some crude crossings-out in red biro.

'Very subtle.'

'No point putting sugar on it,' she said, tossing her hair back.

I wondered what the guest who found herself unexpectedly on the family table made of her elevation, and whether she or the family was more surprised.

We ignored the others on our table, and Suzie's flirtatious badinage with a couple of young waiters resulted in lots of wine flowing our way. She chattered away about anything that came into her head, laughing and slapping my thigh several times, once allowing her hand to linger there for a few seconds.

An uncle stood up to make a speech, and the reception dozed gently through his almost unintelligible recollections of Rachel as a little girl.

Suzie wrinkled her nose. 'She always was an odious little goody-goody. Never missed a day's school, never got a detention, always did her homework; yuck, what a creep.' A few people at neighbouring tables overheard. Some seemed amused, others looked stony-faced. The population seemed split half and half.

John rose to his feet and several people cheered, rattling their cutlery against their wineglasses. John puffed out his chest and hooked a thumb into his grey waistcoat. He had some cards with notes on them in his other hand. Sliding these into the pocket of his morning suit, he surveyed his guests. The room became hushed.

'When the priest asked whether anyone had reason to object to our marriage, I expected all the unattached men in the church to stand up because they'd missed out on marrying the most wonderful person in the world.' He smiled down at Rachel's upturned face.

'I was the luckiest chairman in the world when Rachel agreed to work for me. Now she's married me, I'm definitely the luckiest man in the world.'

There was a ripple of applause mixed with a chorus of 'Hear-hear' and 'Rather.'

'It's always the cleverest men who are the most stupid when it comes to love,' Suzie whispered. 'Boy, will he regret today in the years to come!'

I felt conflicted but I didn't want to put Suzie off whispering in my ear. The sensation had made all the hairs on the back of my neck stand up, and I was beginning to feel aroused.

'I can't bear to listen to any more of this crap.' Suzie didn't bother to whisper. 'I'm leaving. Do you want to come with me?'

Fortunately, we weren't far from the staircase used by the waiters, and I slipped out discreetly. Suzie followed, not caring whether she was seen, and stumbled noisily on the wooden stairs.

'Let's go somewhere open and green,' she said,

swaying slightly, as we emerged in the bright sunlight. 'Hampstead Heath or Richmond Park or somewhere like that; I've had enough of central London.'

She stuck her hand out and a taxi pulled up beside us.

'We haven't got the right clothes,' I replied and she shoved my shoulder with her hand.

'You sound like my Great-Aunt Maude. It hasn't rained for a month, what's wrong with going as we are?'

I looked down at my hired morning suit and highly polished shoes and shrugged.

'OK. Why not? Hampstead Heath? I haven't been there for years.'

'Good choice.' Suzie jumped in and told the driver where we wanted to go. 'I used to take Charlie there when I was fourteen, maybe fifteen,' she added as we seated ourselves next to each other.

'For walks? It's a long way from where you lived,' I said, thinking Charlie was the family dog.

'For sex. He was my lover.' She paused. 'I adored him, or at least I did till Rachel stole him off me.'

I tried to picture the then twenty-six-year-old Rachel stealing her little sister's spotty teenage boyfriend.

'But surely—'

'You don't believe me, do you?' Suzie's jaw tightened. 'You think I'm making it up.'

'No, not at all. It's just that Rachel's so much older. Why would she go out with some pimply youth?'

'He wasn't some youth, he was Daddy's curate, and she didn't know about us, at least not until I told her.'

'Rachel didn't mention Charlie when telling me about her previous boyfriends.'

'I'll bet she didn't. She dropped him like a piece of cat shit, and Daddy had him sacked for sex with a minor. It was the talk of the village, despite Daddy trying to hush it up. I felt a bit sorry for Charlie. He was a virgin when I seduced him.'

We fell into silence as we flashed past Belsize Park tube station, a lustrous red in the bright afternoon sunshine.

'I hate my family,' she said, apropos of nothing.

'I don't much like mine. By the way, is your father all right? He wasn't at the ceremony today.'

'Daddy's a non-person now. No one has anything to do with him, except me. He's shacked up with a former choirboy of his in Poole. Couldn't be happier.'

A lorry cut across our path and the taxi braked hard. Suzie and I were flung forward and I managed to grab hold of her arm to stop her from banging her head.

'He seemed such a contented family man,' I said, releasing her.

'Living a lie, like so many people.' She reached out, placing her warm hand on mine.

Suzie told the taxi driver where to drop us, and set off at a brisk pace until we came to a secluded spot where she sat down. I looked around at the remnants of ancient woodland surrounding us. A green woodpecker dipped past. I'd never seen one at such close quarters. Suzie patted the grass, and I sat beside her.

'The nature here *is* beautiful.' I thought this would ingratiate me with an artist.

'Bugger nature.' She leaned across and kissed me, her tongue pushing vigorously into my mouth. Soon she was undressing me.

'Someone might—'

'My God,' she replied, 'I *have* brought Great-Aunt Maude with me. So what if they do? Who the fuck cares?'

I thought for a moment.

'Yeah, who cares?'

Soon we were naked, the sunshine warming our skins as we twisted and turned, Suzie's long pale legs wrapped round me.

Afterwards she said, 'You're not too bad really. Even if you are a bit on the tubby side, I still can't see why Rachel traded you in.'

'Thanks. You're not too bad either. As for Rachel, she'd need a bloody good memory to remember what sex with me was like.'

Suzie smirked. 'So there is something my brilliant older sister isn't perfect at then.'

'I didn't say she wasn't good at sex—'

'I know what you said.' Suzie pushed me to the ground and lay on top of me. 'And as for you, I'm going to give you a real hard road test to see whether you're worth going out with. I'm very choosy about the men I shag.'

★

I must have passed Suzie's gruelling test because she came back to my flat with me that night. The next day she went to collect her things from wherever it was she'd been staying, I never did establish exactly where, and moved in.

I realised quickly that our lives were very different. Suzie would stay awake all night, smoking dope in my previously smoke-free apartment, drawing or painting or sometimes staring at the wall as she listened to old albums by Pink Floyd or King Crimson. She would come to bed about seven o'clock in the morning, just as I was getting up. Unless she had a commission to paint someone's pet, and these were rare, she wouldn't go out, and, with the central heating at maximum, would wander naked round the apartment or slouch on the sofa, eyes closed.

In the early days, I tried staying up with her and smoking dope. Both activities so drained me of energy that going to work the next day presented an almost insuperable challenge and I couldn't continue with them.

If we had an invitation to dinner or to a party, she would hum and haw whether to come with me.

'They're bound to be boring people. All your friends are.'

Sometimes she disappeared for two or three days, as though to make up for all the time she'd spent in the apartment. I tried asking where she'd been and who with. Her eyes glazed over and she refused to say.

'I come and go as I please,' was her only reply.

Occasionally a young man called Chico would call up.

'Oh, he's a friend from Art College,' she told me, adding, 'not that it's anything to do with you.'

We co-existed amicably, even though we only overlapped for a few hours in the evening. Although I knew she lived by a different code from me, I liked her company and I enjoyed our vigorous and inventive sex life. It wasn't like being in a relationship. It was like living with one of those cats which moves from house to house, eating and sleeping where it pleases, and I resolved not to become too attached to her. I'd learned my lesson from Amelia, and I didn't want to get hurt again.

★

I was in the office when Rachel phoned; it was the first time I'd spoken to her since the wedding.

'Nice do,' I said. 'Loved the dress.'

'Don't give me all that. I saw you sneaking out with Suzie and now I hear she's moved in with you, the bitch.'

'Who told you?' I was genuinely puzzled. Suzie didn't seem to speak to anyone apart from Chico.

'Mummy; Suzie went to stay there for a couple of days. Listen, she's bad news. She's got zero integrity. She'll sponge off you, two-time you, then piss off and leave you in the lurch.'

'Hang on a moment, Rachel. I'm not thinking of marrying her. We're just having a good time, that's all. There's no lurch to leave me in.'

'Huh!' There was silence on the line for a few seconds. 'She only moved in with you to get at me.'

'I thought it might be something to do with my animal magnetism and my rippling biceps.'

'Even though she might appear air-headed,' Rachel continued, 'deep down she's a cunning little vixen. You'll find out.'

'She speaks very highly of you too.'

'I'll bet she does. I hope the two of you are very happy,' she said and put the phone down.

*

Suzie usually remained elusive about her past. It seemed a strange contradiction in one who in other ways was so forthright.

One Friday evening we were sitting on the sofa, halfway through our second bottle of Sauvignon Blanc and watching *Friends*, Suzie's favourite TV show, when, apropos of nothing, she spat the words, 'Uncle Stuart was a complete fucking bastard.' Dragging my eyes away from Monica's lithe form which, clad only in a short towel, was at that moment, filling the TV screen, I was shocked to see her shoulders heaving, tears streaming down her cheeks and her eyes fixed in front of her. I tried to put my arm around her, but she shrugged me off.

'I'll never forgive him.'

'Who was Uncle Stuart?' I asked, uncertain whether Suzie would be prepared to say more. It wouldn't have been the first time she'd said something dramatic and then, on being questioned, clammed up.

'Aunt Charlotte's husband.' She paused, as though deep in thought. 'He molested me from the age of eight. Let this be our little secret, he'd say as he slid his hand into my knickers, then he'd always ask me whether I had a boyfriend. The day I told him I did, he stopped. I was thirteen then. Five fucking years.'

'Did you tell your parents?'

Suzie gave vent to an explosive series of sobs. Finally, she took a deep gulp of air and, still staring into the middle distance, said, 'I thought I'd done something wrong and I'd get into trouble. Besides, I loved my aunt too much.'

'What about your sisters? Didn't you tell them?'

Suzie dabbed ineffectually at her eyes with a tissue. I handed her another paper handkerchief. She took it and blew her nose.

'I was much younger and we didn't talk about it till later. Then I found out he'd done it to them too.'

'Even Rachel?' I couldn't imagine Rachel putting

up with it. She was too strong, too determined. She would have gone straight to her parents, wouldn't she?

Suzie glanced at the screen for a moment, and my eyes followed hers. Joey, wearing a Native American headdress, was standing on a table while Monica, now attired in fluffy pink pyjamas, tried to coax him down. Ross was on all fours underneath the table, wearing a straw hat and pulling a face. Guffaws of studio audience laughter flooded the room.

'She wouldn't talk about it.'

'That Uncle Stuart should be locked up. All cons hate paedophiles, he'd have a hell of a time. Why don't you bring a case against him? If you all testified—'

'He's dead. Heart attack. None of us went to the funeral, though he got a hero's send off from the rest of the family.'

'Did you tell anyone after he died?'

'Yes, but they wouldn't believe me. Aunt Charlotte was in denial and my mother said I'd made it up. Of course, by then, everyone thought the worst of me, so writing it off as a drug-induced fantasy was easy.'

'And your sisters?'

'Brushed it under the carpet.' Her voice was small and childlike. Squeezed into the corner of the sofa, she seemed to have shrunk to half her normal size. I reached out and put my arm around her shoulders. This time she leant towards me. As *Friends* drew to a close with all the central characters sitting drinking coffee in Central Perk, Suzie, oblivious to what was happening on the screen, soaked my shirt with her tears.

Chapter 27
SENIOR PARTNER, 2001

'So, you've made it to the top of the greasy pole.' Richard watched his sliced shot land in the rough about a hundred yards to our right. 'Congratulations. I suppose we'll all have to salute you now.'

I took out my battered old driver. 'If Braithwaite had still been around, I wouldn't have. He never liked me, despite my landing the Beart account.'

I swung at my ball and it ended up a few yards from Richard's. At least they'd be easier to find.

'He never trusted anyone under the age of sixty,' Richard said. 'That's why we've lost all our best young people. You didn't arrange his death by any chance?'

We trudged in the direction of our golf balls, conscious of a foursome gathering impatiently on the tee behind us. Golf was no longer the leisurely game it had once been. Even on a wet Wednesday afternoon the pressure was on us to perform.

'No, it really was a heart attack.' Braithwaite had died on the eighteenth hole at Wentworth, just after missing the putt that lost him the game.

'Stingy old bastard. Anything rather than pay up,' Richard said. 'Still, I'm surprised our fellow partners were prepared to tolerate a callow fifty-year-old at their head.'

'What a bunch,' I said. 'Most of them are just waiting for retirement. Who else could do it? Apart from you, that is.' My bravado masked the deep disquiet I'd experienced since accepting the role. I'd never been very proficient technically and I lacked the intuition that good auditors need, that ability to ask the right question. I knew most of the people working for me were more capable, and more motivated. In fact, my long-term strategy at work had been to avoid any detail and hide my incompetence behind a barrage of questioning, hoping no one would find me out.

Richard's second shot was lying nicely on the fairway. Mine hit a tree, ricocheted and ended up twenty yards behind me. Perhaps it was time to give up golf. We looked back at the four golfers taking practice swings near the tee.

'Shall we step aside and wave them through?' Richard said. 'They look like they know what they're doing.'

'Not on your life,' I replied. 'We're ahead of them, and that's the way it's going to stay.'

*

I met Neil for a drink. His expression was even more jaundiced than ever.

'Congratulations, mate,' he said. 'I always knew you could do it.'

'Thanks Neil. And congratulations on your promotion to Superintendent.'

'Thanks. Sadly, I won't make chief constable now. Too old. All these kids with their Oxford degrees. What use are Latin and Greek in modern policing? Doubt I'll even make chief super, unless I land a big one, that is.'

'Got your eye on anyone?' I asked, not expecting an answer.

Neil tapped the side of his nose theatrically. 'Might have.'

'Who is it?' I was astonished we were having this conversation.

'Can't say, mate. Only thing I will say, strictly off the record, is I hope you're doing a good job auditing Beart.' He winked and I wondered whether he was pissed. There had been several empty pint glasses in front of him when I walked in.

'You're not looking at Beart? Surely he's above suspicion? There's hardly a government committee he isn't on. He spends more time in Whitehall than with Rachel.'

'I'm not saying anything,' Neil replied. 'If you're

covering all the bases, you've got nothing to worry about, have you?' His arm brushed the pile of peanuts heaped in front of him, knocking several onto the stained carpet.

'The only thing that didn't add up was Martin's death,' I said, 'though that was a few years back.' Neil looked around and lowered his voice to be almost inaudible.

'The Met thought he might have known too much, so they called us in. Couldn't come up with anything, more's the pity.'

'I doubt murder is Beart's style.'

'Rich people get others to do their bidding.' Neil drained his glass. 'Want another?'

I looked down at my beer. I'd barely started it.

'No thanks, mate.'

'You wuss.' He hauled himself unsteadily out of his seat while I made a mental note to talk to Alana the following day. A few more irregularities had come to light which we'd satisfied ourselves weren't significant. Now I needed to double check. Even if it was the drink talking, I couldn't believe what Neil had implied. Beart was far too much of a pillar of the establishment.

★

Chapter 28
SISTERS, 2001

When I got home that evening, I found Suzie wrapped in a new black kimono, lying on the sofa giggling. She was completely stoned.

'What's so funny?'

'Rachel,' she managed to say between tear-filled sobs of laughter.

'What about her?'

'Here; she was here.' She bit a chunk off the Mars Bar she was gripping.

'When?'

Suzie shrugged her shoulders. I knew I'd have to wait to get a sensible answer. The next morning, as Suzie was going to bed and I was getting up, I pressed her to tell me what had happened.

'All I remember was Rachel ringing the bell and shouting at me as soon as I opened the door. Don't know what she said, though I don't think it was very nice. Then she fucked off.'

I waited until mid-morning before phoning Rachel at her office.

'When you came here last night, did you want to see me?'

'No, I wanted to speak to Suzie.'

'What about?'

'Nothing to do with you.'

'Come on Rachel, you can't leave it like that. You come to my flat and make a scene. You could at least tell me what it's about.'

'If you must know, Suzie's been going to my mother's house every now and then for a day or two. After she's left, something, a picture or a print or a piece of silver, is missing. No doubt she's financing her drug habit. I hope you've counted your valuables recently.'

Although I knew Suzie was a free spirit, and she'd frequently trotted out the hackneyed 'property is theft' mantra, stealing from her mother was taking it too far. I was always very careful with my own financial matters; I kept all my papers locked in a safe hidden behind a painting and only I knew the combination. I checked my credit card and bank statements regularly. I'd have known if there were any discrepancies. Even so, I decided to double-check my own security.

Shortly afterwards Suzie started to go out more regularly. She said she'd been given several commissions to paint the portraits of famous people's pets.

'Whose pets?' I asked.

'Confidential.'

'Why would a pet portrait be confidential?'

She didn't reply.

Suzie seemed to have plenty of money now. She bought some stylish clothes and her lifestyle became more diurnal. I wondered about the source of her new-found wealth. Was she selling her body? Had she become a drug dealer? Perhaps she'd taken up with a rich sugar daddy who could only see her during the day? As she wouldn't answer even the most basic question, there was no way of putting my mind at rest. I decided not to make an issue of it. We were still getting on well and our sex life was good. What did I have to be concerned about?

★

'Oi! Hang on mate!'

I must have been daydreaming on my way back from the newsagent's, a copy of *The Sunday Times* under my arm, because Neil's disembodied voice made me jump.

'What the hell—?'

'You'll never guess what,' he exclaimed, stepping out of a shady alleyway and falling in beside me. He looked round the deserted city streets and his voice dropped to a near whisper.

'You remember Roberts?'

I must have looked blank.

'From school. In Beart's year.'

I nodded.

'We got him.' His chest visibly swelled. 'I got him. And the rest of them. A child porn ring.'

'How did you get onto him?'

'An anonymous tip off. Then we followed the links from Roberts to the others. Really explicit stuff, children as young as two.'

'Disgusting. Well done for nicking them.' It was difficult to reconcile the jubilant look on Neil's face with this repulsive activity.

'Thanks. Yes, it'll do my career no harm, but that's not the point. Roberts says he was corrupted by old Summerbee, and he's willing to testify against him. Apparently, he buggered all the Mollies.'

Something was niggling inside my brain.

'Since when was Roberts a Molly?'

'He said Summerbee recruited him after we left.'

'Strange. The Mollies were all pretty boys. Roberts looked like a garden gnome.'

'Well, that's what he says.'

'What about Beart?'

'I haven't approached him yet. I'm going to this afternoon. Did Summerbee try anything on with you?

'No, nothing at all.'

'Nor me, thank God.'

On the spur of the moment, I decided to mention my concerns about Suzie. I hadn't heard from her for at least a fortnight, the longest period since the start of our relationship, and I had begun to worry. She was probably all right. But what if she wasn't? And then again, what if she'd gone off with some other man? I recoiled from the idea. Would it be better not to find out?

Neil listened attentively and promised to make some enquiries, though he wasn't sure he'd be able to help.

★

A few days later, the phone rang. It was Neil.

'Strictly off the record, right?'

'Sure. Are you phoning about Suzie or Summerbee?'

'Suzie, although interestingly, on the Summerbee case, Beart denied anything took place. Was quite vehement about it.'

'Strange,' I mused out loud. 'He was definitely one of The Mollies.'

'He was indeed,' Neil replied. 'Anyway, about Suzie.'

My heart fluttered like a caged bird in my chest. I wasn't at all sure I wanted to hear what Neil had to say.

'She was spotted in the company of Ignacio Rodriguez. Looks like she's been spending some time with him.'

I didn't think that confirmation of Suzie's

infidelities would have much effect on me but, as well as experiencing continuing palpitations, I was now beginning to feel decidedly queasy. Nevertheless, I affected a languid drawl.

'Oh, really? Who's he? A waiter in some Tapas bar?'

Neil laughed and I felt relieved he'd been taken in by my feigned indifference.

'Hardly, mate. He's probably the biggest Colombian drug baron there is. Came to London a couple of months back. He's staying at The Mirador, one of those posh places on Park Lane. Suzie seems to have taken up residence there too. That's all I can say; and don't forget, I've told you nothing.'

I instructed my secretary that I wasn't to be disturbed and spent the next hour pacing up and down my office. It had been easier to ignore Suzie's absences while ignorant of what she was doing. Now I'd found out, I was in a quandary. I didn't know whether she planned to return to me, but if she did, I'd have to challenge her. She'd probably evade any questions as usual. I concluded I'd have to go to The Mirador in the hope of seeing her there. Then I'd have a justifiable basis on which to question her.

I marched down the corridor to Richard's office, where I found him preparing to leave for Wandsworth and the delights of a home-cooked dinner. Reluctantly, he agreed to come for a drink. Without saying why I'd invited him, I positioned us carefully in the bar so I would have a good view of the lobby.

‘Everything all right?’ he asked. ‘You seem rather on edge.’

‘Stressful day,’ I replied.

At about 6.30 pm Suzie walked in wearing a three-quarter length mink coat and carrying a cluster of Harvey Nichols’ and Harrods’ bags. She disappeared into the lift only to reappear about an hour later, teetering on very high heels and wearing a sparkly and scanty silver dress. She was accompanied by a fat, balding man of about sixty, encased in a shiny suit. Even when he stood on tiptoes, he barely came up to her shoulder. She stooped to kiss him, and they went into the dining-room, his arm clamped around her waist.

Richard, unaware of what I’d seen, announced it was time for him to go home, leaving me to finish what was left of the crisps.

*

About a week later she walked into the apartment as though she’d never been away, and wrapped her arms around me.

‘What’s wrong?’ she asked as she sensed me pulling away from her.

‘I was at The Mirador last Tuesday with Richard. I saw you there with someone.’

‘You were spying on me?’ A scornful smile twisted the corners of her mouth.

‘No, of course not; we often go for a drink together

after work. We just went there for a change. Who's your fat little friend?'

'That was Ignacio. He's such a sweetie.'

'Looked like a little runt to me.'

'He may be short; he makes up for it in other ways.' Her look challenged me and I had no wish to debate the invidious comparison.

'Is the inquisition over? I'm aching to soak in the bath for an hour or two.' She walked slowly to the door, shedding clothes as she went.

I suppose I could have tried to throw her out, but what if she refused? And, in any case, I was fond of her and liked the company. The door closed firmly behind her naked back, and I was left staring in bemusement.

That night she came to my room, slipping into my bed as though she'd never been away. The warmth of her body soon melted my indifference and I forgot my resentment.

★

Beart buttonholed me in the corridor of his building to give me the benefit of his views on the extortionate nature of audit fees.

'A mere flea-bite to a firm of this size.' I forced a laugh.

'And about as useful.' He shook his head and made for the lift.

A sudden thought occurred to me and I called out. He paused, waiting for me to walk over to him.

'Old Summerbee; you've heard the police have him in custody?'

'What of it?'

'Well, I wondered whether you'd be making a statement.'

'I have. I told Wallington that Summerbee was an excellent teacher and a man of the highest integrity.'

'What about Roberts' allegations?' I stared into John's cold, unblinking eyes.

'Roberts was a fantasist who delighted in getting others into trouble. They won't find anything on Summerbee, but that little nark Roberts will get his comeuppance at last.'

He stepped into the lift and the doors closed, leaving me staring at my distorted reflection in the shining metal.

Chapter 29
HONOURS, 2003

Every so often, Rachel and I would take it in turns to choose a place to meet for coffee. This time I'd chosen The Gardenia, a basic, clean café in Dalston, famous for its Cypriot pastries.

Rachel looked on disapprovingly as I licked my fingers

'Yum. That kataifi was too good to waste.'

Rachel took a sip of her coffee and looked round. The café was empty apart from a couple of elderly ladies in the corner. Their views on the price of vegetables drifted across to us in snatches.

'Swear to keep this secret?'

'Of course.'

'They're going to give John a gong.'

My Greek coffee suddenly tasted very bitter. I didn't want to puncture Rachel's good mood, so I stifled the comments about John's 'knight starvation' which sprang to mind.

'What, you mean like that man from Rank films? Or the sort butlers use to summon people to dinner?'

'Why can't you be serious, you fool? They're giving him the knighthood he bloody well deserves.'

'So you'll be Lady Beart, flouncing around in ermine-edged ball-gowns.'

'Titles mean nothing to me. This is important because it's an official vindication.' She sighed. 'It might stop some of those baseless rumours.'

I adopted my one-eyebrow-raised incredulous look. It often worked well on Rachel, though sometimes it just annoyed her.

'They wouldn't have given him a knighthood if they had any doubts, would they?' she insisted.

'There have been plenty of dodgy knights and even peers in the past. In any case, wasn't it for services to the party, i.e. bunging them a load of dosh?'

Rachel looked affronted. 'How could you say that? You know how busy he is, serving on all sorts of do-gooder committees and quangos. And he's raised millions for that battered women charity he set up.'

I adopted my incredulous look again.

'You're never prepared to give him a break, are you? Just because you didn't like him at school—'

I held up my hand to silence her. 'It's nothing to do with that. Please pass on my congratulations.'

'You'll be able to congratulate him yourself. We've finally finished doing up the Palazzo Urtica, and I'm going to throw a big party to celebrate his knighthood and his birthday. You must come.'

I had no desire to go.

'When is it?'

'We haven't finalised that. You'll find out when we send you an invitation.'

'Can I bring Suzie?' Surely the prospect of Suzie being there would put Rachel off and make my declining all the easier. Rachel's face darkened.

'Do you have to?'

'I am living with her. It seems a bit churlish not to.'

'I doubt she'd come.' Rachel paused, then sighed. 'If you must, then OK. I hope she can be magnanimous enough not to try to steal the show. Or the paintings.'

I ran through possible excuses for not attending while Rachel popped to the loo. On her way back, she settled the bill.

'Very generous,' I said. 'You're obviously practising being Lady Bountiful.'

She jabbed me in the ribs.

'You're incorrigible. I don't know why I put up with you.'

'It's because you're still secretly in love with me,' I replied, as we found ourselves on the street, blinking in the bright sunshine.

'You wish,' she shouted over her shoulder, setting off at speed for the tube station.

⋆

I took Neil's call on my mobile phone. He didn't bother with the usual niceties.

'I hear you're going to Beart's party in Italy?'

'How do you know? In any case, it's not true. I'm going to find some way to wriggle out of it.'

'I'd like you to go.'

'Why? What's it got to do with you?'

'It's important,' Neil said. 'Trust me.'

An invitation arrived a week later, addressed to both Suzie and me. Suzie was astonished.

'What's that cow up to now?'

'Perhaps she wants to make up with you.' I much preferred the idea of going to Italy with Suzie to facing a weekend there alone. Suzie's face twisted into a sneer.

'I suppose I would be a tiny bit interested in seeing what they've done to that poor old building. Bet they've desecrated it with their abominable taste. Rachel never had the faintest idea, that's why she always dresses so appallingly. I'm not saying I will, but if I do decide to come, I'm certainly not staying at their place, and I'll have as little to do with them as possible.'

About a week later, I bumped into Beart strolling casually along one of the corridors in his head office. He hailed me.

'You look as though you haven't a care in the world,' I said.

'I haven't,' he replied. 'I pay other people to do the worrying for me. By the way, I'm looking forward to seeing you at the Palazzo. There are a few things I want to talk through while we're there.'

'Why can't we discuss them here?'

'I don't want to waste your time now and, besides, it'll be much more pleasant there. I'd like you to meet a couple of people too.'

Bearing in mind Neil's exhortation, I didn't feel I could decline the invitation, especially as Suzie had now grudgingly agreed to accompany me.

'We'll be there.'

'Oh yes, Rachel told me you'll be bringing Suzie. Remarkable girl.'

As we shook hands, I wondered why he'd said that. Surely, after exposure to Rachel's incessant character assassination of Suzie, he could only think of her as a scrounging, drug-dependent petty thief?

★

The next few weeks with Suzie were idyllic. She ceased lounging about all night and secured some verifiable pet painting commissions, and one captured the essence of a spaniel so well I could imagine it hanging in the National Gallery.

We started going to the cinema and restaurants together, and Suzie even agreed to accompany me to an AP sponsored charity dinner. My initial doubts as to whether she'd behave herself, especially once the wine began to flow, proved unfounded, as she engaged in polite conversation with the people on our table about their gardens and children.

With some trepidation, I suggested inviting Richard and Sandra round. I'd been to dinner at their house lots of times and had yet to have them back. Surprisingly, Suzie jumped at the idea.

'I could cook bouillabaisse.'

I thought she was joking. I'd never known her cook more than a boiled egg.

'I've got this secret recipe. Well, the main ingredients, bream, monkfish, mullet aren't secret. It's the herbs and spices which count.'

'When did you start cooking bouillabaisse, or anything else, for that matter?'

She didn't reply.

The bouillabaisse was delicious. Sandra raved over it and asked for the recipe.

As we tucked into crepes suzette, Richard said, 'I hear you lucky chaps are off to Italy this weekend.' My face must have fallen, because Sandra asked, 'Aren't you looking forward to it?'

'I'm dreading it. Bloody Beart; I see enough of him as it is, and I'm sure I won't like the other guests.'

'I'm not looking forward to it either,' Suzie said. 'Still, it's a nice place. I reckon we'll be OK if we can do our own thing. Some of the other guests are quite fun, so that'll help.'

'Who do you know who's going?' Richard asked.

I thought through the list of business associates,

bankers, lawyers, and assorted hangers-on who were likely to be there.

'Ignacio Rodriguez,' she replied without hesitation. 'And a couple of his Latino friends. They're a very jolly crowd.'

The twinge in my guts felt uncomfortably like jealousy.

*

The Palazzo Urtica, a magnificent white marble mansion with an extensive water-front on the lake of the same name, dominated the town square. Using John's seemingly endless supplies of money, Rachel had refurbished and considerably extended what had once been an eighteenth-century hotel where Goethe, Shelley and Wagner are all reputed to have stayed.

I'd booked us into the Albergo Ricardo, a hotel down one of the rambling town's narrow alleyways.

We arrived at prosecco time on Friday, heading off immediately to a lakeside café for an aperitif. Overhearing a group of Americans at the table behind speculating over the identity of the owner of the Palazzo Urtica, we stopped talking to listen.

'He runs the biggest investment fund in the world. What else is there to know?' said a gravel-voiced man.

'Someone told me he's behind several of the big private equity outfits and through nominees owns half of the UK's companies, though that doesn't amount to much these days.' A woman's voice elicited a ripple of laughter.

A waiter came with our drinks and we missed the conversation behind us for a few moments.

'...so he worked his way up from nothing, and now he's a billionaire.' A young woman's voice was cool and rational.

There was a moment's silence.

'I don't think so.' It was an older woman, sounding tentative. 'I'm sure I read he inherited it all. He's some sort of aristocrat distantly related to the Queen.'

I sneaked a glance over my shoulder.

They digested the thought of possible royal connections for a moment. The silence was soon broken by a man with a neatly trimmed moustache.

'You're all wrong. I heard he's a front man for Colombian drug barons and the investment fund he runs really belongs to them.'

'No! Really?' It was a different young woman. 'I suppose that makes sense. Apparently, he had a man killed but managed to bribe his way out of it. It was all hushed up.'

'You and your conspiracy theories!' said the gravel-voiced man. 'I don't know where you get them from. You don't read *The Enquirer*, do you?'

'I tell you, I had it on good authority—' the younger woman insisted, before the man with the moustache interrupted her.

‘Well, whatever he does, he sure gives us something to gossip about.’

Suzie’s eyes met mine and we exchanged a meaningful glance at the rumours which were circulating. The Americans paid their bill and left.

We looked at each other again and sighed. The air was fragrant with the scent of jasmine, and the clear water of the lake lapped softly against the quay.

I leant across and kissed Suzie gently on the cheek.

‘I’m so glad you came.’

We finished our drinks and left to change for dinner at the Palazzo. Rachel had told us Friday’s gathering would be a relaxed affair for twenty close friends. The real festivities would start on Saturday with a formal dinner for forty, and would culminate in Sunday’s party, which fell on Sir John’s birthday.

The dinners on Friday and Saturday at the Palazzo Urtica, held in a vast candle-lit ballroom, passed off uneventfully. Suzie and I found ourselves relegated to the lower reaches of the table on both occasions, struggling to make small talk with local luminaries. Apart from ritual greetings and farewells, we were largely ignored by our hosts who concentrated their efforts on a couple of the fund’s biggest investors, who both sucked on six-inch cigars and swilled champagne like cold lager. Ignacio Rodrigues had yet to make an appearance, though Suzie told me she’d received a text saying he would arrive on Sunday.

Chapter 30
TRAVELLING BACK FROM URTICA, 2003

The return flight from Turin took off two hours late. Once airborne, I sat back and reflected on Sunday evening's party. It had all been very strange. Beart had seemed unusually friendly with Ignacio Rodriguez, whom he had introduced as a major food exporter and investor in his fund. There were various technical issues relating to the accounting treatment of Rodriguez's investments, which we cloistered ourselves in an adjoining room to discuss.

Although I'd been concerned that Suzie would be all over Rodriguez, she acted in an uncharacteristically demure fashion, indulging in no more than a peck on the cheek.

I'd also been shocked to meet Simon, Amelia's ex-husband, outside the marble-clad lavatory. He was equally surprised but, after a moment's hesitation, we shook hands in an almost friendly way.

'No hard feelings?' I asked.

'Frankly, you did me a favour, old boy. I couldn't bear having that bitch around any longer, whingeing and whining. Gather she's shacked up with some other woman now.'

'Are you sure?' Amelia had so often commented on men's bottoms or speculated on their lunchboxes, it was difficult to believe she hadn't meant it.

'Absolutely. John met her and her partner the other day; a real pair of lovebirds, apparently.'

Amelia's rejection had made me feel a failure, and now this information cast it in a different light; I just wasn't the right sex.

'Great to see you again, Simon. It really is.' I slapped him on the back and made my way towards the ballroom, a new lightness in my step.

Narrowly avoiding colliding in the doorway with a couple of Arabs, he strode off in the direction of a slim, dark-haired young man, whom he touched affectionately on the arm, earning a dazzling early-in-a-relationship smile. Later, I saw them leave together, the younger man leaning heavily on the older.

I was roused from my reverie by the aircraft crew clattering along the aisle serving greasy croissants and scalding, tasteless coffee. Suzie appeared to be asleep. I looked at her, wondering about the true nature of her relationship with Ignacio. She stirred and I thought for a moment she'd woken up, but she merely twisted in the narrow seat, mumbled something and settled down again. I decided against waking her for breakfast, took a bite of my croissant and gazed out at the white candyfloss clouds, my thoughts returning to the party.

It still rankled that I'd been dragged in from the comfort of the fringes of the proceedings to give tax advice. Beart refused to entertain my protests that a clear conflict existed between the roles of adviser and auditor and steamrollered me into doing it anyway. But why had it been so important to discuss those matters during the party, when any competent accountant could have given them the answer over the phone? And how come Beart was mixing with those Colombians anyway, when he must have known they were drug barons?

Suzie opened her eyes, looked first at me and then out of the window.

'It's really boring up here,' she said, shutting her eyes.

'What did you think of the party last night?'

'Dull.' Suzie stretched languorously as her eyelids flickered open again. 'John and I had a good long chat, though. He's quite cute.'

'I bet Rachel loved that.' I could imagine her fuming as Beart neglected his other guests to heap attention on her despised sister.

Suzie looked at me coolly. 'I don't give a fucking monkey's what Rachel thinks.'

We parted at the airport.

'Are you going back to the apartment now?' I asked.

'I've got to see some people about a few things first. I'll catch you later. Bye.'

She hugged me.

I didn't see her for several weeks.

*

Neil was waiting at my office when I arrived.

'This is a nice surprise.' I ushered him in and asked my secretary to make two coffees.

'I'm here on business.' His voice was unusually terse. I scrutinised his expression trying to discern his mood. I could make little of it.

'I gather you took my advice and went to Urtica.'

'My goodness, society news travels fast these days. Been reading *The Tatler*?'

He didn't smile.

'Meet anyone interesting?'

I told him about Ignacio Rodriguez and his companions, recounting the conversation as accurately as I could.

'Beart's a slippery fish,' Neil said. 'We're sure he's up to something.'

'What I can't understand is why you lot are so interested in Rodriguez. Isn't that Drugs Squad business?'

'Everything's connected, isn't it?' He frowned.

'What's that theory? You know the one where the butterfly flaps its wings in Asia and there's a hurricane in the US.'

'Chaos Theory?'

'Could be; anyway, there's a lot going on, and we probably don't know the half of it. Your friend Beart seems to be at its centre.'

'He's no friend of mine.'

A belligerent look came into his eyes.

'You've done very well for yourself thanks to him.'

'You did too – for a while. How much of a friend of yours does that make him?'

His voice softened. 'Just make sure you don't blow it. By the way, you know Beart's mother has just gone into a hospice?'

My heart missed a beat. 'Where?'

'The Alison Rose in Abbotsford. Why are you so interested?'

'Don't forget I was her gardener. I knew her quite well.'

Neil stood up.

'This Beart business could be serious, you know. I hope you auditors really have done your stuff properly. By the way, I wouldn't be surprised if you get a visit from some heavy-handed colleagues of mine.'

'Are they from B6 too?'

'No, just about everyone has a finger in this pie.'

We shook hands and he left. I didn't know what to do with these persistent warnings about Beart.

The time-honoured letters CYA came to mind; cover your arse. I summoned Alana and told her I'd decided to call on the services of a couple of the other more experienced partners to carry out an independent review of what we'd done and the decisions we'd made about irregularities. I didn't mention the police's suspicions to her and I wouldn't share them with my colleagues. I'd choose the most biddable and was sure, with a little subtle prompting, they would see our largest client in the same light as I had and confirm the appropriateness of my actions. If later we found something amiss, they'd have to shoulder some of the blame and support me.

Chapter 31
ANOTHER DEATH, 2003-4

Abbotsford was an old walled city, famous for its fourteenth century cathedral, historic centre, and its numerous teashops. It would have been charming had it not been drowned by traffic trying to force its way through the narrow streets like blood through a sclerotic artery, and dwarfed by modern office blocks, thrown up on land made available by bombing. At the fringes of the indeterminate urban sprawl which surrounded the redeveloped business area, lay a few suburbs of tall gabled Victorian houses built in stark red brick. Every so often, one or two of these had been demolished to make way for a close of several modern two-storey town houses. Most of those remaining had been converted into flats. One, extended significantly by the addition of a modern concrete wing, was the Alison Rose Hospice, standing in its own tree-lined grounds.

As I entered, I felt full of trepidation, although I wasn't sure why. The corridor leading to the reception desk smelled of floor polish and Dettol. The duty nurse looked up at my approach.

'Mrs Beart, love? Room seven, third door on the left.'

I signed the visitors' book and found the room easily. A small tabby cat sat on the linoleum outside as though it couldn't decide whether to go in. I stepped carefully round it, holding my handkerchief to my face. I sneezed and the cat flinched.

'Sorry moggy, not your fault.' It stared at me with disdain before strolling down the long corridor, its tail raised in some form of feline semaphore.

'I suppose that means "fuck off" in cat,' I muttered to myself.

The perfume from the numerous large vases full of lilies and roses surrounding her was almost overpowering. Mrs Beart, grey and waif-like in the metal-framed bed, was lying with her eyes closed. I hesitated, not wanting to wake her. A nurse came in and, seeing me dithering, brought over a chair which she placed quietly by the bedside. I sat down and gazed at Mrs Beart's crumpled face and almost hairless head. She didn't move. Just when I'd decided to get up quietly and go, her cloudy eyes opened and looked vacantly at me. I smiled and said 'hello'. Her look of puzzlement only deepened. I felt myself grow hot under my shirt and regretted being there at all.

She continued to stare at me, the intensity of her eyes trapping me like a deer frozen by an on-coming lorry's headlights.

'Mrs Beart, I…., er I…..' Words were congealing in my brain.

Wheezing with effort, she pulled herself up onto her elbows and peered more closely at me.

'Oh, it's you.'

'Yes. You remember me.'

'John?'

'No, it's me. You probably remember me when I had hair, a lot more hair.' I spoke with forced jollity, thinking to myself she was almost unrecognisable with so little.

'John.' She sighed.

'He's not here. I wanted to come before—'

'After all this time—' she said weakly, slumping back onto the bed.

I didn't know what to say; I didn't even know why I'd come. Was it that I was sorry for my behaviour all those years ago? Was it because I'd never been able to forget her, even though our emotional entanglement had been so brief?

'I wanted to see you again,' I mumbled feebly.

'You took your time. Where have you been?' Her voice was a hoarse whisper. She shut her eyes and stretched out a hand as cold as marble.

After a few minutes, she slipped her hand from mine and groped for something on her bedside table.

Clasping it, she passed it to me. It was a large silver crucifix with a distinctive cluster of emeralds at its centre.

She made as though to speak, and I craned over her to catch what she said. Her voice was almost inaudible.

'Want you to have this.' She pressed the crucifix into my hand.

'But why?'

She lay down with her eyes closed, shaking her head almost imperceptibly. Her hand hung down beside the bed. Then she half-coughed, as though clearing her throat, exhaled deeply and her body went limp. For the first time since my arrival, her face looked serene. I placed her hand gently on the bed beside her and went to the end of the corridor where the duty sister was sitting. She returned quickly with me and confirmed Mrs Beart's death. It was only then I realised I still didn't know her forename. I glanced at the whiteboard above her bed. It read 'Josephine Beart.'

Numb, I left the hospice and eventually found myself on a bench in a park, the smell of new mown grass in my nostrils and the clamour of children playing Frisbee in my ears. My hands, arms and legs were shaking. I took the crucifix out of my pocket and examined it, the emeralds glinting in the waning sunshine of early evening. I flipped it over, noticing a minute inscription on the back. I strained to read it, holding it this way and that, before finally discerning that it said, 'To Mummy, with all my love for ever, John.'

Why had she given it to me? Had she had a soft spot for me all these years, or had she been deluded by pain, drugs and the imminence of her own mortality into mistaking me for Beart? I slipped the crucifix into my suit pocket just as a Frisbee rapped my ankle. I stood up and threw it back. It veered off course, bouncing off a push chair. I waved my arms in apology, only to be given the finger by a young mother busy comforting her bawling brat.

★

I wasn't invited to the funeral. I heard from Rachel no expense was spared, even though it was only attended by half a dozen of John's closest work colleagues. The coffin was polished bronze lined with red velvet, and the funeral cortege consisted of five black Rolls Royce limousines draped with black crepe. Josephine's body was buried in a cemetery outside Abbotsford, and Rachel said a life-size statue of the virgin and child in Italian marble had been ordered to mark the grave.

A couple of days after the funeral, my phone rang.

'You were with my mother when she died.'

'Yes. How did you know?'

'The nurse told me someone was there. I got her to look in the visitors' book.'

'Sorry, I should have mentioned it. I've been meaning to call you, John,' I lied.

'Where's her crucifix?'

'Crucifix?' My brain froze.

'The nurse said it was on the table beside her. Then it disappeared.'

I felt a moment's panic and a strong desire to lie again. Instead I took a deep breath.

'Yes, I've got it. She gave it to me just before she died.'

'She gave it to *you*?' His tone was scornful. 'Why would she give it to you? You hardly knew her.'

'I used to do her gardening,' I said, realising how limp the explanation sounded.

'You could have created the hanging gardens of Babylon for all I care. I want it back.'

'Of course, John; I was going to talk to you about it after the funeral.'

'Have it sent round to my office tomorrow morning.' I heard the click of his phone disconnecting, followed by a dialling tone. I felt as though I'd been caught stealing. I went to my jacket straight away – I hadn't worn it since and it hadn't been to the dry cleaners. But there was no sign of the crucifix. Even though I turned the pockets inside out, it remained stubbornly absent. I tried to cast my mind back to the day Josephine Beart had died. After my sojourn in the park I'd gone to a fashionable bar, one of those with wooden floors and exorbitant prices, and had drunk myself steadily into a state of near oblivion. I thought I could remember hanging the jacket on the back of a chair. I might even have gone to the toilet and left it there, unguarded. I felt sick. I picked the phone up and dialled Beart's number.

'Yes.' His voice was harsh. His phone obviously had a number recognition function.

'John, I've lost it. I think it must have been stolen while I was in Bar Barollo.'

'You fucking idiot,' he said quietly. 'You absolutely stupid fucking idiot. That crucifix meant the world to my mother. She clung onto it through the worst of times, prayed clasping it in her hands, bathed it with her tears. Then you come along, God knows why, and walk off with it before the breath's even left her body, just because you used to cut her grass.'

'I didn't walk off with it. She gave it to me and I put it in my pocket—'

'You must think I'm a fucking simpleton. I won't forget this.'

'John, I, I—' I started to say before realising he'd hung up on me.

★

I suppose I should have been expecting a visit from the police after Neil's tip-off. Even so, it still came as a surprise, not least because they arrived at my apartment one Saturday morning at five-thirty, insisting I accompany them to the station. Soon I was sitting on the chill back seat of a police car being whisked through empty streets.

I found myself in a small, windowless interview room with a metal table and two metal chairs. One had a cushion. I was told to sit on the other one, and the cold seat froze my buttocks through my thin linen trousers. A uniformed female constable stood between me and the door. After twenty-five minutes, a youngish man in a short leather jacket and ripped jeans came in carrying a cup of coffee and a half-burnt cigarette. He sat down and stared at me, swigged at his coffee and drew heavily on his cigarette.

'You attended a party recently at the Palazzo Urtica. Correct?'

I resolved not to be intimidated.

'I believe the correct form of address to a member of the public who pays your salary, and the upkeep of all this,' I looked around for dramatic effect, 'is "sir". What's more, you should have the decency to introduce yourself before peppering me with questions.'

His upper lip curled. 'I'm terribly sorry, *sir*. I'm Inspector Barnes. Now would you mind answering my question, *sir*, as I haven't got all day, *sir?*'

'Of course, Inspector, but you realise I was asked to attend the party by Superintendent Neil Wallington in B6, and I've given him a full debriefing.'

'Never heard of him,' Barnes replied. 'And I wouldn't pay those tossers in B6 in bent washers.'

The interview lasted two hours, during which I was asked to name everyone I remembered from the party and was shown several photographs. Every time I denied recognising someone, it was greeted with looks of exaggerated disbelief. I recounted the conversations I'd had, and the people with whom I'd had them. A small silver device recorded every word.

'You may think me naïve, Inspector,' I said after about an hour's interrogation. 'Beart is an extremely intelligent man. Why would he invite dodgy characters to a high-profile party unless he had absolutely nothing to hide?'

Barnes looked down his nose at me.

'For the same reason leaving something out in the open is the best way of hiding it.'

At the end of the conversation Barnes said, 'I trust you'll keep this discussion confidential, *sir*.'

Once home, I showered, shaved and brewed a cappuccino which I sipped as I sizzled bacon and toasted bread for my traditional Saturday morning breakfast. The door opened and Suzie walked in as though she'd returned from a ten-minute stroll. She'd been away for several weeks.

'Hello.' She kissed me lightly on the cheek. She exuded the salty-sweat and sunshine aroma of someone who's been sunbathing. She pulled out the grill pan and inhaled.

'That smells good. Got enough for me?'

I threw another couple of rashers under the grill.

Although I was aching to, I knew I mustn't ask where she'd been.

'You're up early for a Saturday,' she said. Without thinking, I mentioned my visit to the police station.

'Are you in trouble?' She was wide-eyed with disbelief.

'I'm sorry, I can't tell you anything but it's nothing to do with me.'

'Why did they take you there?'

I could tell from her terrier-like expression it wouldn't be easy to fob her off.

'They wanted some information.'

'From you? You never go anywhere exciting or do anything remotely dodgy. The only interesting person you know is me.' Her expression became thoughtful.

'It's nothing to do with Ignacio, is it?'

'I can't say.' I pulled out the grill pan and checked the bacon slices. A small globule of fat spat out and landed on the back of my hand.

'Oh, you're so irritating. I hate you.' She sat quietly for a moment, reflecting. 'Hold on. You only met him in Urtica, so it must be connected to that party.' Her eyes lit up. 'It's something to do with Ignacio and John, isn't it?'

I didn't reply.

'I knew it, I knew it,' she sang as she pirouetted around the room.

She wolfed her bacon sandwich and, giving me a

big slobbery retriever-like kiss, told me she had to go out and would be home for dinner.

'Can we have lamb chops? I really fancy lamb chops.'

I nodded. 'If you like.'

Even though I went shopping that day, I didn't bother to buy lamb chops. I wasn't expecting her back.

*

It was a wet, grey Sunday morning. Torrential rain beat against the windows and formed puddles in the road through which the traffic ploughed, making a continuous slushing noise. It was not a day for venturing out. I was watering my house plants when the front door bell rang, and rang and rang. I hurried to the intercom, unable to imagine what was so urgent. Perhaps it was a bunch of schoolboys playing games, or a tramp looking to be bought off. Both seemed unlikely given the conditions outside.

'Yes, hello?'

'Let me in.' The voice hissing down the line was unmistakably Beart's. I pressed the release button and the buzzer sounded. A few seconds later his fist thundered on the apartment door. He must have bounded, almost flown up the four flights of stairs. I put down my silver watering can and released the catch.

He barged in, a look of fury on his face and, without greeting me, produced a battered tome from under his soaking coat. I recognised it from all those years before as Mrs Beart's diary.

'You bastard, you fucking bastard, you screwed my mother.' His whole body was rigid and his hands were shaking. He lent slightly towards me and I was sure he was about to hit me. I took a step back.

'Look, John, calm down, I'll explain—'

'I won't calm down, and I don't need you to explain anything.' He thrust himself towards me, pushing his face against mine. His breath had the sourness of rotting vegetables. 'It's all here, in her own writing, everything. About you, and him too. Let me tell you, you're finished. I made you and I can break you. I'm taking Beart Enterprises away from Andrews Postlethwaite.'

He stuffed the diary under his coat and stormed out leaving a trail of water behind him. I heard his feet slapping their way down the first flight of stairs as I closed the door quietly and slumped to the floor. I wondered how she'd recorded our brief encounter and, for one blissful moment, I had a vision of how lovely she'd been, stretched out naked beside me.

Then my stomach started churning and I felt sick. I'm not sure how long I stayed there; dusk was already falling when I finally got up. I poured myself a strong whisky and phoned Richard. I'd no doubts about Beart's resolve, so I decided to warn the partners.

One thought kept niggling in my mind. Had I heard Beart correctly, or was it my imagination? 'And him too?' Why had he added this reference to Smallwood, if that was what it was, to his tirade against me? Or had someone else been her secret lover? Could it have been Ronald Carrot-Top, after all? Recalling the blankness of Ronald's expression when I'd mentioned her name all those years ago, I dismissed the thought. Then my mind threw up an image of Neil, lying on that same sofa, flicking post conjugal peanuts into his mouth. I shook my head. It was ridiculous. Neil hardly knew her.

*

I expected the world to collapse around my ears, so on Monday morning I was surprised to see everyone at their workstations with their heads down or scurrying along the corridors with files or folders in their hands. It was almost as though it had been a bad dream. Richard called the senior partners together and I addressed them. Of course, I couldn't tell them why Beart was taking the account away, so I fabricated a story in which he'd attacked me for questioning his business practices and I'd defended the auditor's integrity. Led by Richard, the partners agreed I'd been left with no alternative; I'd had to resist the blandishments of an aggressive and arrogant client. As I scanned the room, I could see the fear in their eyes. They knew the consequences of losing this audit account and hoped the matter would blow over.

I decided to talk to Rachel before calling Beart. She was curt. I didn't know whether he'd managed to turn her against me, or whether she was just in her normal overstretched and stressed state.

'I don't know what you've done to upset him. As far as he's concerned you're a non-person now, and the audit's as good as dead. A resolution to change the auditors will be put to the next Board meeting and ratified by the shareholders a few weeks later. What on earth did you do? I've never seen him as angry.'

I didn't feel up to confessing my youthful peccadilloes to Rachel, so when she said, 'It's not still about that bloody crucifix, is it?' I grunted.

Beart refused to take my calls. Richard also phoned him and was rebuffed. I visited Beart's offices in Victoria, only to be told he was away on business, even though his Lamborghini was parked on the forecourt. I tried to use Rachel as an intermediary.

'You're going to have to sort this one out yourself,' was her blunt reply. 'Something here doesn't add up. I'm not going to get involved.'

A few months passed and, true to his word, Beart took his business away from us. It was a calamitous blow. More than half our staff was billed to his account, and we had to institute a savage round of redundancies. Our younger more promising staff, as well as the more experienced and capable ones, deserted us for other accountancy firms. We were left with the unemployables, those we should have weeded out years before.

Worse still, a few months later, someone, I can only surmise it was one of Beart's henchmen, told the Inland Revenue we were aiding and abetting tax evasion, naming some of our larger remaining clients. The Inland Revenue carried out dawn raids on my home, those of other AP personnel and on our offices. The tax inspectors installed themselves in our boardroom, where they remained for several weeks, disrupting our normal business activities and carrying out a campaign of harassment and intimidation. As one of them explained, these operations were so high profile and so expensive, they had to stay until they uncovered something, so even after the firms about whom the initial allegations had been made were found to be clean, they moved onto others.

Most of our remaining clients abandoned us, fearing they would be the next to be picked on. We tried hard to find new ones to fill the vacuum, slashing our fees and offering extravagant dinners. They must have smelled our desperation because no one showed any interest. Then I started to receive reports that Beart had been poisoning the market with tales of our incompetence.

We sold the lease on our glass and steel office in the famous Bell-Jar building and moved to run-down premises near Holborn that were so dingy the only plant I could keep there was an etiolated dracaena, which clung to life in a thin shaft of light that snaked its way in from between two neighbouring office blocks.

Apart from soliciting new business, there was little to do. At about 11 o'clock I would head to The Magpie, returning about 3.30. In the evenings, I'd go home and drink myself to sleep. I'd given up cooking and lived on kebabs from the late-night take-away.

*

'We can't go on like this anymore,' Richard said as I limped into the office one morning. 'I've been looking at the figures. We're insolvent. We're going to have to wind the firm up.'

I stared at him. 'I don't understand.'

'We're broke. Can I put it any more clearly than that?'

I shook my head and slumped onto the chair behind my desk.

'No, I suppose you can't.'

'You'll have to call a partners' meeting straight away,' Richard said. 'We can't delay. We're trading while insolvent.'

'Like fuck I will. Most of them won't even look me in the eye when we pass in the corridor. They can go to hell.'

'Look,' said Richard, reaching across the desk and

putting his hand on my forearm. 'Beart has put it about that the real reason for our dismissal was you went off with something valuable of his mother's and won't give it back. Says he could have lived with our incompetence, he's grown so used to it. What he can't tolerate is your dishonesty. It isn't true, is it?'

'A load of balls. I told you why he sacked us.'

'I believe you,' Richard replied. 'The trouble is, no one else does.'

I didn't bother to go through the pretence of working. Instead I rushed to the pub as soon as it opened. After four pints and a large scotch, I wended my way back into the building and found it seemingly deserted, though everywhere were clues of recent occupation; a still-warm coffee cup here, a half-eaten pizza there. Then I became aware of raised voices coming from the boardroom. Not wanting to face a confrontation with the partners, I made for my office via the vending machine, where I was collecting a cup of coffee when Richard approached me.

'Someone spotted you coming back and they want you to join the meeting. I think you'd better.'

With my heart fluttering, I walked slowly to the boardroom and pushed the door open. The room, full of sullen faces, fell silent.

'Nice of you to turn up.' It was Andrew Liversedge, a red-faced man whose rank incompetence made me look the acme of professionalism. 'It's Captain

Disaster, finally deigning to spare us a few minutes of his valuable time.'

Several of the partners muttered profanities. A few started a slow handclap.

Staring at their puffy faces and aggressively scared eyes, my initial impulse to turn and bolt for the door gave way to the desire to take them all on.

'Who's got something to say?' I demanded, hands on hips.

There was a moment's silence. Brian Alcock broke it.

'Through your incompetence, you've thrown away the Beart account, we're standing on the edge of the precipice, and you ask whether anyone's got something to say? You're bloody lucky we don't rip you limb from limb.'

Several partners waved their fists and yelled abuse. I raised my hands and shouted over the noise.

'And what have you ever done, Brian, to bring in new business? What have any of you done? At least I landed the Beart account and hung onto it for sixteen years. You've all done bugger all except grow fat on the back of my success.'

'Not true. I brought in the MasonMurray account.' Alcock's jaw jutted out as he spoke and I experienced a strong temptation to punch it.

'And what a dog of a business that is,' I retorted. 'Just about every worthwhile account, apart from Beart's, we inherited from Braithwaite and his crew.

You, collectively, have done nothing to grow this firm.'

'You bastard,' Liversedge yelled, his face now purple, his veins like fat slugs. 'We were doing all right. You got us into this mess.'

'By defending our integrity,' I shouted back, to a chorus of cat-calls.

'Like fuck you were. You nicked something from Beart's mother and won't give it back.'

'I didn't—' I protested, but was drowned out.

'Now we're all ruined, thanks to you. What about the Limited Liability Partnership you promised to set up?' It was Ted Evans, a man with a Neanderthal's sloping forehead and an IQ in the low teens.

There wasn't much I could say. Braithwaite and his cronies, in their time at the helm, had refused to follow the major accountancy firms when they converted themselves into Limited Liability Partnerships. They took the old-fashioned view we should be prepared to back our judgments by putting our own wealth on the line, rather than, as they saw it, hiding behind limited liability. I'd always thought Braithwaite was deluding himself and promised to make the change when I took over. However, I hadn't got round to it, and so we partners found ourselves jointly and severally liable for all debts.

'I always did what was best for the firm,' I said above the partners' baying. 'It's—'

I experienced a sharp pain as a Blackberry struck

me behind my right ear, a clammy trickle of blood oozing slowly down my neck.

'Steady on!' Richard shouted. It was too late. A fusillade of Blackberries was unleashed. I covered my head with my arms and the missiles bounced painfully off them. I edged towards the door and, when the bombardment abated, ran for it. Thank God no stones were available, I thought as I bounded down the corridor to my office, otherwise I might have faced the same fate as Saint Stephen. I stuffed a few things into my briefcase and raced towards the exit. Richard intercepted me as I was about to leave the building.

'Sorry; no idea it would get so ugly. Are you all right?'

'They'd give hyenas a bad name. I'm finished with this bunch of wankers. Tell me what I need to do to wind this firm up and I'll do it.'

I could hear feet pounding along the corridor which led to the foyer, and wondered how many years, or centuries, it had been since a businessman was lynched by his colleagues in London.

'I'll let you know what you owe. Oh, and take care.' Richard gave me a pat on the shoulder. 'Keep in touch.'

I ran for the door as a horde of panting middle-aged men burst into the foyer, sweating and swearing in equal measure. With a bit of luck, a couple of them might suffer coronaries I thought, as I puffed and wheezed down the road.

*

Some weeks later Richard phoned and told me my share of the liabilities. It wasn't as bad as I'd feared. AP's out of London property estate had been sold quickly to an expanding firm of lawyers which took care of a large chunk of debt. If I sold my flat and liquidated all my assets, I could cover my own share of the liabilities and even keep my cherished black BMW, the sole tangible reminder of my time as an accountant.

Shortly after, I received a Civil Court claim form from Beart alleging misappropriation of his mother's crucifix. I phoned Rachel.

'He can't be serious, can he? He knows it was stolen from me and I've reported it to the police. What more can I do? What does he want, blood?'

'He wants you arrested for theft. The police say it's a civil matter. He's still in a frenzy. My advice is make yourself scarce. I don't think it'll blow over, exactly, but some of the heat might go out of it. I still don't understand why he's so angry though. I know it was his mother's crucifix. Even so, it seems a bit over the top.'

I scrunched the form up into a tight little ball and dropped it into a bin in the park. I decided to take Rachel's advice. If he wanted to pursue his case he'd have to find me first, and I wasn't going to make that easy. With money I'd stashed away for emergencies, I rented a room in a crumbling concrete tower block in Bermondsey which was scheduled for demolition.

★

I was sharing with three thirty-something-year-olds, one male and two females, all working in the charity sector. The only person I'd told of my new address was Richard, and I knew he wouldn't let on to anybody. I doubted whether anyone would be able to track me down.

Less than a week later, while heating a can of baked beans and scorching some toast under the grill, I had a visitor. It was Neil.

'How the hell did you find me?'

'Easy-peasy, mate. You stick out here like a pimple on a tart's arse. Let me buy you a drink.'

★

'Not going so well, I hear,' Neil said, and I was sure I saw a flicker of satisfaction cross his face. 'Too bad mate. Still, I'm sure it's only a temporary setback.'

Even though I couldn't imagine anyone ever wanting to employ me again, I wasn't going to expose my self-doubts to Neil.

'Something will turn up. By the way, I had a funny old interview with some of your friends in Scotland Yard a while back. I'd have thought you'd have shared what I'd fed back to you, but they said they'd been told nothing and grilled me like a pork chop.'

'I asked them to go easy on you.' Neil sat back in

his chair, relishing my discomfiture. 'No more than a light going over.'

'They said they'd never heard of you,' I retorted. 'And they didn't have a good word for B6.'

'Mind games, mate. We all do it.' He picked a peanut from the pile lying on the torn packet and flipped it expertly into his mouth. It was the third time in a row he'd accomplished this trick.

'Very impressive. So, they did teach you something at Hendon. Anyway, what progress are you making?'

'We know Beart's up to something; it's just a case of finding out what. I can smell a wrong'un, and believe me, he's rotten to the core.'

'Perhaps Beart is playing mind games of his own, Neil. Personally, I wouldn't give him a drop of water if he were dying of thirst and I owned a reservoir. However, the rest of the world thinks he's a model citizen. Sits on lots of committees, gives bundles of money to charity and visits No 10 more frequently than the milkman.'

'I didn't know you were part of his fan club. In fact, I thought you disliked him as much as I do, especially since he's nicked all your women off you.'

The loud noise of fellow revellers in the Prince of Wales seemed to die down to a background hubbub and everything moved in slow motion.

'What do you mean, all my women? He only took Rachel off me, and that was because I was fool enough to let her go.'

Neil took a swig of beer, keeping his eye steadily on me. He wiped his mouth on his sleeve.

'If that's what you choose to believe.'

'What do you mean, Neil?'

'You really want to know?'

I nodded. 'Spit it out.'

'I have it on good authority he was shafting Amelia while she was living with you.'

'Unlikely, Neil. She's a lezzie. Came out shortly after we split up and moved in with another woman.'

'I don't think so. She's Beart's creature, always has been. I heard he arranged for her to move into a nice house, all expenses paid and visits her on the quiet from time to time, just as he did when she was supposedly married, and just as he did when she was living in what you thought was bliss with you. In fact, if you believe the rumours, Beart is the real father of her daughters.'

Jealousy clamped my chest, squeezing the breath from my lungs. I finally managed to force some words through my constricted throat.

'What about her husband? Didn't he object?'

'Beart probably had something on him, otherwise he wouldn't have married her in the first place. It was the classic marriage of convenience, only in this case it was all for Beart's convenience.'

We sat in silence as this new information sank in. It was all so implausible. However hard I tried, I couldn't make sense of it. My mind flitted back to what had seemed halcyon days when she, her daughters and I had taken on the semblance of a happy family.

'Water under the bridge,' I said. 'It was all a while ago.' I reached for a peanut.

'And now he's shagging Suzie.'

I choked on the nut, coughing uncontrollably and he slapped me on the back. When I recovered, I looked at his face to see if he was joking. His expression was grim.

'Are you sure?'

He nodded gravely.

'Sorry mate. I take it you didn't know. He's set her up in some nice little love-nest too. He's got quite a harem of your ex-women, hasn't he?'

'Does Rachel know?' I couldn't imagine Rachel tolerating his philandering, least of all with her own sister.

'Know what, mate? About Suzie, or Amelia?'

'I don't know, either, both. Amelia would be bad enough. Finding out about Suzie would really crack her up.'

'Not yet, mate. Soon will though, I can assure you of that.'

'How will you tell her?'

'Tell her? Interfere in the private lives of the nation's citizens? What do you take us for?' He grinned broadly, tossed three peanuts into the air together and caught them all.

★

The story only made the inside pages of the *News of the World,* which I'd bought because Neil tipped me off. Though the photographs were grainy and the headline – 'Knight of Passion' – corny, the evidence was incontrovertible.

It didn't take Rachel long to phone me. Her manic work ethic and relentless pursuit of success meant she'd acquired few, if any, true friends. Her tone was brisk and I could imagine the firm line of her jaw as she spoke unemotionally into the receiver.

'I don't suppose you've seen the *News of the World*?'

'As a matter of fact, I have. I bought it to read why Andre Albakken paid well over the odds for Igor Ludochenko, then left him festering on the bench.'

'Never mind all that. Did you see the article about John and Suzie?'

'Couldn't really miss it.'

'Think it's true?'

I was struck by how unemotional Rachel seemed.

'How would I know?'

'Because you live with Suzie, for one reason, you dumb cluck.' Her voice had changed suddenly from steely to angry.

'Well in a manner of speaking, though I haven't seen much of her recently. Anyway, I suspect it's true. I'm sure he'd sue them if it weren't, so we'll only have to wait a short while to find out.'

'I'm not waiting ten seconds. John and I are

through.' She paused. 'He'll live to regret it, the bastard.'

'What are you going to do, Rachel? Nothing silly I hope.' I couldn't imagine Rachel throwing herself off a cliff; she would be more likely to hurl Beart to his death.

'I'm getting out of here, I'm quitting Beart Enterprises, and I'm going to get even.'

'I read of a jilted woman who cut the crotch out of all her partner's pairs of trousers. Perhaps that might be the place to start?'

'I don't think a little sartorial vandalism is going to do much to satisfy me. No, this is one I want to get absolutely spot-on.'

'Well, if you want to go out for dinner and talk about it—'

'Thanks. I'll let you know. Sorry, better go now; I've got lots of things to think through.'

Chapter 32
RACHEL DISAPPEARS, 2004

I thought I'd better let Rachel sort herself out after the traumatic experience she'd been through, but when I hadn't heard from her for a few weeks I started to worry. Could even the self-sufficient Rachel be depressed? She wasn't answering her mobile and I wasn't sure how to contact her. I knew she must have moved out of the Belgravia home she'd shared with Beart and, from what she'd said, would no longer be working for Beart Enterprises, so I tried calling her mother. An unfamiliar female voice answered.

'Could I speak to Edwina, please?' I said.

The voice sighed. 'Sorry, there's no Edwina here.'

'That is the Vicarage, Wintlesham?'

'Yes, and we're the new owners, and no, I'm afraid I don't have a forwarding address. You must be the umpteenth person to ask.'

I puzzled over what to do. I telephoned Rachel's old office hoping to speak to Wendy, her secretary, but was informed she'd left the organisation, and they didn't have contact details for her or Rachel. I didn't want to ask Neil. That smug tone of voice he'd barely suppressed when he told me about Suzie still rankled. That only seemed to leave one avenue, and I recoiled from taking it. Finally, however, with my concerns mounting, I found myself on the steps of Beart's Belgravia house. The door was opened by their Filipina maid, Bing. Her usually sunny expression clouded over when she saw it was me.

'Bing, I wondered whether you had a forwarding address for Lady Beart,' I said.

'Who is it, Bing?' A female voice I recognised asked in the background. Seconds later Suzie, wearing a short white silk dressing-gown, padded barefoot into the hall.

'Oh, it's you,' she said, as though greeting a troublesome neighbour. 'What do you want?'

Bing retreated.

There were so many things I wanted to say, so many questions I wanted to ask, so many insults I wanted to unleash that they wrapped themselves around each other, strangling my brain and paralysing my vocal chords. It took me some moments to straighten out my thoughts, and even then I stumbled in getting the few words I could articulate out.

'R-R-Rachel's address.'

Suzie folded her arms. 'Thought I'd cured you of that prissy cow.'

The anger in me prevailed over the hurt and the shock.

'She's worth a million of you.' As I mounted the last step and pushed myself forward, she slammed the door in my face, missing my nose by millimetres.

'Go away! This is private property,' she yelled through the letterbox. I thundered on the gleaming brass knocker.

'I'll call the police,' she shouted.

I dropped to my knees and pushed the flap open. 'You fucking hypocrite. What happened to property is theft and all the other shit you spouted? Let me in. I want Rachel's address.'

'Go away, you pathetic little man. I'm calling them now.'

I heard a telephone number being dialled as a shadow loomed over me. I looked round, shielding my eyes from the sun's glare, to make out a policeman's pointed helmet.

'Everything all right, sir?'

I stood up and brushed the dust from my knees. The policeman was a couple of inches shorter than me and, fleetingly, I felt the strong desire to push him down the front steps.

'Bloody hell, you were quick. Suppose you're part of his personal protection squad, paid for out of my taxes.'

'No idea what you're talking about, sir. Is this your house?'

The door opened. Suzie stood there looking at me as though I were her least favourite form of invertebrate.

'No, it isn't,' she said. 'He's stalking me.' Suzie's gall rendered me speechless. She could switch between social codes with the ease of a chameleon changing colours. The free-wheeling socialist who'd sponged off me had changed into the protector of property rights, albeit someone else's.

'In that case, I suggest you move along now, sir.'

As I walked away, I cast a bitter look in Suzie's direction. I'd always expected her to abandon me, but never to turn against me. She was still standing on the steps, talking to the policeman. She noticed me looking and gave a cheery wave, accompanied by a hearty 'goodbye'. Resentment clogged my chest as I made my way to the Beart Enterprises Head Office, only a few yards away in Victoria.

The doorman knew me well from my auditing days.

'Morning, George,' I said.

In place of his usual stiff smile, I was greeted by a grimace. Suzie must have warned them. He stood on the top step before the revolving doors, barring my way.

'Sorry sir, I have instructions not to admit you.'

I glanced behind him. He was a flabby sixty-something, with a sizeable paunch. If I pushed past him, I could be through the doors, up the stairs and into Beart's office before anyone could stop me. At that moment, the lift doors opened and Beart emerged. He strode towards us, eased the doorman aside and stared down at me. He looked lean and strong in his pale blue shirt, his gold cufflinks glinting in the sun. His arms hung loosely by his sides, and his mouth was twisted into an expression of disgust. I stepped up to his level. His body tensed and I saw his right arm twitch.

'You—' he snarled.

I puffed my chest out. Although he would beat me in a fight, at least I wouldn't give him the satisfaction of seeing me back down.

'Give me Rachel's address.'

The doorman was joined by three men in dark glasses and security officers' uniforms. One of them must have been six feet four and the other two not much shorter; the muscles in their necks bulged above their tight dark blue collars.

'Doesn't exist.' Beart spat the words and I felt a fine spray of saliva on my face.

Despite the trembling in my arms and legs, I forced myself to square up to him. Memories of adrenaline-charged playground fights came flooding back.

By now a crowd, breathless with excitement, was gathering around us. I recognised one of them, Leigh Rosenberg, a truculent young Finance Manager from Ilford, with whom my audit team had had several run-ins. He yelled, 'Don't put sugar on it, boss, gob him,' and made a punching motion with his right arm as several people picked up the chant of 'gob him, John,' and waved their fists.

'What do you mean, doesn't exist?' I shouted above the mounting clamour.

Beart, his face now impassive, said to the security men. 'Our friend is leaving. Please see him off the premises.' The three stepped between us. Then he turned to the onlookers and said, 'OK folks. Show's over. Back to work.'

Past the three broad chests ranged in front of me, I glimpsed him stroll back into the building as though nothing untoward had occurred. One of the security men put a hand on my shoulder. I shook it off.

'I'm going.' I swivelled on my heel and walked quickly across the forecourt and around the corner. Once out of sight, my legs buckled and I slumped against a wall, where I stood shaking with a mixture of disbelief, nerves and exhilaration. Although I hadn't found out where Rachel was, for the first time since schooldays, I'd stood up to John Beart.

It was Richard who suggested a private investigator. I found Arnold Trippier's name in Yellow Pages and visited his Hackney office.

A week later I was back in Arnold's office to hear his report.

'She's either disappeared or been disappeared. I traced her to a rented apartment a couple of months back. After that, nothing. I've tried my police contacts. Another blank. Maybe she's in hiding somewhere. If so, she's made a professional job of it.'

'No surprise there. Rachel makes a professional job of everything.'

'Disappearing without trace isn't that easy. Most people leave some clues, unless they've been trained by the security services or Special Branch.'

I sat forward on his leather sofa.

'Could she have hired someone, perhaps someone like you, to help her?' I sipped my macchiato.

'Unlikely. I don't know anyone legit who's in the business. There are a few criminals who do it for a living. Is it possible she had contacts?'

I shook my head.

'And her mother?'

'Had a stroke. Can't remember a thing, and the care home doesn't have Rachel's details. Two other daughters had power of attorney and sold the house to pay for care.'

'Her sisters?'

He shook his head. 'Don't know anything.'

'Any point going to the police?'

'Absolutely none. They won't pay any attention to you.'

'Must be something I can do.'

'I'd wait. Missing people usually turn up sooner or later, alive or dead.'

When I shared Arnold's advice with Richard, he

pronounced it sound, advising me to get on with my life and sort out my own problems.

I tried repeating the phrase, 'I'm sure she's fine' and, with plenty of help from my old friend Johnny Walker, did my best to put thoughts of Rachel out of my mind.

*

Richard hadn't worked on the Beart Enterprises account, and he quickly managed to find a job as Finance Director of a drinks company. More confident of the future, he and Sandra gave a house-warming party when they moved from Wandsworth to a much larger property in Esher and insisted I come.

'Could be a new start. Perhaps you'll meet someone,' Sandra said.

The house was enormous with a sizeable garden surrounded by laurel bushes. As I gripped the antique bell-pull, memories of Thorpe Barton flooded back, stirring up deep feelings of failure.

Richard was very good at keeping in touch so I was hoping some of the people I'd known in my younger days would be at the party. I propped myself in a corner, sipping a glass of red wine, and was quite enjoying trying to recognise old male acquaintances, despite their balding heads and thickening waists, when Alison and Mark arrived.

'Hi, how are you? Long time, no see. We almost

didn't recognise you with your bushy beard. You look more like an artist than an accountant.'

'What are you two doing here? I didn't know you were friends of Richard's.'

'I treat Sandra,' Alison replied. 'Rachel was very good at recommendations.'

'And how are the fitness and herbalism businesses going?' I asked, proud of my ability to dredge up their occupations. It suddenly occurred to me they might know Rachel's whereabouts. 'Are you still ministering to Rachel, Alison?'

'I am, or rather I was,' Alison said, 'only it's, or it was, shiatsu and reiki. Mark's given up fitness coaching and is now wholesaling biodynamic food.'

'Trouble with my knees,' Mark said, almost apologetically.

'What do you mean, you were?'

'Rachel seems to have vanished. We're quite worried about her.'

'Yes, I can't imagine her surviving without her daily dose of qi,' I said, though my heart was beating faster and my bowels twisting and contorting.

They didn't smile. Perhaps they believed Rachel really did need daily reiki and cosmically enhanced vegetables to continue with the arduous process of living.

'When did you last see her?' I continued.

'Must be a couple of months or more ago, I think,' Alison replied. 'She seemed scared.'

I couldn't picture Rachel scared of anybody or anything.

'Of what?'

Alison shrugged. 'Don't know. She wouldn't answer the door, the blinds were down, she kept looking out at the street, you know, a million little things.'

'The atmosphere there,' Mark added, 'smelled of danger, of fear. I was in overload when I was with her.'

I looked at Mark's brawny frame and the deep scar on his cheek. He would easily have passed as a rugby prop forward or a nightclub bouncer.

'What was she doing?'

Alison looked around as though concerned we might be overheard.

'Eating chocolate bars and analysing figures on her computer.'

'Chocolate bars! Are you sure?' I couldn't believe this of a paragon of the virtues of exercise and wholesome food.

'Absolutely! She ate two in front of me.'

I mentioned the name of the apartment Arnold had found.

'That's it. It's one of those fully equipped service apartments. After Rachel, a Japanese businessman rented it. Said he knew nothing of her. The company that runs the block couldn't or wouldn't tell us where she'd gone.'

'I fear the worst,' Mark said. 'My sixth sense is

telling me something bad has happened. We went to the police, but......' His voice trailed off and his shoulders hunched. Alison gave a little squeal.

'Don't say that, Mark.'

Mark put his arm around her and produced a small phial.

'I think we both need some more rescue remedy.'

I left them tending to each other. I needed some air. Queasiness gripped my stomach and, after a few palpitations which left me breathless, my heart started racing. Rachel was in danger, or, worse still, may already be dead. A shudder shook my whole body. I'd been a fool not to go to the police myself. She needed their protection. I overcame my reluctance and phoned Neil's mobile number. It rang through to voicemail. I left a garbled message, asking him to call back urgently.

Two anxious days and two sleepless nights followed with Neil neither answering his phone nor returning my calls.

On the third day, my phone rang.

'What's the panic, mate? You won the lottery and want to share your winnings?'

'Rachel's disappeared.' I told him the details, blending Alison and Mark's account with my own and adding in Arnold Trippier's conclusions.

'People disappear all the time, then they reappear. She's a jilted woman, thrown over for her own younger sister. You wouldn't expect her to sit around at home doing macramé, would you?'

'Neil, how can you be so relaxed? You told me Beart might have disposed of other people who crossed him. Rachel probably knows more about his business, and him, than anyone else alive, if she is still alive, and you don't seem to care. I thought you wanted to get the goods on Beart. If that's true, Rachel is your best bet. You can't put her life at risk.'

'Being a bit melodramatic, aren't we? Why don't you leave it a few days and see what happens?'

'Neil, I can't believe you're being like this. If you won't do anything, I'll go to the ordinary plods and see whether they can help.'

'Please yourself, mate. However, I'd appreciate it if you didn't refer to my esteemed uniformed colleagues as "plods".' The line went dead.

I went to Scotland Yard and asked for Inspector Barnes. After a two hours' wait, I was seen by a young officer with a lop-sided face and acne. He seemed more perturbed that an ex-husband should be reporting his former spouse as missing than he was about my suspicions, and I had the uncomfortable feeling I'd unwittingly edged myself into being prime suspect.

Chapter 33
DITTINGTON, 2004-2005

Even though I went through the motions of job hunting and approached my contacts in other accountancy firms, I always was greeted with polite, slightly condescending smiles and told I was too senior. I applied, to no avail, to several blue-chip companies for roles as Finance Director, and then as Financial Controller or Head of Internal Audit. Although they never admitted it, it was clear I was damaged goods. I was even rebuffed by the consultancies I approached.

Sharing a living room, kitchen and bathroom with three other people was proving difficult. From their frowns, they disapproved of my drinking a bottle or two of red wine each night, and from the lulls in the conversation when I walked in, I knew they talked about me, so, after a while, I found it less unpleasant to stay in my own room in the evenings. Meanwhile, I looked around for somewhere cheap but more private and more permanent to rent.

It was probably a chance in a million; I found *The Wattock and Dittington Bugle*, on the tube, picked it up and took it home. Leafing through it, my eye was caught by details of a small thatched cottage which was available to rent. Too far from London, I sighed and threw the paper onto the sofa. The next day, I picked it up and looked at it again, searching Google and the public library for everything on Dittington. There wasn't much. The place sounded ideal.

The next day I drove there and its picture postcard charm seduced me; the narrow, cobbled streets, the timber-framed Elizabethan cottages with honeysuckle and climbing roses wrapping themselves round each front door. Every garden was ablaze with flowers. Children's voices floated on the light summer breeze, wafting across from the playground of the old stone village school. A pub, The Jolly Throstle, its rusty sign depicting a thrush catching a worm, and a shop with small panes of old fashioned glass in its window, stood side by side at the village's heart. Although the cottage for rent was easily the most dilapidated, the garden more than compensated. Without a sign of a weed, it was planted out in different hues of pink and blue, interspersed with the occasional blotch of sparkling white. Around the back, I could make out neat rows of lettuces, beans, peas and carrots.

'It was Old Bob's passion. In fact, he died right there.' The letting agent pointed to a cucumber frame. 'Odds-on favourite, he was, for first prize at the village fete. He was cruelly robbed.'

I agreed to take the place on the spot; I could manage without creature comforts if it meant having access to this magnificent garden.

Within a month, I'd moved in even though I'd no idea how I was going to earn a living there. After all, I had my plants and vegetables to console me. The only thing which continued to worry me was that I'd still heard nothing from Rachel.

Dressed in old brown corduroy trousers and a faded denim shirt, I'd managed to work up quite a lather digging in the hot sun one afternoon. I was leaning on my spade contemplating my efforts when I became conscious of a high-pitched, nasal voice.

'Are you the gardener?'

I looked round. A man, aged about forty and dressed in a cream linen suit, was leaning against the cottage's peeling white picket fence. A lock of dark blond hair hung down across his forehead.

'Might be.'

'We've just bought the place down the lane, Honeysuckle Cottage, and need some help. If you're not fully booked perhaps you'd consider keeping our place tidy. We only use it at weekends.' He looked around at my garden. 'You've certainly done a great job here.'

‘All down to Old Bob. I’m new here. If you’re still interested, I’d be happy to do some work for you.’

‘How much do you charge?’

I peered down the lane and, just past the massive beech which towered over it, I could see the gate to Honeysuckle Cottage, with the boot of a Maserati protruding. I thought of a figure and doubled it, regretting I hadn’t asked for more when the man didn’t quibble, or even express surprise.

‘Name’s Anton, Anton Guillard.’ He extended a hand, then half withdrew it when he saw the dark mud staining my own.

‘Bit mucky,’ I said, declining to take it. He breathed a soft sigh of relief, pulled a silk handkerchief from his pocket and dabbed at his brow.

‘When would you like me to start?’ I asked.

‘Sooner the better, old sport.’

We ran through some formalities and agreed I’d start the next day.

*

Anton was a bond trader, and his wife, Clarinda, a corporate lawyer. Some weekends they would invite me to join them in the shade of their old apple tree, and we would drink Sancerre and discuss ways to improve their garden. My initial reluctance to make expensive suggestions evaporated when I realised that for Clarinda cost was not a consideration, and I could refashion the garden by bringing in mature trees and shrubs. Within a few months, it was transformed. Delighted with the results, Anton and Clarinda invited me round one hot and sunny Sunday for Pimms and a celebration meal. We sat on the terrace I'd created in the shade of plants which had, only recently, been growing in Italy. In the woodshed beside the cottage lay neat piles of apple wood logs, now drying out for use in the winter.

It seemed that the village was made up of Anton's City colleagues and acquaintances. Through him, and even more so Clarinda, my reputation spread and my services were soon in demand.

Though most of my new clients' ambitions, initially, were modest, over time my work grew in scale and complexity. From being someone who did a bit of lawn cutting and hedge trimming, I graduated to laying out sizeable chunks of ground with plants, and from that to fully fledged garden design.

I also found, to my delight, I could live on the proceeds from my horticulture business and even have enough left over to run my black BMW. I became a regular in the pub and, while the old locals who'd been born and bred in those parts were still reserved, the more recent arrivals in the village welcomed me, buying me drinks and including me in their conversations. I took up darts, at which I made a fool of myself on numerous occasions, and even tried my hand at shove ha'penny and dominoes.

I didn't have a television and I'd given up reading

newspapers. I'd changed my mobile phone number and was in contact with no one, except, very occasionally, Richard. I'd even lost track of the length of time I'd been in Dittington; it felt as though it was forever, so it came as quite a surprise when I heard a visitor had been asking after me.

'Said his name was Neil,' Colin, the landlord, told me as I raised my pint of bitter to my lips. 'Said you'd know how to contact him. He wants to speak to you; says it's important.'

A twisting in my gut told me it could have something to do with Rachel. I slipped out of the bar and stood in the frosty night air, my breath pluming in front of me as I called his number.

'Oh hello,' Neil said in a tone that suggested we might have been speaking only a few hours ago, rather than the year or more that had elapsed. 'I hear you've buried yourself in the darkest countryside. "Budding Genius"? Not a very original name for a gardening firm, is it? Would have thought you could have come up with something better, but I suppose as you were an accountant, imagination can't have been your strong point.'

'Wonderful to talk to you too, Neil. However, I doubt you sought me out to tell me your views on the names of horticulture companies. In any case, I now pay for my own phone calls, so it would be good to get to the point. Is it about Rachel? How is she?'

'Rachel's OK, but I think it would be better if we

met. There's quite a lot to tell you. I'm in Wattock, staying at the Beetle and Pulpit. If you've still got a car, why don't you motor over and I'll buy you dinner? It sounds as though you could probably do with a square meal.'

'My business is doing pretty well, thank you. Even so, I'll take a meal off you any day.'

Chapter 34
TRIALS AND TRIBULATIONS, 2005-7

The fourteenth century Beetle and Pulpit was replete with low, dark wood beams, bottle-glass windows and a battered sign saying, 'Duck or Grouse'. I pushed open the heavy oak door and looked inside. Something about the regularity of a lot of the wood, the horse brasses scattered liberally across the walls and the rows of too-shiny Toby jugs whispered, 'cynical restoration' to me. Neil was in the corner of the snug, engrossed in flipping peanuts. I paused to watch him as he executed this trick seven times perfectly before the eighth bounced off his nose and dropped into his beer. It was an appropriate point to make my presence known.

'I see you haven't improved despite all the practice you've doubtless had.'

'That peanut just wasn't aerodynamic.'

'A poor craftsman—'

It was the sort of thing we used to say to each other when we were messing around in the old days. He stood up and we shook hands.

I settled down with a pint and we exchanged further pleasantries as we placed our order for food.

'What news of Rachel?' The words burst out of me almost involuntarily.

'Steady on, mate. All in good time. I've got some other hot news for you first. Did you know your friend Beart's in the slammer?'

'What for?'

'Looks like his famous Investment Fund was laundering Colombian drugs money and siphoning off chunks to unsavoury third parties like Al Qaeda.'

'Why would he do that? He had everything to lose.'

Neil gazed at me levelly.

'Greed.' He put his mug back firmly on the table.

'Surely he can't have been convicted already? I know I've been out of circulation for a while, but these trials take ages to come to court.'

'We're in the process of putting the case together, thanks to Rachel. Concerns raised by the new auditors had started to arouse her suspicions. Then when Beart went off with your woman Suzie, Rachel declared war on them both. She's dedicated herself to the task of unearthing what was going on, despite heavy intimidation. We had to whisk her away and give her a new identity.'

'So, you knew where she was all along, you bastard! You could have told me, or at least hinted.'

His eyes slid away from mine and fixed on the ceiling.

'Sorry mate. Level five classified. Couldn't breathe a word.'

'And Beart—?'

'He'll be out on bail in a jiffy. Only until we get him convicted, of course. I really think we've got him this time.'

I sank back into my chair. It was worth having paradise invaded to hear this news.

'Don't know what you're looking so smug about,' Neil said. 'You're going to be called by the Crown as a witness. It seems a lot of the things Beart was getting away with were quite basic and should have been picked up long ago, or at least that's what the new auditors say.'

I felt myself blanch. 'They're not really going to call me, are they?'

'Star witness, mate, star fucking witness.'

'What about Rachel?'

'We'll protect her until the trial's over. Then it's up to her. She can continue with the false ID or resume her true identity.'

The chump chop, new potatoes and peas I'd ordered arrived. I stared at them. I'd lost my appetite.

‘Cheer up mate,’ Neil said. ‘You’re the person who’s brought him down, you and his ego that is. If you hadn’t been such a crap auditor he’d never have sacked your lot and we’d never have got a toe-hold, and if you hadn’t been such a woeful boyfriend, Suzie wouldn’t have dumped you for him so Rachel wouldn’t have got on his case. We couldn’t have done it without her, you know. She’s sacrificed a lot. She’s close to broke and virtually unemployable now. Isn’t jealousy a marvellous motivator?’

I cut a small piece of lamb, put my knife and fork down and pushed my plate away. I couldn’t face eating anything.

‘Could I speak to Rachel?’

‘Sorry mate, it’s beyond my powers to allow it. She’s hermetically sealed.’

‘I’m an old friend—’

His expression was enough to make me realise my request was hopeless.

‘By the way, as well as some of my colleagues, you can expect the DTI to be in touch shortly. I daresay your institute will also have something to say to you.’

I had the uncomfortable feeling Neil was enjoying my discomfort even more than his rare T-bone steak, from which a thin trickle of blood had found its way into the blue-grey stubble on his chin.

★

Unfortunately, Neil's predictions were all too accurate and my life over the next few months became peppered with uncomfortable interviews with the police and assorted regulatory bodies. Each interview exposed my incompetence more starkly.

'Stupid child! I knew you'd fuck it up. You're even worse than your brother.' My father's imagined words echoed frequently in my ears, and many were the times I cursed him for pushing me into accountancy.

Not knowing what else to do, I kept my head down and continued with my gardening business, deriving great satisfaction from the growing beauty – in both senses – thanks to my efforts, of the village. It wasn't difficult to persuade the bankers and city lawyers who owned most of the second properties to part with sizeable sums to improve their investments. As beneficiaries of six or seven figure bonuses every year they hardly noticed the cost, and it gave them something to talk about at dinner parties in town.

I had broadband installed and bought a laptop, the first I'd used since leaving work, and started to follow the news online. I read that Beart had been released on bail. Not much else was reported, which surprised me. The police really must want to keep a tight lid on this one if they weren't talking off the record to their journalist paymasters.

Even though I'd prepared myself, it came as quite a shock when I received a subpoena requiring me to testify at the trial.

*

The trial lasted only four months, a short time for such a complex case. It was a tribute to the quality of Rachel's two-year dissection of the data that the jury appeared to understand something of what had gone on.

My own appearances, which lasted a couple of days, were inglorious and I was pilloried in the media for my incompetence. Martha Grant was called to give testimony, telling the court I'd been in Beart's pocket because we were old school friends. Even though Bedlington House was hardly Eton, the press had a field-day. 'Toffs stick together' was one red-top headline, 'Old Boys, Old Tricks,' another.

During my interrogation, it took me some time to recognise the two identical solicitors sitting behind Beart's barrister, and providing the QC with her ammunition, as the Kray twins.

Beart didn't look at me once throughout my testimony, though I thought I detected a faint smile on his face as I was grilled for several hours by both prosecution and defence counsel. My words were twisted so many times that even I lost track of what had taken place. I was on the verge of tears when my inquisition drew to a halt and I left the stand shaking so hard I had to cling onto the rail to avoid collapsing.

My heart had barely stopped thumping when I bumped into Neil in the Court's hallway.

‘My God, that was hell. It felt as though I was on trial, not Beart,’ I moaned, relieved to see a friendly face. ‘I’d hate to think what it’s like actually being in the dock.’

‘You were lucky you weren’t. The Crown Prosecution Service tried to put a case together against you. There wasn’t quite enough evidence. That, and the fact Rachel said you weren’t bright enough to be in league with Beart.’

The insult stung, though I suspected Rachel had said it to protect me. It was painful enough to be portrayed as an idiot by the press. It was worse when it was a close friend and ex-wife.

‘In fact, her theory,’ Neil continued, ‘is that Beart relied on being able to fool you whenever he needed to. You were his patsy.’

Rachel’s performance in court was, apparently, outstanding and the jury hung onto her every word. Despite defence counsel trying to bully her into contradicting herself or admitting to the existence of guesswork or gaps in her account, she remained unruffled. I wondered what expression had played across Beart’s lips as she set about destroying his life.

I only saw her fleetingly as I was called and she stood down as a witness and we coincided briefly outside the courtroom. I flashed her a nervous smile. She was so calm and self-assured; it was as though this was the big match for which she’d been preparing for years, and now she was ‘in the zone’.

Beart was convicted at the end of the trial and sentenced to fifteen years in prison.

If I thought it would be all over when the trial concluded, I was sadly mistaken. I was pursued by petty officials from diverse Government departments and regulatory bodies, as well as being hounded by the press, who plastered my name and career details over their pages with little regard to truth or accuracy. I wasn't in a financial position to sue even though much of the comment was libellous. After an assortment of humiliating hearings, I was struck off as an accountant and told I may well be personally liable for losses sustained by investors in Beart Enterprises.

*

The day after the trial I walked into the village shop. A couple of locals, one with a baby, were chatting and laughing with Maria, the shop assistant. The conversation died immediately.

'Morning all,' I ventured. Only the baby responded, and that was with an incomprehensible gurgle. The mother inspected the cereal packets and the other woman started rummaging through the cabbages.

I picked some reduced fish fingers out of the deep-freeze, and handed them to Maria. She took them silently.

'How's Brenda?' I asked. Normally any reference to her three-year-old triggered an avalanche of information about every aspect of her health and well-being.

'OK.'

'And how's Bill?' She didn't ever say much about her husband, except how busy he was.

'OK.'

I put a note on the counter. Without a word, she rang up the till, laid the change down and pushed the packet towards me.

'Thank you, Maria,' I said brightly. 'Have a good day.' Her eyes were fixed on something below the counter.

'Bye.'

I looked back through the glass door as I walked away. The three women had converged, their heads inclined towards each other in the unmistakable gossip pose. It didn't require great intelligence to guess the topic.

As I hurried down the lane I bumped into Rod and Marjorie, two of the village's older inhabitants.

'Morning,' I said. They ignored me.

Having deposited my shopping at home I wandered into the pub.

Three locals were sitting at their usual table. I sensed the group tighten into a circle to exclude me, like wagons defending themselves against marauding Apaches.

Colin was behind the counter.

'Morning,' I said. He nodded.

'My usual, please Colin. I seem to be the village leper today.'

He took a glass, gave it a perfunctory polish, filled it and put it down in front of me.

'Are you surprised?' he said, unloading the dishwasher and stacking the still-steaming glasses on the shelves above the bar.

'I've done nothing to hurt them.'

'They're pissed off with you. You told us you were a gardener. Now it turns out you weren't. People don't like being deceived.'

'Can't they see I was trying to re-invent myself?'

'What they see is you lied to them.'

'Am I welcome here still?' I didn't know what I'd do if I weren't.

'Your money's as good as anyone's. Besides, I know what it's like to be down on your luck after my marquee rental business folded a few years ago.'

Being shunned by the locals was bad enough. Being pestered by the City folk to re-live my experiences so they could derive enjoyment from my incompetence was worse. One day I overheard Anton and Clarinda, their voices carrying from their back garden, exclaim to some friends,

'Hiding down here like some war criminal… No one could be that incompetent… Must have been in cahoots with Beart… Should be in jail.'

'There should be a national gullibility award. He'd walk it,' came the reply, 'if he isn't, as you say, bent.'

‘Perhaps he’s the cleverest one.’ It was Clarinda’s dark chocolate voice. ‘After all, he’s got away with it while Beart’s in jail.’

I was horrified at my public dissection. I shaved my beard off to make me less recognisable and became a virtual recluse during the day. In the evening, even though all the locals ignored me, I would take up my position alone in the corner of the public bar, only moving from it to replenish my glass or visit the gents.

One evening a group of farm lads nudged each other, pointing in my direction and sniggering. I ignored them. I was settling in for my fourth pint when one of them I’d heard called Josh approached me.

‘Are you the accountant who doesn’t know the difference between right and left let alone right and wrong?’ He was quoting a press headline and I shouldn’t have risen to the bait. I tried to ignore him, to control myself, to think of something, anything else. Suddenly, it became too much; his idiotic straw-coloured fringe, his buck-teeth, his inane grin. I lashed out, catching him on the jaw. As he sprawled across the bar, I surged forward, my fist clenched. I was pulling back my arm to unleash another punch, this time at his nose, when a couple of local farmers grabbed my arms and pinned them to my sides.

I shook myself free of the farmers, though they stood close enough to grab me if necessary.

Colin was standing in front of me. ‘You’ve given me no choice. You’re banned until further notice.’

To the sound of the youths' jeers, I stumbled outside.

The next minute Josh was ejected from the pub and I heard Colin say, 'And you're banned too, Ballantyne.'

We looked each other up and down as we stood under a cloudy night sky. Josh shivered, perhaps fearing I might resume hitting him.

'No offence meant,' he said backing away down the lane. 'Only joking.' I made a feint towards him and he jumped back and sprinted away. I started to walk in the other direction, beaming broadly. I'd shown that young pup. The smile on my face faded as it struck home that through one stupidity on my part, my only refuge from the world would now be denied to me.

Now I had to make do with huddling by the wood-burning stove in my damp cottage while being kippered by the thin trail of smoke leaking through the faulty seal around the burner's door. To console myself I would drink cheap supermarket lager until I subsided into oblivion, often awaking the next morning still fully clothed, my throat parched and a severe crick in my neck.

One day there was a rap on the front door. There was no one I wanted to see so I ignored it. When there was another, louder knock, and a voice saying, 'I know you're in there,' I crawled out of bed and, after peering out of the window first, opened the door.

‘Registered delivery.’ The postman reminded me of a smaller, squatter version of my father. He waved a brown envelope in front of my nose and handed me a pen to sign for it.

‘Not for me.’ I handed the pen back, my hand shaking uncontrollably. The letter was addressed to me and looked ominous.

‘Yes, it is.’

‘Well I’m not signing for it,’ I said, steadying myself against the door-frame to avoid keeling over.

‘Please yourself.’ He adjusted the glasses perched on the end of his nose, and looked me full in the face. ‘You look terrible. Next time I’ll probably find your corpse.’

‘Cheery old soul, aren’t you?’

‘Happened to me again only the other week. Ninety-two-year-old over at Lower Hadsham. The smell was indescribable.’ He stuffed the rejected letter back into his bag and sauntered down the path.

⋆

When summer gave way to autumn and the nights became cold and damp, I picked up a persistent chest infection, coughing and hacking continually. After a couple of days, I was beset by a raging fever which left my sheets sodden with sweat. There was very little to eat in the house and I felt too weak to go shopping.

The symptoms lingered for a few weeks, disrupting

my sleep and leaving me overwhelmed by an all-pervasive lassitude, which deprived me of the will to get out of bed for several more days.

I missed appointments to work on people's gardens. A few times I showed up still drunk. One morning, in late autumn, when the ground was thick with red-gold leaves and the air was assuming a crispness presaging the onset of winter, I was asked to go home by a worried young mother who said I reeked of alcohol and was unsteady on my feet.

'I'm fine,' I insisted, toppling into the soft earth of one of her half-dug flowerbeds. She picked up her child, packed it into her four-wheel-drive and sped off down the road while I sat up, spitting soil and brushing the manure and leaves off my clothes. That evening her husband phoned. Ignoring my excuses, he told me that I was a disgrace, that I was sacked and I wasn't to go near his wife and child ever again.

Word got about, several others dispensed with my services and my income dwindled to close to subsistence level. When I looked in the mirror, the lank and scrawny face which stared back was testimony enough of my poor diet. There seemed to be no purpose to life and, a few times, in my darkest moments I even contemplated doing away with myself. I might have followed through with it had I been able to come up with a painless method.

The russets and golds of Autumn faded into the greys of winter and I spent the next few months foraging in the garden for vegetables and eking out my paltry savings on lager. Despite the beer, the bones stood out from my emaciated body. To economise, I gave up toothpaste, using salt instead, and my teeth took on a dull brown appearance. A little later, I developed mild toothache but had to put up with it as I'd no money to see a dentist. I couldn't even afford fuel for my wood-burning stove; instead I fossicked in the woods for old boughs.

I hadn't bothered to follow the news on my laptop, and probably wouldn't have that day, had my cupboard not been bare and the stove fuel-less, leaving the cottage damp and me cold, hungry and in desperate need of distraction. Fortunately, a neighbouring cottage had unprotected wi-fi, so I connected and ran though the news items, which all seemed strangely familiar; similar conflicts, scandals, and disasters populated the screen. Except for the one saying there was still no news of the runaway prisoner John Beart, who'd faked a heart attack to make his escape while being rushed to hospital.

I read the back story in previous bulletins. There wasn't much to add except that Beart's knighthood had recently been rescinded by the Honours Forfeiture Committee. The newspapers' headlines exulted in his downfall: 'Asset stripper's honours stripped,' 'Knight-fall' and 'Not-so-good Knight.' The more of the stories I read, the better I felt.

It was typical of Beart not to allow himself to be

incarcerated, and I grudgingly admired his chutzpah in escaping in such an old fashioned, schoolboy-adventure way. My admiration was, however, dwarfed by my relief that the establishment had disowned him so publicly. It took a lot to have one's honours removed but, as with so many other things in life, Beart had achieved the near impossible.

Thoroughly invigorated by these events, I walked slowly into my neglected garden and dug into the vegetable patch, stopping every couple of minutes to catch my breath and wipe the sweat from my forehead. Trembling from exertion, I unearthed several winter turnips, as well as some swedes and carrots which had surprisingly survived the cold weather thanks to the heavy mulch and straw I'd laid down. I boiled about half, salivating as the smell of food teased my nostrils. It was my first proper meal for several days. After eating, I steeled my nerves and bathed and shaved in cold water. Then I put on my least scruffy clothes. I was going to try to get my ban at the pub lifted.

The bar fell quiet as I entered. Everyone's gaze was on me, anxious to see what I would do and how the landlord would react.

Colin stood impassively behind the bar, eyeing my approach. Customers parted to let me though.

'I almost didn't recognise you. You look like you've been in a prisoner of war camp.'

'Sorry, Colin. I've been an idiot. Please give me another chance.' Before he could reply, I produced a brown paper bag filled with mud-encrusted root vegetables and placed it on the counter in front of him.

'Peace offering, straight from the garden. I just ate some myself; absolutely delicious.'

Colin's face softened. 'Accepted. You're back for now. One more incident like that and you're barred for life. Understand?'

'Understood, Colin.'

'What are you going to have?' Colin asked.

'Nothing tonight thanks.' I didn't want to confess I had no money.

'Have one on me,' a gruff voice behind me said. 'You deserve it for putting one on young Josh Ballantyne. He's had it coming for years.' It was one of the farmers who'd pulled me off the youth.

'I'll have to return the favour another day,' I said.

'Thought as much. Oh, by the way, we need some work done to the gardens of those little cottages we rent out, if you're interested. It's only weeding and grass cutting mind. Still it'll pay enough for you to buy me a drink.'

'I'm interested. Can I start tomorrow?'

'Sure. One other thing. We know some village folk have taken against you. We,' he slapped his two friends on the shoulder, 'were talking about it the other day. We think you've had a rough deal and you don't look like you've come out of it too well. If you were fooled by these slick City types and lost your job, then we should feel sorry for you. These bankers and the like,' he waved his hand to indicate the world outside the pub, 'they're not doing us any good. Our children can't afford to live in the village and we can't find farmhands because there are no homes for them hereabouts.'

By then another three or four farmers had walked in and heard the end of this speech. They all nodded and one spoke.

'You're right, Jack. It's not our village anymore. It's part of Chelsea or Kensington or somewhere posh like that. Soon even we won't be able to afford to live here.'

'Pay no attention to the Country Code, they don't.' It was a small wiry man with a thin moustache and large ears. 'Leave gates open, let their dogs run anywhere. Downright inconsiderate, they are.'

We stood by the bar, drinking our beer, as their list of grievances grew. While I might be a failed auditor and I might have misrepresented myself, at least now I wasn't a City type.

The next day there was a definite smell of spring in the air. All around me a delicate white carpet of snowdrops was in full bloom. Under the apple tree a small army of daffodil buds stood to attention, ready to unfurl and unleash their colour. I looked around my garden and realised what a state of neglect it had fallen into; nettles were marching across the potato patch, deadly nightshade had insinuated itself through the fence and around some of my pear trees, and ivy was choking the open soil where I'd planned to plant carrots and beetroots. Only the cucumber frames remained inviolate. I determined to put things right as soon as I'd earned my morning's money at the rental cottages.

★

I was in the pub, sitting two tables away from one of the oldest locals, whose family claimed to have lived in Dittington for at least eight generations, and who'd never bothered to do more than nod at me until now. He was staring at me.

'How's it going then?'

'Not so bad, Frank.' I put down my pint and wiped my mouth with the back of my hand. 'Had a good day yourself?'

'So-so,' he replied, moving to sit opposite me. 'The old beech was about to lose a branch; had to take it down afore it fell on someone's Ferrari.' He wheezed with laughter at the thought. While it wasn't much of a conversation, it marked a breakthrough, a sign of acceptance. As his cronies came into the bar they found us sitting together, silent for the most part, exchanging the odd word now and then, and followed suit. My integration into the community of old buffers was underway.

Although I could barely afford it, I stood all five of them a round and my new-found acceptability was confirmed.

*

The next few weeks saw me energetically re-approaching the clients I'd lost. Some rebuffed me; about half said they'd use my services again. When I wasn't working, I set about my own garden, hacking back or rooting out the weeds and nurturing and feeding my most favoured plants. The nightmare was over and I looked forward to a life of tranquillity again.

Surrounded by locals, I was slowly drinking my second pint of the evening when the pub door opened and Neil sidled in. I introduced him to my new friends as a 'mate from schooldays'.

'Any chance of a quiet word?' he whispered in my ear.

'Sure.'

I ordered two pints and a packet of peanuts and we retreated into the corner of the bar.

'You've got to keep in practice,' I said, chucking him the nuts.

'Given them up, mate.' He patted his extended gut. 'Getting too fat; you have them, you look like you need feeding up.'

'Who is she?' I couldn't imagine Neil would take the slightest interest in his appearance unless some woman was involved. He tapped the side of his nose in an irritating way. 'Need to know basis, mate.'

'Well, if you don't want to tell me. Anyway, I doubt

you've come all the way down here to let me know you're getting laid for the first time in years. What do you want?'

'Beart's still on the loose. The lag sharing his cell said he was nursing quite a grudge. Kept saying you'd shagged his mother and you'd pay for it.' He looked at me quizzically. 'You didn't really slip one to poor old Mrs Beart did you?' The open packet of peanuts proved irresistible and he flicked one in the air, catching it perfectly without even looking at it.

'Bravo,' I said. 'I told you all you needed was practice. Shame it was flicking peanuts and not golf you took up. You'd have a scratch handicap by now.'

'Anyway, I came to warn you. The uniform boys and girls will keep an eye on you. With any luck, if you do lure him here, we may be able to nab him.'

'That's a great consolation. The nearest police station is over ten miles away and that's only open every other Wednesday afternoon between two and five. Now I know how a tethered goat feels when the tiger's breath is hot on its neck and the marksman is quaffing his third G and T in a faraway clubhouse. Anyway, how's Rachel? Is she safe?'

He took a moment too long to reply. My heart leaped. 'She's all right, isn't she?'

'Yes, still under police protection.' There was something tinny about his tone, like the sound of a false coin falling through a parking pay machine. I stared at him hard, and he looked away. I thought I'd caught sight of a slight blush. Suddenly I realised.

'God, Neil, you're not shagging Rachel?'

He reddened again and refused to meet my stare.

'You are, aren't you? You bastard! That's hardly ethical is it, having an affair with someone who's under police protection? It's a bit like a warder sleeping with a prisoner.'

'Actually, she's not under my protection. She's being looked after by the Serious Crime Squad and, in any case, we became very close when we spent so much time working together to assemble the case.'

'That's no excuse.'

Neil, his eyes still focused on his beer mat, swigged the rest of his pint.

'Better be on my way then. Look out for Beart. If you see or hear anything suspicious, let us know immediately, OK?'

'Say hello to Rachel from me,' I said as he got up to leave, and I felt the deep thrust in my bowels of jealousy laced with self-pity.

'Neil, one more thing.' I couldn't suppress the question which had been gnawing at me. He stopped and looked over his shoulder, an eyebrow raised.

'You didn't ever dabble with Mrs Beart, did you?'

'What could ever have given you that idea?' A blast of fresh air fanned my face, and then the pub door clicked shut behind him.

As I walked home, I half expected to encounter Beart waiting in the shadows to waylay me. Or perhaps he would be waiting for me in my cottage. Would he kill me outright, or would he want to talk first? Would he execute me cleanly, or would he want me to suffer? The more I thought about it, the less I cared. Life wasn't so great so giving it up wouldn't be too much of a loss. I'd be missed by no one. My mother sounded, in the few telephone conversations I'd had with her since she moved to her Spanish love-nest, to be perpetually stoned or drunk – I couldn't work out which – and I hadn't seen my brother since my father's death. And as for Josephine Beart, my only regrets were how I'd behaved after our brief sexual encounter. I'd never regretted making love to her. In fact, as I reviewed the patchwork quilt of my life, it stood out as one of the more beautiful and worthwhile, if brief, experiences. If Beart wanted me to grovel in apology before he pulled the trigger or wielded the knife, or whatever he planned to do, I'd tell him straight that I wasn't sorry, and what I did was motivated by love.

Dittington was generally a very safe village and I wasn't accustomed to locking my front door at night. My hand hovered over the bolt that evening before I retracted it. I wasn't going to do anything unusual because of Beart.

Even though I'd determined to act normally, over the next few days I experienced a raised consciousness of all that was going on around me, noticing cars passing and people standing around talking in a way I'd never done before. I carried on with my work for others and laboured in my own garden.

I also continued looking at the news on my laptop. The BBC and newspapers remained silent on Beart's disappearance, until one Saturday morning I was greeted by the headlines: 'Plane Crash. Escapee John Beart and four others killed.' I read the article avidly. The six-seater aeroplane had been chartered under false identities to fly to Northern Cyprus. It had taken off in thick fog and exploded just after crossing the North Sea, the debris scattering widely over the Normandy coast. Several body parts had been recovered and, such was their poor condition, dental records had been used to confirm their identification.

'Thank God for that,' I said aloud to myself. 'Celebration time.' I left the cottage and strolled down to the pub.

'Your usual?' Colin reached for my pewter tankard as I walked through the door.

'Hell, no, I'm celebrating, Colin. Give me a large pink gin and a packet of salted nuts.' As I sipped my drink, it dawned on me that there should now be no obstacle to seeing Rachel again. But how could I contact her? The knowledge of Neil's involvement with her put me off using him as a conduit. Then the thought struck me that if Rachel were emerging from hiding, she would be likely to contact Alison and Mark. All I needed to do was track them down through the internet when I got home.

I finally found a website for Alison and Mark called Total Zen Solutions with an email address and a phone number which I scribbled down.

I went to bed confident my search for Rachel was nearly over.

Chapter 35
RACHEL, 2007

'I'm afraid I don't know where she is.' Alison's voice wavered slightly as she spoke, and I could imagine the discomfort clouding her face. She was poor at lying, even over the phone.

'I was sure she'd be in touch with you Alison. I know how close you two are and how much she values you.'

Alison didn't say anything. I waited for a few moments.

'Perhaps you could tell her, if she does make contact in the next few days, that I'd really love to see her. I'll give you my new mobile number to pass on.'

'Right.' Alison still sounded doubtful.

Rachel phoned me that evening.

'Thank God, Rachel,' I said. 'You're all right. I was so worried about you. It's been so long.'

'I'm so sorry. I wanted to contact you. It was the police who insisted I remain incommunicado.'

'By police, you mean my old chum and your new lover Neil?'

'He's not my lover, well not any more. Too many shavings in the washbasin and toenail clippings on the bathroom floor. The man's barely housetrained.'

'I think he's missed out on the civilising influence of a good woman.' I was secretly delighted at this turn of events. 'Any chance of our getting together in the next few days?'

'Have you still got a car?'

'Yes, why?'

'I want to go to John's funeral tomorrow and I'm struggling to think how I can get there without taking a taxi, which would cost a fortune. The bus service has atrophied and there's no station nearby. I know it's a long way for you to come.'

'Only three and a half to four hours, depending on the traffic.'

'Is it really? That's too far. Please forget I asked.'

'Not at all. I'd be delighted, although I'm surprised you want to go. Are you planning to drive a stake through his heart to stop him re-incarnating?'

'Might be a sensible precaution, if they found his heart. In fact, I'm not sure how much of him is in the coffin. They probably shared out the body parts as most of them were pretty well unrecognisable.'

'So why do you want to go? To dance on his grave?'

She hesitated as though pondering my question.

'Do you know, I'm not quite sure. It's a terrible phrase I know, though it does seem to fit what I feel. I guess I want closure. He was such a big part of my life, and I know he ruined me, but still—'

'Well, we can talk about it tomorrow,' I interrupted. All this nonsense that people talked about closure irritated me. As far as I could see she didn't have a sensible answer. Perhaps she could come up with one overnight.

'Where are you living?'

She gave me an address.

'Solhurst High Street?' I said. 'Sounds like the arsehole of the universe. Has it got any redeeming features?'

'It's cheap,' she replied, 'and very anonymous.'

*

After we'd returned from Beart's funeral and demolished Rachel's wine, I was on the point of leaving when, with the smell of spices and onions from a nearby restaurant tantalising my digestive juices, I decided to invite her out for a curry instead.

'You're offering to buy me two meals in one day,' she said, 'and you still run a BMW. This gardening business must pay pretty well.'

'It's had its ups and downs.' I saw no need to share the vicissitudes I'd experienced. 'Now it seems to be on a bit of an up. In fact, I could do with some help. Do you fancy coming in with me?'

'Me? You know my gamma ray fingers kill any plant I touch.'

'Could be very handy for weeding. In any case, you'd only be hacking, hewing and trundling wheelbarrows full of muck.' I looked her up and down. She'd put on some weight since we were married, though nothing a bit of exercise wouldn't shift. 'You still look pretty fit. I reckon you could handle it.'

'You're seriously offering me a job as a gardener's mate? You must be joking.'

'Why, have you had a better offer? I didn't see any head-hunters queuing at your door.'

'I'm planning a book about everything I've been through, a full exposé. You wouldn't believe the way these guys stick together.'

'Sounds very worthy,' I said. 'I still can't see why you couldn't help me during the day, part-time if necessary, and write your memoirs in the evening. Anyway, let's go and discuss it over a jalfrezi. I'm famished.'

★

'The strangest thing,' Rachel said, spooning curry onto her pilau rice, 'is the way Suzie's been behaving recently.'

We were sitting in one of the dark alcoves of the

otherwise empty restaurant and, had it not been for a guttering candle and the night-lights keeping the dishes warm, I would have struggled to see the food in front of me. A waiter lolled behind the counter, absorbed in his smartphone. While the décor was traditional, the music was discordantly modern pop. I tried unsuccessfully to catch his eye to order another glass of lager and had to resort to calling out. He seemed surprised we were still there and strolled over to take our order with an air of cultivated ennui.

'I'm sorry, what were you saying about Suzie?' It was odd to think Suzie and I'd once been in a relationship. When I looked back, like my marriage, like so much of my life, it was like a distantly and imperfectly remembered film.

'My sisters say she's got lots of money now and won't say how she came by it. She's also talking about emigrating.'

'Emigrating? Where?'

'South America somewhere though she wasn't very clear exactly where. She mentioned Paraguay and Uruguay interchangeably and didn't seem to know the difference. They think she meant Paraguay because she kept referring to a place she called "Ascension". She says she wants to make a new start after John.'

'Perhaps she does.'

'I'd be surprised if she could organise a weekend in Brighton. What's she going to do when she's out there? Is there a big market among geriatric ex-Nazis for having their dobermans' portraits painted?'

Rachel stabbed at a chunk of Bombay potato.

'But the really intriguing questions are why is she doing it, and where is she getting the money? She's a tapeworm. She's spent her life sponging off others. Who's she going to latch onto in Paraguay? And how can she afford to set herself up in any style? Only a couple of months ago, she was trying to borrow money from my aunt.'

'Perhaps she discovered John's secret cache and helped herself. The reason she's emigrating to a country without an extradition treaty is she thinks the law will catch up with her and confiscate it unless she makes herself scarce.'

'Similar thoughts went through my head,' Rachel said. 'Do you think we should tip the police off?'

'You could always exchange some pillow talk with your friend Neil.'

'Oh, for goodness sake!' Rachel looked needled. 'He's not sharing my pillow. We spent a few nights together, that's all. It's all over now. Anyone would think you were jealous.' She calmed herself. 'I like your suggestion of telling Neil.' She pulled out her smartphone. 'In fact, I think I'll e-mail him now.' I kept a serious expression fixed on my face. Inside I was jubilant. It was great fun winding Rachel up and her denials were very reassuring.

'Go ahead,' I said, ignoring the fact she was already

keying in letters furiously. 'Not a moment to lose.' I took a deep draught of my lager. It was turning out to be a most enjoyable evening.

★

It was a surprise when Richard knocked on the door of my cottage. I'd just got back from a hard day's work planting a garden composed completely of pink flowers for a balding young bond trader and his blonde, pink wife. Every muscle and every sinew ached. I couldn't wait to run myself a bath and sink into the hot water.

He didn't smile when I opened the door. More portly than ever, his stomach protruded so far you could have balanced a pint of beer on it, and the thought went through my head that he'd been indulging too much in his company's products. His hair had receded to a clump around each ear, with only a few outlying wisps clinging doggedly to the weather-beaten scalp in between.

As he followed me into the low-ceilinged sitting-room, my warning came too late to stop him bumping into the oak beam that ran across its length. He rubbed his head.

'Can I offer you tea or coffee?' In my endeavour to clean up my life I'd stopped keeping alcohol on the premises.

'No thanks.' He was still massaging his skull. 'I've

come to warn you. Some of the investors in Beart Enterprises are planning to sue AP for negligence, and the former AP partners think you should be the one in the firing-line, not them.'

'Is that what you think too, Richard?'

'I'm not joining them, or anyone else in any action against you, if that's what you mean, but you did make a right mess of it, didn't you?'

'I certainly did. I wasn't alone in that; several other partners agreed I was doing the right thing. I'm not going to hide behind them though. The truth is I wasn't up to the job.' I paused, feeling a weight lifted from my shoulders by the admission. 'Look, you can tell whoever's interested I take full responsibility, but do make it clear I'm the proverbial "man of straw". I own the clothes I stand up in, I've a few hundred pounds in the bank and an ageing BMW. Other than that, nothing. Even the cottage is rented fully furnished. If anyone sues me, I'll declare myself bankrupt and continue with my gardening jobs as though nothing happened. It won't benefit them at all.'

Richard looked around, his eyes flitting across the sofa, the stained carpet and finally fixing on the damp patches spreading up the wall.

'God, you have made a mess of things, haven't you?'

I patted him on the shoulder. 'On the contrary. Do you know, Richard, I've never been happier. I feel fulfilled when I plant something and see it thrive and grow, when I see a beautiful garden which existed only in my mind's eye unfold in front of me. I get on well with the locals, and I've even started seeing Rachel again from time to time. There's no need to feel sorry for me. It's those, like you, who have managed to claw your way back into stressful jobs and are clinging on who deserve pity.' I looked at my watch. 'If you give me fifteen minutes to have a bath, I'll take you down to the Jolly Throstle. They serve a lovely pint. Besides, I'd like to hear all about your family, and how they're getting on.'

'All right,' said Richard. 'I'm in no hurry. I quite fancy a beer.'

*

Rachel's flat in Solhurst High Street was awash with paper, huge piles heaped on the table and chairs, and random pages lying thick on the floor or spreading like dust-sheets across the carpet.

'What's all this?' I asked. Rachel was normally such a meticulously tidy person.

'Sorting out what I want to put in my book. I've finished the first draft, still can't quite decide on the order.' She pointed at the piles. 'These are sections; several of them could fit in any number of places.' She looked down at the sheets lying on the floor. 'And those are rejects.'

'Was writing it easy?' I was impressed that Rachel

had knocked out the first draft in just over three months.

'Not too bad. Editing will be the hard part. Once I've assembled it, you wouldn't like to help me proof-read it, would you? For some strange reason, I tend to read what I thought I'd written not what I actually wrote.'

'Happy to help.' I put the kettle on and scanned the local free newspaper while Rachel wandered around rearranging wads of paper. Finally, she declared herself to be happy with the order.

'I'm surprised so many parts of it are interchangeable. That's unusual in a book, isn't it? I thought there was always a beginning, a middle and an end. Something to do with some Greek chap or other.'

'Aristotle. No, they're all designed to link together. I've written it with an eye to serialisation in a Sunday newspaper, so each pile constitutes a self-standing story. You can make big bucks. And, even better than that, you get fantastic exposure.' She noted down the sequence of sections she'd decided on and pushed the fat draft into my midriff.

'Bloody hell, Rachel,' I said weighing it in my hands. 'You've written more than Tolstoy did in his whole career. This'll take ages to plough through.'

'Happy reading!' She patted me on the back.

I didn't start proof-reading until the following evening, planning to work on it for an hour at most and then drop in on the pub.

I didn't put the book down until five o'clock the next morning. I wouldn't have given Rachel any prizes for style. The whole work was written in a stilted, sometimes staccato manner reminiscent of a business report. In certain places, she'd even resorted to using bullet points. Nevertheless, the content was riveting. I don't know how she'd managed it. She'd got hold of Beart's diary and overlaid the timing of several of his appointments with UK Government ministers, with subsequent meetings with terrorists, in such a way as to suggest he might have been acting with the connivance of the British Government. I felt less comfortable when I came to the section dealing with the role of AP in the debacle, and extremely unhappy when I read Rachel's account of my own part in the proceedings. She hadn't been kind and I was exposed as a biddable incompetent in awe of my client. She'd even included reference to my affair with Mrs Beart, and cited it as the real reason why Beart, in an irrational fury, had decided to sack us as auditors

'She can't include this!' I shouted, hurling the draft at the wall. Papers flew everywhere and I left them where they fell, scattered around my room.

During the day, the starkness of my recollection softened, and I allowed myself to imagine I hadn't read those things or, if I had, they weren't as blunt and brutal as I'd first thought, so I carefully collected the pages up, arranged them in order and put them aside. A day later I read and re-read the work. It was worse each time.

I arrived unannounced at Rachel's flat the next day with the marked-up pages in my hand.

'That was very quick. Thank you so much. What did you think of it? Would it make you buy *The Sunday Times*?'

'It was great, Rachel, really well researched and very powerful, but—' I paused.

'Yes?' she said, raising an eyebrow and fixing me with a stare, 'but what?'

'You can't print all this personal stuff.'

'You mean the bit about you?' She gazed at me impassively. 'It's all true, isn't it? He always thought you didn't know what you were doing. When we got together, he assured me he was just trying to help you out even though I suspected he didn't like you very much. Then he let slip he'd always wanted to make sure he had tame auditors who weren't going to bark. And later still, of course, when he'd read that diary, he just wanted to destroy you. Unfortunately for him, his anger sowed the seed of his own downfall. He should never have sacked AP. It was the beginning of the end.'

'No. That's not what's bothering me, though it does make me sound feeble. Do you really have to include those reference to poor Mrs Beart?'

'What does it matter?' Rachel replied. 'She's dead, and you don't exactly have much reputation to lose, do you?'

'Kick me when I'm down, if you must. Just take the passage about Josephine Beart out. Please.'

She looked at me quizzically. 'Why, I do believe you're still carrying a torch for her after all these years. Talk about three in a marriage. I suppose she was the one you really loved when you married me.' She gave me a gentle shove. 'Come on, admit it.'

'I don't see any reason to drag her name through the mud, that's all. What's she done to hurt you? We had a very temporary fling, which should by rights be consigned to history.'

'Because she's the reason the whole edifice came tumbling down. If it hadn't been for her involvement with you, John wouldn't have acted so irrationally and he'd still probably be the darling of the establishment.'

'My take on it is that the reason his empire crashed was your jealousy of Suzie. As soon as he took up with Suzie, he was done for. You'd be bound to get even.'

Rachel sat back.

'You're probably right. I would have gone for him, with or without the new auditors' help, and I'd have found out what he was up to. It's funny though. Even before he found the diary, he seemed to have some sort of grudge against you, though he always denied it. I really believe the only reason he took up with Suzie was to get at you, like an alpha wolf proving all the females are at his beck and call.'

'So, you admit Mrs Beart wasn't pivotal to his

being found out. Then you can leave the part about her out.'

Rachel's eyes narrowed. 'Sorry. I'm not changing my book for anyone, not for you, and certainly not for Mrs Beart. What I've written is my unvarnished, honest and complete account of what transpired. If I'm attacked for writing it, and I expect to be, what defence do I have if I've deliberately falsified some aspects?'

'Don't be so bloody pious.' I slammed my hand on the table. 'You're the author. You can do what the fuck you like. You're choosing to drag your ex-mother-in-law's name through the dirt. No one's making you do it. There are plenty of ways you could get round it. Leave the stuff in about me and what an arsehole I was. I don't care, but take Mrs Beart out. It's not a lot to ask, is it?'

Rachel fixed me with her gimlet stare. 'The truth is the truth. It stays in.'

'There must be more to it than that. What have you got against Mrs Beart?'

'If you must know, I loathed the woman and she detested me because I stood up to her. John was always in awe of her, always doing her bidding. I persuaded him to do what he wanted for a change, so she excommunicated us both. John had barely seen anything of her in the weeks before she died, and the guilt nearly cracked him up.'

'I can't believe it. She was so sweet, so understanding—'

'Even though you slept with her, you didn't know her. She was a manipulative bitch.'

I must have looked incredulous.

'You don't believe me?' Her voice was harsh. 'John rarely confided in me. She was his real confidante, and she pulled his strings.'

'What, even his business decisions?'

'Not exactly. She didn't have a business brain, but when it came to people, he often consulted her and she told him what to do. She was ruthless, calculating.'

'What about Smallwood? He sorted him out.'

Rachel sighed. 'You've been listening to John's version. She planned Smallwood's demise, John merely followed instructions.'

I fell silent for a few moments. I couldn't reconcile this portrayal of Mrs Beart with my own experiences. The traffic outside groaned slowly by.

'I can't believe it. She was such a lovely person.'

Rachel got up and walked across the room. When she came back she was holding Mrs Beart's diary. 'It's all in here. And more. Her real problems started when she got religion again. Apparently, she'd been devoted as a little girl. Then the guilt and the bitterness set in. She hated John having female friends. If he did, then they had to be Catholic, and, of course, I wasn't.'

I stared at the diary, aching to read what she'd said about us.

'Could I look at that?'

She looked as though she might be considering the request for a moment. Then she shook her head.

'No, I don't think so.'

Almost involuntarily, I extended my hand.

'Not a good idea. It's just possible I might let you read it one day, though I think you'll regret it. In the meantime, you and Mrs Beart stay in. The sex angle will definitely sell copies.'

'Then I have nothing more to say.' I stood up and walked slowly to the door. I grasped the tarnished brass handle to let myself out, not looking over my shoulder and half hoping Rachel might call me back. She didn't. I got into my BMW before seeing the large sticky notice across my windscreen telling me my car had been clamped. I'd have to make my way by public transport to some remote location to pay an extortionate fine.

'Shit, shit, shit, fucking shit,' I shouted, hopping from one foot to the other.

'Don't say rude words. It's not nice.' I looked down to see the unblinking brown eyes of a little girl. She tossed her hair back before running off to join her mother who was nearby on the phone.

Chapter 36
DEVINE TOWERS, 2008

The Old Manor House stood in two acres of ground, about half of which was laid to gardens. Owned by the Throgmortons for over three hundred years, as the family fortunes declined so the house had fallen into disrepair and the garden became a wilderness inhabited by badgers and foxes. When Emily Throgmorton died at the age of ninety-seven leaving only second cousins as heirs, the property was sold to Charles Devine who'd made his fortune opening fashionable boutiques specialising in cashmere scarves, jumpers and bed socks. Charles set about restoring the house and called me in, on the recommendation of a neighbour, to re-design the garden. I drew up three very different options for him, which he took away to consider.

He greeted me warmly when we met again a fortnight later.

'I love this one. It combines elegance with flair, and it's so original. I've never seen anything like it before.'

I was delighted with his choice, which involved conjoining a Japanese garden and an English wild flower meadow. At the heart of the design, like an oasis in a flowery desert, was a traditional walled garden, which housed fifty-six different varieties of roses, some selected for appearance, others for fragrance. The plan would also necessitate bringing in twenty three-quarter grown British beeches and the same number of Japanese black pines.

I told him what it would cost, erring heavily on the generous side for contingencies, and expecting he would trim the budget as severely as I trim hydrangeas in the spring. He waved his hand, saying, 'If you need more, let's discuss it.'

I selected three sub-contractors, all specialists in different aspects of landscaping, and negotiated contracts with them. We then set about the task. I was filled with joy as I saw it taking shape in front of my eyes, and my pleasure was compounded by Charles's obvious delight.

Charles was extremely well-connected, and very soon a reporter from *English Stately Homes*, dressed in a brown tweed suit and sturdy brogues, came to interview me. We met at the Jolly Throstle, where I was disconcerted by her rapidly fluttering eyelids until I realised she suffered from a tic. She slow-bowled benign questions at me while vigorously attacking the rare steak and salad in front of her. I answered each one fully, relishing the veal and ham pie she was paying for and the interest she was showing in my work. After lunch, I took her on a tour of the village so she could see the many other smaller designs I'd implemented.

'Charming,' she boomed repeatedly as I recounted the story behind each, and her photographer busied herself taking pictures.

Charles, breathless and trembling, showed me the article that appeared in the next quarter's edition. In addition to the extensive coverage of the work in hand at Devine Towers, ample space had also been accorded to my work in the village. The headline read 'Capability Brown Mark 2 redesigns Dittington'. I felt a glow of satisfaction as I recalled my father's views on my potential. I realised that it was I who had been at fault over my choice of career. I should have stood up for myself and done what I wanted. In his own way, and by his own standards, his own code of professional respectability, my father may even have had my best interests at heart.

I remerged from my thoughts to find Charles was still talking.

'What's more, they're going to follow up with another article when the job's finished. My friends in Islington are distraught with envy. I'm sorry, I'm keeping your contact details a secret, otherwise they'd all be trying to lure you away.'

I shivered. If my fame spread too widely perhaps the many putative litigants who'd held off because of my penurious circumstances would decide it was worth suing me after all.

'I'm very happy to keep a low profile, Charles. It's the work I enjoy, not the fame.'

★

I was so absorbed with the task I didn't give much thought to what was going on in the outside world. My laptop, succumbing to a virus, had ceased functioning and I hadn't bothered to get it fixed. While I regretted my rift with Rachel, it was never enough to make me take the initiative and seek a rapprochement. However I looked at it, and whatever their relationship, I considered her treatment of Mrs Beart in her memoirs shabby, even vindictive, and I'd no intention of backing down.

At the end of the project, Charles threw a party and invited me. I hesitated before persuading myself it might lead to new work. The contract with Charles had been lucrative and my financial position had eased. A few more jobs like that and I might even be able to buy Old Bob's cottage from his family.

Sipping my glass of champagne, I surveyed the guests now filling the cream and gold ballroom and spreading noisily through the French windows into the garden. Charles walked up to me, clapping me on the shoulder.

'Ah, the star of the show! I'm delighted you could make it. Now you've finished here I can introduce you to my friends.' I was led around the ballroom and my hand was pressed enthusiastically by a host of expensively dressed people, each parroting the same glowing comments.

I soaked up the compliments before Charles, consummate at working a room, deposited me with a small woman with a retroussé nose and hazel eyes, whose name I failed to catch.

'What do you do?' I asked, purely out of politeness.

'I'm an accountant with Pears Montague,' she replied, naming the firm which had taken over from AP as Beart Enterprise's auditors. My stomach felt as though it had started crawling away from me. The last thing I wanted was to talk about the Beart Enterprises' audit and my fears looked like being realised when she added, 'I've been working on winding up Beart's businesses. It's been fascinating.'

She was joined by a tall man wearing an unfashionably droopy moustache and sporting a tuft of beard on his chin. After looking me up and down, he directed his gaze at the woman.

'Beart, did you say? What a rogue. Incredible no one saw through him.'

'Fancy his turning up in Brazil like that when everyone thought he was dead,' the woman said.

I spilled some champagne down my only presentable shirt, and dabbed feebly at it with a paper tissue, leaving small scrunched white clumps on the dark blue cotton.

'You mean Beart's not dead?' I mumbled. The man nodded.

'Quite a stunt, faking his own death like that, and then trying to kill his woman.'

The conversation was moving too fast for me.

'What do you mean? His ex-wife Rachel?'

'No, not her. The other one,' the man said.

'Have you been living in a cave?' the woman asked. 'It was on TV, radio and all over the newspapers. Beart salted away a small fortune, leaving this woman Suzie to look after it until they met up in Paraguay. Then she did the dirty on him and met up with her lover in Brazil instead. Beart had just enough cash to hire a cut-price hit man. Unfortunately for him this buffoon got caught and pointed the finger at him. The British Government is trying to have Beart extradited. Could take years, if it happens at all. Meanwhile he's languishing in a jail near Sao Paolo and this Suzie has made it to Paraguay with a Latino boyfriend.

'What's his name?' In my confusion, I slurred my words, and had to repeat them.

'Chico, I think, or something like that,' the man said. 'According to the paper, he's another right shady character. It's like the plot of a second-rate film.'

The woman looked at me.

'And how long have you been a landscape gardener?'

'All my life, though I sometimes had to do other less interesting jobs to tide me over between gardening assignments.'

'What sort of jobs?' the man asked.

'Office jobs, that sort of thing.'

'I really envy you,' she said, 'always being out in the open air and doing something really creative.'

'Wouldn't change it for the world.' I lifted another glass of champagne from a passing tray, placing my old one on the mantle above the fireplace. 'My father wanted me to be an accountant, but my heart was always in gardening.'

Chapter 37
THE REMAINS OF MY LIFE, 2008-2009

Despite my promise to myself that I wouldn't contact Rachel again, I found myself dialling her number later that evening.

A sleepy voice answered.

I looked at the clock on my wall and realised, in my inebriated condition, it was past one o'clock in the morning. Following the news about Beart and Suzie, the rest of the evening had slipped by in a welter of meaningless conversations with unmemorable people, made even more so by copious quantities of champagne.

'Sorry Rachel, did I wake you up?'

'Yes, you bloody well did. You sound drunk. Are you?'

I looked at my reflection in the mirror; a rumpled stranger with big dark circles under his bloodshot eyes stared manically back at me.

'Maybe just a tiddly bit tiddly.'

'What the hell are you phoning me about?'

'Heard about John and Suzie tonight. About the murder attempt and his being in jail. Did you know about it?'

'Is that really what you've phoned me up to tell me?'

I thought for a moment and understood how ridiculous I was being.

'Sorry. I'll call you tomorrow. Goodnight.'

Rachel put the receiver down without responding. I stood up and did a lively jig around the room, gyrating my arms vigorously. Beart had been stitched up good and proper by Suzie. Who would have thought the girl had the nous? I now knew what I'd always suspected; Suzie must have been two-timing me with Chico as well as, probably, lots of others. It didn't matter. She'd always made it plain we weren't an exclusive couple, if you could even describe us as a couple. Perhaps a better description would be 'sometime lovers'. Exhausted, I collapsed fully clothed onto the sofa and dreamed that Beart was a pirate who attacked the ship I was sailing and made me walk the plank.

*

The crick in my neck prevented me from turning my head to the left, and my bloated tongue seemed to fill my mouth. Otherwise I felt surprisingly healthy despite the amount of champagne I'd consumed. I got up, had a quick shot of orange juice and prepared a bowl of instant porridge. I took the first mouthful without the slightest sensation of nausea and wondered whether I was still drunk, or whether the elation I'd experienced on hearing of Beart's humiliation had protected me.

I texted a grovelling apology to Rachel and asked her to meet me. I wanted desperately to hear what she had to say. Had she suspected Suzie of double-dealing, or had she consigned her too firmly to the 'too thick' category? Rachel took her time replying, and by the time she did so a dull throb played around my temples. So much for the myth you can't get a hangover when you drink top quality champagne.

The text was brief: 'CU Wed 2pm. My flat. x'

*

The next couple of days dragged, although I was pleasantly surprised to be contacted by two of the guests from Charles's party who said they were following up conversations of which I'd no recollection.

I awoke early on Wednesday feeling energetic and put in a brisk couple of hours' work at The Parsonage, now owned by a hedge fund manager, before embarking on the four-hour journey to Solhurst.

Rachel opened the door. Her hair was swept back and she was wearing horn-rimmed glasses.

'You look like a librarian,' I said.

I lifted the glasses and peered at her.

'Why, Miss Jones, without your spectacles—'

She snatched them back from me.

'What do you want, you silly ass?'

'It's customary to invite all except Jehovah's Witnesses, double glazing salesmen and vampires to cross the threshold before peppering them with questions,' I replied.

She stepped aside and made a sweeping gesture with her right hand. I walked past her into the dingy sitting-room. It was unchanged from my last visit, except perhaps for the thick carpet of dead flies' carcasses lying on the windowsill and the large pile of unopened brown envelopes, which looked like bills, by the door. I plonked myself in an armchair and, in the thin shaft of bright sunlight coming from the window, a cloud of small dust particles lifted around me.

I pointed to the piles of papers which surrounded me.

'Even after all this time you're still working hard on that villainous book? You're a persistent little blighter.'

She nodded. 'You haven't come to pester me again about that horrid old flame of yours, have you? Because if you have, you might as well leave now.'

I shook my head slowly.

'No, I know when I'm beaten. I wanted to talk to you about John and Suzie and what happened.'

Rachel's face creased into a smile. 'Marvellous, wasn't it? He's gone and landed himself in even more trouble, and she's stuck in Paraguay with nobody but this Chico character and a handful of living-dead Nazis for company. I can't think of a better outcome.'

'Any luck finding a publisher for your book?'

She shook her head. 'Only one chance left; I should hear soon.'

'How come? You've got the inside story.'

'Too slow. A couple of journalists made any missing details up and got their books out already. I keep reworking mine hoping I can generate some interest. Unfortunately, everybody seems to have moved on from John Beart, so the odious Josephine's sexual exploits may have to remain secret.'

I sighed with relief. 'It was only one indiscretion and a very long time ago.'

Rachel's jaw tightened. 'Well, actually, there's more to it than that, though you probably don't want to hear.' Rachel could be cruel, and this was the expression she wore when she was doing it.

'Try me,' I said as confidently as I could.

Rachel's mobile phone rang. She pulled it out of her handbag.

'Oh yes. Thanks for calling.' She walked into the corridor to continue the conversation, leaving her papers, and Mrs Beart's diary on her desk. The temptation was overwhelming. I grasped its tattered spine and spun it open, leafing quickly through the pages until I came to her entry for that day.

'Saturday, 18th.

Shopping, then lunch with C. RS came round in the afternoon with emerald ring. Said he was sorry, wouldn't happen again. Let him MLTM. Then big row about where I'd been on Friday. Told him we were finished and wanted him to put the flat in my name. Refused. Told him had enough to have him put away for years and flung ring in bushes. Stormed off. Boy Gardener, J's old school friend, appeared like a genie from between the floor boards, tongue hanging out like a big puppy. Angry with RS so let BG MLTM. Clumsy and clueless, but sweet. Funny. Suddenly said he had to go home for supper. Left buttoning himself as ran down road. Showered and met M and C for late night drink in the Albion, and went on to boring party in boring Dean.'

Feeling slightly sick, I flicked over onto the next page.

'Sunday 19th.

Got up late. M and C came round and we went to the Albion. Came back for coffee. M suggested film, so we went to Abbotsford and saw Carrie. Piper Laurie brilliant as Margaret White. V Scary. Afterwards, had curry, probably cat. Felt queasy. M came back with me and brought a bottle of Tequila. Cured nausea and both fell asleep on the sofa.'

I read the entry several times. Its contents

remained indelibly the same. She hadn't thought about me at all. I flicked on a few pages and read, as a footnote to a litany of complaints about the weather, the post and the launderette, a brief reference to my letter.

'Received funniest love letter from BG. Almost forgotten our brief fling. Would like to frame it but it would upset J. Nice to have an admirer, even if so gauche. Very different from father.'

The muscles in my neck became rigid and a steel band tightened round my head. My father? She knew my father? I scrabbled frantically though her diary until I found an entry from a couple of months earlier.

'April 14th
Saw Bank manager. Pompous. All eyes and hands. Said loan would be very difficult, no security but could work on it with Head Office. Would need more information. Touched me up on way out and asked whether I'd meet later for a drink to discuss further. Suggested he drop in for a cup of tea instead. Arrived at 5.30 sweating like a bull waiting to enter the ring and put hand up my skirt. Secretly checked TR before letting him MLTM, objecting, but not enough to put him off. Over in seconds. Asked whether loan now possible. He said v unlikely still, and that we would need to meet again tomorrow and left. Hateful man. Needs sorting.'

An image of Mrs Beart spread-eagled under my father, his purple-veined bottom pumping up and down as she stared impassively over his shoulder waiting for him to finish, filled my mind. That bastard! Feelings of loathing and contempt consumed me. I wished I'd hit him that evening, I wished I'd killed him. Though my hands shook, I forced myself to read on.

'April 15th
Took copy tape into bank. Suggested BM listen to it before I decided whether to pursue with police and the Bank. Suggested as well as loan he might like to make personal donation to my relocation fund. Most accommodating to both and most generous. Once secured, lectured him on his disgusting behaviour and sexual inadequacy, then gave him two copies of tape. Still have one. Insurance."

Rachel was right. Mrs Beart had been a ruthless woman. While no doubt she'd had little choice if she wanted to survive in a world populated by the likes of Smallwood and my father, she wasn't the woman I thought I knew.

I let the diary slide onto the floor. She, or at least my idealised version of her, had haunted me throughout my life while I had barely been a footnote in hers. I heard Rachel's footsteps and the door handle turning. I plucked the diary up and thrust it back on the desk.

Rachel was talking. I had difficulty concentrating on what she was saying. 'Another bloody publisher… last hope… shit…'

Rachel sat down heavily. 'Shit, shit, shit, shit.'

I stood up, staggered to the window and pushed it open, breathing the stale Solhurst air deeply into my lungs.

'You all right?' she asked.

'Feeling a bit faint.' I walked back to my chair and slumped into it.

'Would you like a glass of water?'

I shook my head. She looked at me intently.

'I think I'll go and make us a cup of tea. You look as though you need it and I certainly do.'

That image of my father, more graphic every time I replayed it, kept recurring.

'Where were we?' she said, coming back with two mugs. From the pale colour of the tea, it looked as though we'd shared a teabag.

I drew a deep breath. It was essential I acted normally. I needed to make Rachel do the talking while I steadied myself.

'Catching up on John and Suzie. Did you have any inkling what Suzie was up to?'

Rachel looked out of the window at the grey, cloud-laden sky, and then down at her hands, which she spread out in front of her.

'I've told you what she did to Mummy over the years. It got worse. She managed to find Mummy's PIN at my sister's house and emptied her bank account before she buggered off. She took over £6000 in all. So, in answer to your question, no I didn't know what she was up to but I'm not surprised. She has the morals of an alley cat so it's also in keeping with her code of behaviour to two-time people, or was it three-time, counting you?' She smiled again. She was enjoying her cruelty.

I remained expressionless, refusing to be hurt by her taunt. 'Probably more than that, but hey, who's counting?' I decided to twist the knife a little myself and looked at the pile of brown envelopes.

'Looks like you've got some debts mounting up. What are you living on?'

'What's it got to do with you?' Then her face softened. 'Well, actually not a lot. I was banking on getting an advance for this book. I lost most of what I had when Beart Enterprises' shares cratered and now I've spent what was left. In short, I'm broke and unemployable.'

A tear had formed in the corner of Rachel's eye. She was sitting so stiffly upright it looked as though the slightest breeze would have sent her toppling. I moved over to her and put my arm around her shoulders. She let my hand rest on her for a moment, and then shrugged it off. The tear rolled slowly down her cheek.

'I'm fine.' She wiped her face with her finger. It was the closest I'd ever seen her come to crying. 'Well, actually, I'm not fine. I've made a complete mess of everything. I should never have allowed myself to be taken in by John. Deep down, I never trusted him. He was so charming, so persuasive and I was a fool, a complete bloody fool. Now I'm nothing and I've got nothing, and it's all I deserve.'

She stood up slowly, walked over to a kitchen cupboard, and pulled out a bottle of white wine with about quarter of an inch left in it.

'I haven't even got enough to offer you a drink.' She slopped the wine into a tumbler, and drank it in a single gulp. She inclined her head towards the pile of bills. 'It'll just be my luck if the government brings back debtors' prisons.'

Her movements were deliberate and clumsy and I wondered whether she'd been drinking before I arrived. However, the dampness around her eyes had disappeared and, drunk or not, Rachel was back in full control of herself.

'The offer of a position in my firm is still open,' I said. 'You'd be doing the donkey work, all the heavy lifting and carrying. The orders are flooding in though, so at least you'd have a crust to eat at the end of a hard day's toil, and you could shack up in my spare room, so there'd be no bills. Of course, there'd be one condition.'

'If you think I'm going to sleep with you, forget it.'

I laughed. 'No, you wouldn't have to do that, unless you wanted to, of course. It's something you might find even more disagreeable. You'd have to take directions from me.'

She screwed her face up into a grimace. 'I see what you mean. Difficult to shut your eyes and think of

England when you're lugging half a hundredweight of soil.'

*

The grey Toyota with the crumpled wheel arch had been parked just down the lane for half an hour and, even with my binoculars, I couldn't make out who was sitting in the driver's seat.

I got on with the housework. I'd put it off for long enough already. Every so often I would find myself near the window, glancing out to see whether the car was still there. It was. Finally, I switched off the vacuum cleaner and pushed it to one side, before opening my front door and stepping out. The smell of freshly rained-on vegetation and cow manure filled my nostrils. I walked slowly, avoiding the cow-pats covering the road surface like an outbreak of warts. As I approached, I heard the car's engine start. The driver turned neatly and sped off. Despite his cap and glasses, his face, through the steamed-up window looked familiar.

'No, too dark, too thin, chin was wrong,' I muttered to myself. 'But still…'

I fumbled as I pulled out my mobile phone, nearly dropping it in a large puddle. Even though it was almost noon, Neil's voice sounded sleepy.

'Didn't wake you, did I Neil?'

'Been up for hours. What do you want?'

'Beart *is* still in Brazil, is he?'

'Probably being sodomised by some swarthy crime king from the favelas as we speak.'

'Are you sure?'

'That he's being sodomised?'

'No, that he's still behind bars. Can you be absolutely positive?'

Neil sighed. 'Yes. Why?'

'I've seen someone who looks a bit like him outside my cottage. He drove off when I went to confront to him.'

'You must be imagining it. We still haven't managed to get them to extradite him, but he's definitely still banged up.'

'But Neil, that face—'

'Paranoia.'

'He feigned death before and got away with it. Could you double-check? Rachel's moving in here and I don't want her to be in any danger.'

'Rachel?' Neil's voice was icy. 'Moving in with you? Why would she do that? She thinks you're a plonker.'

'Never mind that,' I said, 'what about Beart?'

'Beart's out of the equation. Say hello to Rachel from me.' Neil hung up.

*

A crimson canvas laced with purple and pale blue streamers; sunset over the Wattock Hills was famous amongst visitors though barely noticed by residents who'd grown accustomed to its magnificence over the years.

Even though I was now trying to pass myself off as a local, I was still awe-struck by its beauty and would stand on the old coppice gate and stare at it whenever I had the opportunity.

The day she moved in, I took Rachel to Lewer Ridge, the best place to witness the sunset and, as the dark mantle of night gradually pressed the red glow beneath the horizon, I stretched out my hand to touch hers, and felt her cold fingers curled into a ball. She turned in the fading light, a half-smile on her face.

'Don't get any ideas,' she said, withdrawing her hand gently. 'I only agreed to be your tenant.'

'And my labourer,' I added. 'Didn't you realise that droit du seigneur is still part of the feudal code?'

'In your dreams,' she replied. 'If you had a castle, or at least a sizeable manor house, I might consider it, but I don't think letting me stay in your spare room makes you much of a seigneur.'

'You may have a point,' I conceded. 'OK, in keeping with more modern management techniques, I'm going to propose an incentive scheme. We'll go to the Jolly Throstle on a Friday evening. If we have a good week, we'll have the rump steak and a decent bottle of wine. If it's a bad one, it's burgers and beer. Agreed?'

'Perfect,' she said. 'I do hope this is going to be a good week. I don't much like beer.'

We stood in silence for a few minutes breathing in the cool night air before Rachel cleared her throat and looked up at me.

'Actually,' she said, 'I've been thinking a bit about the business and I can see a way to reorganise how we do things, and maybe even bring in some hired help. I'm sure with your horticultural knowledge and my business acumen we can grow this into something really profitable.'

'It's getting a bit chill. I think we should go back now,' I said as a shiver danced the length of my spine.

THE END

Acknowledgements:

Cover design concept by Hilary Thripp

My thanks to the following for their advice and encouragement:

Tony Allen, Mohamed Asem, Ross Baglin, Michael Fleming, Mark Goldthorpe, Eva Hoffman, Roger Kohn, Cosimo Lopalco, Kevin MacNeil, John Marks, Tamzin and Meli Pinkerton, Iain and Ruth Richardson, Lissette Roberts, Dave Russomano, Fiona Sampson, Jane Wallace, James Whittaker, and students and faculty (Creative Writing course 2012-14) at Kingston University, London.